# Harlot's fire

L.M. Pampuro

**Harlot's fire**


This book is a work of fiction.
Names, characters, locations, and events are either a product of the author's imagination, fictitious or used fictitiously.

Any resemblance to any event, locale or person, living or dead, is purely coincidental.



Cover design by Grateful Publishing
**ISBN: 978-1-7344990-8-7**

L.M. Pampuro

*For the dancers and dreamers and*
*the music makers.*
*Peace.*

The Connecticut Daily

## Gray Death Trial Set For mid-July.

By D. Rob Porter, Daily Staff

On July 20, Salvi Giovani will stand trial for the manufacture and distribution of illegal substances along with kidnapping charges stemming from his detainment of a federal agent against their will. Giovani, 36, of Hartford, Connecticut, along with Harlot Grace, age and address unknown, both will be tried in Hartford Superior Court. According to Attorney General Curry's office, both face charges relating to multiple counts of drug trafficking and manufacturing and possession of illegal firearms. Grace was employed in the area as a popular local adult entertainer.

The Attorney General's office would not go into detail. A spokesperson said, "At this juncture, the federal drug task force and the great state of Connecticut have combined efforts to discover sufficient evidence to bring multiple charges in the case of the *Gray Death* street drug. We want the public to know that this harmful product has been eradicated, and those responsible will be given a speedy, fair trial. We will release more information as it becomes available, and we are able to do so without compromise," in a statement released earlier today.

When asked if the defendants will be charged with murder, the attorney general's office spokesperson responded, "At this time, the attorney general's office is focusing on the manufacture and distribution of illegal substances, along with the ancillary charges of illegal firearms. This case is complex. There is much more to this case that will be discussed at a later date." The charge of murder is being pursued by the families of the 146 victims of an overdose on the grounds that both manufacturer and distributor knew the substance to be unstable.

A spokesperson for the families responded, “that although they understand that the added charges will not bring back their loved ones, they feel that the addition of murder might dissuade others from partaking in this industry in the future.” He also added, “there are other options available to the families, and at this time, they are exploring the vitality of each.” Although no one involved would speak on the record to confirm, The Connecticut Daily obtained information for a pending civil suit. (More information to come at a later date.)

On May 29, a drug task force of federal and state officials raided a property in Lyme, Connecticut. A drug manufacturing lab was found in an outbuilding on the premises, along with multiple unregistered firearms and small bill currency stacks. Multiple sources confirm that the substance found in the lab had a similar chemical compound to the *Gray Death* street drug responsible for over 146 overdoses earlier that month.

Two men, both unidentified, were taken into custody by federal agents. A spokesperson for the federal drug task force has confirmed that both men are the chemists responsible for the compound. The same source also confirmed that at least one of the two men are in the country illegally. At this time, the person's country of origin cannot be confirmed.

The property is owned by a series of shell corporations that ultimately lead authorities back to Giovani through forensic science and cybersecurity breaches. Giovani was on the premises at the time of the raid. He fled through the woods in an all-terrain vehicle. Authorities arrested Giovani later that day in Salem, Connecticut.

During the raid, federal agents shot and killed Lester A. Yongst, 37, last known address West Hartford, Connecticut, after he threatened officers with a firearm. Yongst is believed to be the primary distributor of *Gray Death*. Officials believe that he set up a distribution network in conjunction with local and regional drug dealers. Yongst was known to frequent many area establishments during the day and could often be found at various bars and coffeehouses along the I-91 corridor.

Yongst's older brother, Louis A. Yongst, is the co-owner of Lucky Lou's, the adult entertainment establishment on Airport Rd in Hartford. A further connection to his brother's business, Harlot Grace was recently employed at Lucky Lou's. Upon departure, she joined the Matteo Corporation as Salvi Giovani's personal assistant. Salvi's family owns the Matteo Corporation. Victor Giovani, Salvi's father, is the current C.E.O.

At this time, both companies have been cleared of any wrongdoing. Lucky Lou's remains closed until further notice.

Jury selection for both defendant's trial is scheduled to start next week. Currently, the proceedings will be open to the public, although *The Daily* has been informed this may change as the trial start date draws closer.

Look for further updates in the The Connecticut Daily and online at ConnecticutDaily.com.

L.M. Pampuro

Urine and tobacco made sense. Every alleyway in every city possessed this stank. Yet the soft, faint haze of a Cuban cigar threw the entire scene off. That and the directions in his hand. *Go to The Alley of Whores. There will be a sign.*

Before venturing out, he searched city maps on Google along with the bureau's database. No such street existed in New Haven, Connecticut. He glanced back into the mirrored windows for anyone suspicious who may be following. His feet marched in cadence along the main drag.

And there it was, not a street sign in the traditional sense, just a photograph of Harlot Grace, the stripper from Hartford, tacked up on a brick wall, alongside posters that advertised a Kung Fu and The Meadows Brothers Band show at a famous music hall a few blocks over.

He turned into the alleyway—junkies scattered in the shadows. Moans rose into the harmonies of a drunk acapella choir. A melody of desperation filled the air. Along with his handwritten directions, he clutched an 8.5 x 11" manilla envelope so tight, sweat from his palms soaked through to the pages.

The pages of his new retirement plan. Screw his pittance of a government pension.

The walls stopped at a soft glow in the middle. Intelligible voices weaved within the junkie's chorus. A hint of marijuana and ammonia tangled with the smell of burning wood filled in the distance to an old Airstream covered with the faded graffiti of Picasso-esque palm trees and rolling waves. Outlines of humans appeared in the curtained windows next to the trailer's entrance.

He counted four heads yet knew there could be more out of view. The false bravado held by a service revolver tucked in his waistband started to fade. The human waste around the fire acknowledged his approach with faint interest. The door opened before he could knock, temporarily causing blindness.

"Come in, comrade, come in." A solid hand covered with scars grasped his shoulder to move his body inside a fog of cigar smoke. "How good of you to make it. This is—"

"No names, please," Morris Webb interrupted.

" – my friend, no names, please. For tonight, we call him Judas," the leader smiled in his direction, "okay?" A small nod from the visitor returned the slight. "Okay, good. What have you got for me?" The well-built man who opened the door removed the envelope from his hand. With a similar build, another male reached over the table to accept the container before transferring the package to a wiry man in the center. Without even a nod, he opened the envelope.

"The deposit– " Webb started to say.

"Will be made when we verify this information," the wiry man scowled.

"That wasn't– " a rod slipped against his back. The stale smell of ammonia crept over his neck. "that will be fine," Webb replied, adding, "To the Cayman account, please." The please came out more of a habit than of politeness.

The man at the table mumbled something incoherent as those around him nodded. "When can we get our Harlot Grace back?"

"All of that is in the file. She was shot– "

"That isn't what I asked," Yarok Yarokov's voice remained steady, yet eyes turned dark. Although physically more imposing, the men at the table leaned away from their leader.

"She is under a 24-hour watch at the hospital. Armed guards—" Webb's voice rose an octave.

"Who is in charge of this—" Yarokov barked back.

"I guess I am—"

"You guess?" Yarokov leaned forward on the table. "You get me time. We will take care of the rest."

"There can be no violence," Webb wagged his finger for emphasis. "I mean it. Enough people—"

"Comrade Webb, if you gave a damn about other people," Yarokov held the envelope up, "then this would not be in my hand, no?" Webb returned a slight nod. "Good. You call my friend here with time, and we will escort my Harlot Grace out of your hands. Okay?" Another slight move of Webb's head followed to affirm. "Now, here is a little something for your troubles, okay?"

The greeter handed Webb a small package. The plain brown wrapper gave zero indication of the contents. The phrase, *a pound of twenties,* whispered as Webb's lips rose into a full grin. He butchered, "Blagodaryu vas," thank you in their native language. At the same time, he fell back out the door. His hand tapped the package, nestled safely in one breast pocket, while his other, out of sight, clutched the handle of his service revolver.

His business was completed. He walked with purpose through the mixed smoke, passed the concert of addicts' hum, to slip back on to the crowded streets of New Haven.

Alia Price sat in an authentic 1930's green high-back, leather chair across from her boss, the illustrious Alister Otis Reed, Assistant Executive Director of C.C.R.S. (Criminal, Cyber, Response and Services). Every item in Alister's office had a story. Her chair came from his grandfather's law firm. His desk was his father's, an investigator as well. Books lined the shelves behind him, some real, some that hide the secrets of this room.

Hands folded on her lap, her black LL Bean flats connected to the floor, Alia sat up straight in her chair. Without expression, Alister typed vigorously into his computer. To Alia, the computer always seemed out of place with the rest of the space. Each tap of Alister's fingers echoed in the paneled wood cavern. "We have a problem," his hands stopped moving as his eyes met hers, "the mob is after you."

Alia's laughter bounced out of the room. "After me? Whatever for, Alister? I didn't shoot Salvi!" Her amusement spilled into the hallway. Alister narrowed his eyes. Alia ran her hands over her face, sat up even straighter, then brought her hands back to her lap. Her face showed zero emotion, both shoulders shook. Alister took a long inhale off the lit cigarette before placing the burning embers back to smolder in the ashtray. Since before Alia's arrival almost ten years ago, the building had been nonsmoking, yet Alister didn't think the rule applied to him.

If anyone dared to complain to human resources, they got his standard answer, "this is not a kindergarten class," although some days, Alia wondered.

"I'm not joking," he took another long inhale. "And for the record, Salvi doesn't have the right background for this mob."

"I don't understand," Alia started to fidget in her chair. Her legs bounced below her. "No one knew about my assignment except," her eyes opened wide, "the people on the case with me. Alister?"

"I don't have an answer."

"DeLuca?" Alia moved to the edge of her chair.

"Definitely not," Alister brought his gaze back to the screen.

"How can you be so sure?"

"Because I trusted him with your life." Alister's comment is met with silence. Alia got a bit over sensitive that Johnny DeLuca ended up on the team who saved her during their drug raid last month. The two somehow got into a sibling type competition back at the academy. Johnny always bested her by the smallest margin. Alia should be over it, yet her competitive side wouldn't let him win her one-sided competition.

"Someone here?"

"Possibly," Alister snubbed out what remained of his cigarette in the overflowing ashtray. A few ashes escaped onto his desk. "Probably. I haven't got to there yet."

"Haven't got there yet?" Alia repeated. She twisted in her chair. "How far have you gotten?" She waited for a silent beat before she continued, "Really, Alister. I have already been drugged, detoxed, and debriefed. Plus, had that hospital stay, don't get me started on that." She turned her head away. Foot bounce harder against the wood floor. She turned back to Alister, "What the heck do I do now? Go undercover again? I have a life I would like to get back to."

Alister diverted his gaze. He shuffled a few papers on his desk. He then repositioned his body to take up his executive chair's entire space. Alia bounced, yet her expression never went beyond neutral.

She crossed her arms and asked, "What are you not telling me?"

"An hour ago, Harlot Grace disappeared from the hospital," Alister said.

Harlot Grace, the former stripper, who somehow got connected with Alia's ex almost fiancée, Salvi. Her hand flew to her stomach. A bocce ball game started in her gut. Although Alia still hadn't fashioned a connection beyond sex with her ex, Harlot was involved in their current case. What reasons would a gunshot victim have to leave a medical facility? She raked her teeth against the inside of her cheek. "How did Harlot Grace disappear?"

"No one has that answer. The word I got was that Grace walked out."

"Could Salvi have helped her?" Salvi had kidnapped and drugged Alia, along with performing other travesties; to move Harlot would be less complicated for him than ordering at Starbucks.

"I doubt it. As I mentioned earlier, wrong mob." Alister moved a few more papers on his desk. He surveyed one with the state seal on the top with care. "His trial, along with the others, is scheduled for the end of the month."

"Alister," Alia cleared her voice. "How does the FBI lose a person?"

Alister gave his employee the death stare across his desk. He spoke as if she hadn't. "Alia, I need you to do me a favor. Might you consider a little vacation?"

"Vacation or disappear?"

"Both. Mostly the latter," Alister answered.

"Is this one of those practical vacation situations where the company will cover my expenses because I am not really on vacation? Like the last time?" Alia recrossed her arms and legs to still the rest of her body. Right before this case, the company paid for a Florida adventure that had fun in the sun in the middle of a turf war between two rival Miami gangs. Alister reached for another cigarette and rolled the cylinder between his tobacco-stained fingers. With his other hand, he pushed a piece of paper across the desk with his free hand.

"What's this?" Alia took the offending document in her left hand, holding it at arm's length, she squinted to read the faraway type. A bunch of cities is listed under the heading *The Flying Monkeys.*

Alister watched her hold the paper like a dirty diaper. "Please, read it and find out."

"I don't understand." Alia brought the document closer. "What the hell is a flying monkey. Is this the list of sightings?" She laughed at her joke. Her boss's expression didn't change.

"Alia, you are one of the best at digging up people's secrets."

"Thank you. I believe that is why you hired me."

"You have a gift that allows people to trust you, a great attribute in our line of work. However, your attitude," He watched as Alia re-crossed her arms and legs in the opposite direction, "is probably going to get you killed someday."

The Howard Miller Schoolhouse clock to her left beat one loud tick at a time. Behind her, she could hear co-workers as they laughed, gossiped, and took on the days growing list of unthinkables. Without thought, her top leg began to bounce again, this time to the beat of the clock. Alister's typing brought in a second rhythm, one that matched up perfectly with the other sounds before it drifted apart into the chaos in the room.

"I think you should leave town until after the trial. You don't need to testify. We have people to represent your findings." Alia opened her mouth to speak, yet Alister kept on going, "This here is a band of musicians who have got a lot of threats lately. Most have been online, yet last week someone threw a bottle filled with explosives at their tour bus. The bus was empty at the time, and no one got hurt, but the chemical combination of nitro-methane with ammonium nitrate-- "

"Says whoever is responsible, they knew what they were doing." Alister shook his head. "Are there any buzzes about a motive?"

"The exact motive is what we are still searching for. The Flying Monkeys have a following who enjoy a lot of marijuana with a bit of alcohol. For the most part, the band draws a pretty mellow group…"

With only two years on the job, Alia picked up on situations faster than most veterans. Her head moved to meet his eyes. "I am going to find out anyway, so you might as well—"

"Attorney Curry's son is their guitar player."

Alia's mouth dropped open. "Attorney General Curry of the great state of Connecticut?"

"The same. The same guy who is prosecuting your friends on the drug manufacturing charges—"

"Holy shit!" As the words escaped, one hand rose to cover her mouth.

"Alia!"

"Whoops. Sorry. I mean, oh my gosh! Curry's son is a rock star?" Alia took out a pen from her bag. She immediately began scribbling notes on the once offensive paper. "Why isn't Curry's office handling the explosive investigation?"

"Good question that I don't have an answer to. My theory is Curry's office believes the incident ties to his present case, and turning it over to us limits their distractions. How would you like to be a groupie for a few weeks?"

"Groupie? Seriously? What is my cover going to be, tour slut?" She folded her body in half to lean one arm on the desk while resting her head in her hand. Alia mouthed specific phrases, underlined others, and placed question marks all around the page. "The report reads as if it is a slam-dunk that the drug mob is after the kid."

Alister knew better than to speak. He watched Alia stand, the file still in her left hand, pen poised in her right. "What else is Curry involved in?" she asked, rhetorically. Her boss sat back to observe her analysis process. "Let's consider beyond the case that involves me."

"Why?" Alister sat up at this observation.

"That case is too easy." She flipped over to the last page to start to read backward. An old college trick used to edit papers, concentrating on every word, circling to add those to question. The pen tapped against her front teeth incorporated the clock's tempo.

"You are wearing out my rug," Alister pointed down to the well-worn Indian rug. Alia stopped to give a death stare back to her boss. Her facial expression matched his earlier. "By all means, continue," he gestured in her direction.

"I have questions," she said.

"You are a journalist," he kept his face neutral. "You will have full access to all areas wherever they play. You are taking Miranda Silver's place as she is going undercover amongst the fans to try and shake out whoever is making the threats."

"So, she is focused on the mad bomber?"

"She is looking for the mad bomber." Alister pushed another file across the desk.

Alia reached across Alister's desk to grab a new pen out of the BOSS mug. She made a couple of notes on the file. "You want me to write a column? Are you joking?" she laughed.

"About that. Miranda is doing some weekly articles under Miranda Stone. Write under her name, so people will think you are legitimate." Alister waved his hand in the air in an attempt to magically just move forward.

"I can't write under my name."

"You understand that you are not really a writer, right?" Alister smirked.

"Yeah. But…"

Alister brought the unlit cigarette to his mouth to take a drag before opening every drawer of his desk. "Polly!" he screamed.

"We have a non-smoking office," came back from the hallway.

"Am I in charge?" Alister directed the question to Alia. She shrugged in return, "You do what you need to keep the illusion going. Make sure nothing happens to Curry's boy and, in a few weeks, come back to a new assignment.

In the meantime, try to avoid getting kidnapped by hippies."

"Is the mob really after me?" Alia gave a half-smile.

Alister blew out a breath. "Alia, someone is making threats and noise. You uncovered one too many secrets. Harlot's disappearance adds to all of this." Her eyes watered, "While you are out there, you may want to keep your eyes open for Harlot or Yarok Yarokov. His photo is in the second file." Alister brushed a few pieces of ash off his tie. "You are a good investigator, yet more importantly, you are an exceptional person. Could you please..."

"Fine. I will tour with The Flying Freakin' Monkeys, but let me warn you," she pointed her finger at Alister, "If I find out who gave me away..."

"Not if I find out first. Miranda's on her way to some festival in Pennsylvania. Curry's band is on the bill. She's expecting you tomorrow." Alister held up his cigarette, "and Alia, when you find these idiots, call me. Another division took over the undercover on the premises, and they are ready to jump in with your go-ahead. Don't be a hero - give the word."

"Are the others on my team listed in the file?"

"No. For now, we can't compromise your identity, or Miranda Stone's. The situation dictates for you to appear on your own if you understand." Alia nodded. "Recognize that you are surrounded by both those who will help you and—"

"—those who will kill me." Alia stood up, raised her hand to give a full salute.

"I'll make a call." Alister picked up his receiver. "Oh, and Alia, I need your current laptop. You can pick-up another one downstairs before you leave."

"No problem." Alia walked across the office to her now former desk. An empty cardboard box sat on one side with a note attached: for personal items. She had no personal items. In the corner hung one old Calvin and Hobbs cartoon. *You know, Hobbes, some days even my lucky rocket ship underpants don't help.*[1] She reached out to remove the comic with care and murmured, "You are so right, Calvin."

---

[1] Bill Watterson Calvin and Hobbs quotes

Her computer bag lay on the chair out of sight, under her desk. One pull on the strap, a few clunks to her shoulder. Back in Alister's office, she placed the bag and cardboard box on the empty green leather chair. "I don't need the box," she said. Alister handed her a receipt for the computer.

"One more thing, any updates go directly to me. Do not have Miranda send anything in and please do not speak to anyone else in the office." She nodded. Alister added, "Stay safe" as an afterthought.

As Alia made her way back to the employee exit, co-workers typed away as they stared at bright-lit screens. Phones rested in between ear and shoulder. Others stood in groups. All pretended to be someone other than themselves. She scanned the entire room. Amongst this group of people, there was a distinct possibility that someone broke the code. Someone gave up her undercover identity. Right now, that person could be in her presence.

"I heard Alister fired her this morning," came out of the employee lounge. The gossip already started. Part of her wanted to listen and a possible clue about who betrayed her. Her practical Virgo side forced her straight through the lobby. She slammed her hands into the bar that opened the door. Sunlight blazed around her shadow. She walked across the dusty employee parking lot, then turned back towards the massive brick building.

"This isn't over," she mumbled while shaking her fists. Alia got into her Outback and drove towards Pennsylvania. She was now a music journalist. Her mind quickly assumed the identity necessary to complete the job.

Brendan Curry's body slumped against the hard cushion on his tour buses couch. Outside, his former college roommate stood in perfect view, soaking up the bright sunshine while resting each of his pale, bony arms across the shoulder of a matching set of long-haired brunette beauties. One threw her head back when she laughed while the other just stared at the gravel.

The quiet one glanced at the bus window. Brendan imagined she had blue eyes. When she turned ever so slightly away from him, the thin white strap of her barely-there bikini top slipped down her shoulder. For a brief second, she exposed a soft white breast. He let out a gasp.

"No," Wally's voice broke his spell. His road manager had strict rules about Brendan speaking with anyone outside his bandmates and Wally.

"No, what?" Brendan already knew the question. And the answer had been preached since the start of the tour.

"No strange women on the bus," Wally spoke as if he memorized a script. "We have to be careful about who we allow close. Your father…" Brendan groaned. His father. Blah. Blah. Blah. Wally picked up empty to-go containers, old newspapers, and other garbage as he lectured. "Do you understand?"

Brendan nodded. "All too well," he mumbled. He turned his attention back to the female sandwich his bass player enjoyed. The quiet one had recovered the strap. Her eyes bounced between the bus and the stage. The other's hands motioned in all directions while Marv stared down into her ample chest.

Brendan caught Marv looking back towards the bus window. His friend's lips morphed into a Cheshire cat grin. Brendan knew that look all too well. It usually met complications for any close by. The bus door shushed shut. Alone, he cracked the window open.

"Come on, doll. Let's take a stroll, perhaps check the view out back?" The view out back line. Brendan laughed. It never worked, yet Marv kept trying.

"I want to go on the bus," the loud one-pointed with her chin. "I want to see what a tour bus looks like from the inside."

"Ah… The bus." Marv stroked his naked chin. "We could go on the bus— "

"Is Brendan Curry on the bus?" Her friend joined the conversation.

"Yeah, is Brendan on the bus?" The loud one repeated.

Marv let out a deep sigh. "I don't have a clue who is on the bus," Marv said. "I do know that behind the bus, we have a quiet spot under a shade tree. The air back there is much better than our tour bus occupied by smelly men for two weeks."

The quiet one pulled her friend out of Marv's armpit. "Let's go back by the stage," her voice had changed from sultry to annoying, at least in Brendan's mind. "I want to see the band that is playing." She crossed her arms as her lips pursed into the perfect combination of duck and pout.

"Oh, Bella," her friend cooed.

"Don't oh Bella me," she barked back.

Brendan's laugh escaped through the window. The quiet one turned towards the bus.

"I thought you said that Brendan wasn't on the bus." She narrowed her eyes.

"I believe I replied I didn't know," Marv raised his middle finger over the girl's shoulder, in the direction of the bus.

"I heard someone laugh. It sounded like Brendan." Her right foot tapped.

Brendan placed a pillow over his mouth to snort inside. When he brought his attention back to the group outside, Marv was back at square one.

"Are you a friend of Brendan or not?" Marv's voice took on the shrill of a man about to lose a sure thing, "Because if you are, I can have our tour manager track him down for you. We do that for our good friends." The girls gave each other a slight head nod then brought their attention back to Marv.

"It was nice to meet you," the quiet one extended her hand. Marv took it in his, brought it to his lips, then ran his tongue from her middle finger almost to her elbow. She pulled her hand away.

"Yeah, nice to meet you," her friend repeated. She backed out of Marv's range. Both Marv and Brendan stared as the two swing their barely covered asses toward the stage. Within minutes Marv's skinny body stretched across the entire couch opposite Brendan.

"How long do we have mother Walter on tour with us?" Marv asked.

"I don't know." Brendan blew out a loud breath. "He's part of my parent's paying for the tour expenses."

"He's cramping my style." Marv glanced back out the window. He added, "Those two were a sure thing on the bus."

"I'm sorry." Brendan shrugged. "At least you—"

Marv jumped up and hit his head on the ceiling. "Ouch." He slumped back down. "And we need a taller bus."

Brendan brought his attention back out the window. The two girls found another musician to rest his armpits across their shoulders. "Nothing but tour sluts," he mumbled.

"But what would a tour be without 'em," Marv sighed. "Ah, speaking of our tour necessities."

Wally opened the door and motioned with one finger to follow. "Showtime, boys."

Alia stood on the side of the massive stage. The people up front screamed and danced to The Flying Monkeys. The band had high volume, and from her position, it did not sound like they played actual music, just a set composed of feedback and muffled vocals.

"This must sound better in front," she said to no one. Alia played the part well with press credentials hung around her neck, pad, and paper in her hand. Across the way, a man from Rolling Stone, at least he claimed to be when he asked her to meet him for a drink later to discuss the line-up, spoke into a small recording device. "I should have one of those."

"One of what?" Alia's attention went to her right. Sweat ran in all directions on the young man's body. His hair wet and stringy slid down a overtly thin and bony physique. "One of what?" he repeated. In his hand rested a beautiful mahogany base guitar. Alia pointed to the man talking into the recorder. He added, "The dude or the phone?"

"What phone?" Alia squinted for a better look. "Damn."

"All the aliens have them." Now the guy smiled. His teeth had something green, possibly kale, nestled in between. Alia returned a toothless smile and nod. "I'm honest, you see. Some of us are aliens, and some, like you, are not."

"Aren't you the bass player for The Flying Monkeys?" Alia said, trying to change the subject.

"I am the cosmic traveler for the monkeys. Here on earth, they call me Marv." Marv extended his hand to shake.

"As in Marvin?" Alia gave a quick squeeze.

"Close. Marvelous." He tilted his head back to let out a loud laugh. "You'll keep my secret, right, Alia?" He winked.

Before she could ask how Marv knew her name, his body bounced back towards the crowd to arrive with a loud audience roar.

Alia noted Brendan Curry turned his back to the audience and rolled his eyes to his drummer. Both men's head shook side to side. Curry turned back towards the crowd to pull their focus from his alien bassist. She waited for the set to end. The band moved in different directions, yet Brendan immediately went over to pack his guitar.

A big, burly man followed.

"Who is the person standing by the Marshall amplifier?" Alia asked Marv as he passed.

"That, my dear, is our guitar player extraordinaire, Mr. Brendan Curry," Marv dropped his voice to add, "Not an alien."

"Not him," Alia pointed to the six-foot, muscular man boarding the bus behind Brendan, "Him!"

"Oh, you mean Wally." Alia motioned her hands for him to continue. "Wally travels with us. Also, N.A.A. He mostly hangs with Brendan." Behind her, two striking women posed in neon bikinis and giggled. "I, uh, gotta go," Marv moved past her.

"Wait, Marv, I have questions. How did you know my name?"

"I identify all my fellow-creatures," he replied.

"And it is written on your pass," one of the neon's pointed.

"And N.A.A.?" Alia shouted after. Marv ignored the query.

Alia eavesdropped on the whispers and giggles behind her. "Sorry, ladies, no tour bus as we are having septic issues. The smell is overwhelming. But I am happy to venture to your place…" Marv continued in his attempt to sway the ladies.

She wrote down the "no tour bus response" along with "who the heck is Wally?" in a small note pad.

She walked down the back steps over to the journalist's lounge, a fancy name for a tent with folding chairs and a couple of tables. The promoter did supply a WiFi connection. In exchange for a few bucks, the security detail would release the day's password to anyone.

Alia slipped the guard a twenty. "Just type in *Festival20.* All one word," he gave a wink. She clicked on the agency's secure browser. With a quick hit on the send button, all her notes were forwarded to Alister. Her fingers tapped to the muffled beat the current band expelled. After five minutes, her computer dinged. *Call me a.s.a.p.* She looked around to see that a few others, including Mr. Rolling Stone, started to take up space around the tables and chairs. Around the back of The Flying Monkey's bus provided both seclusion and a strong signal. Music floated by in stifled notes. Alister answered on the first ring.

"I have some news," he started.

"Is it bad?" Alia countered. Alister's laughter produced a bit of bile in her mouth.

"A little. Not much." Alister stalled. Alia could taste his trepidation. "There is a bit of confusion between our office and the A.G.'s."

"Really," Alia replied.

"Curry already took care of his boy with a babysitter," Alister said. The shush of papers moved in the background. "What the hell is his name?"

"Wally?"

"Yes, Wally - wait, did you meet him?" Alister's voice registered a bit of surprise.

"Not exactly. If you read my notes, I asked about Wally's position," Alia answered.

More paper shuffling followed by keyboard pounding. "Oh, yes, right here. Walter H. Whiting, former Navy, Seals I believe, and Curry hired him to watch out for his boy."

"So, what am I doing? Watching out for Wally?" Alia listened to forced laugh bellow from Alister in response to her question. When he didn't answer she added, "I am not smiling. What is my function in this case?"

"Alia, I need you to pay attention. Pretend to be a reporter still. Be discreet. Stay out of sight…"

"Alister," Alia did her best to steady her voice. "I am already pretending to be a reporter. Are you telling me now you want me to take a vacation by hiding out with hippies?"

"Yes."

"Alister, W.T.—"

"Alia! Language!" A wheezing intake of breath followed. "The Flying Monkeys are leaving tonight for another festival. Instead of following the band, you will stay in Pennsylvania and continue to report from the festival. Use your gift, Alia. People tell you their secrets. There is more going on here than meets the eye."

"Alister, What if—"

"There are no what-ifs. This is now your assignment. I want you safe, and if this means hanging out with hippies, well, you will damn well hang out with hippies." Alister took another long inhale. "Oh, and keep an eye on Miranda Silver too. Her new identity is fitting a bit too well."

Alia jumped at a rustle behind her. On a close branch sat a fat, brown squirrel gnawing on an acorn. The squirrel stopped to stare. With two whisker twitches, it went back to his lunch.

No sounds came from the tour bus. "So, I am stuck here?"

"You are to stay undercover at the festival for now. If there is another opportunity, I will be in touch. Any questions?" Alister used his no-nonsense, commander voice. Based on Alia's experience with commanding officer's, this left zero room for negotiations or questions.

"Have you found the mole?" she asked.

"Not yet." The call disconnected. Alia laid back on the picnic table. Above her, the tree branches traversed against the bright blue sky. The crowd noise faded in the distance.

The yellow school bus leaped side to side along the steep mountain road. Alia's head hurt from too much sun, way too much mandolin, and too little healthy food. It didn't help one of the bands played her old favorite, *Scarlet Begonias,* with a hard edge. Alia knew the second she twirled her old shoulder injury, ironically caused by spinning, popped.

The sun went down, and the shoulder throbbed with a faint pulse. Miranda referred to her as a wuss. "The whole point of going to a festival is to push your limits," the woman lectured. Alia wanted to remind that they were not actually attendees. Yet, her counterpart's dilated eyes and metallic smell stopped her lecture. She circled the later in her notebook, adding a few exclamation points on the side.

She jerked her thumb in the direction of the shuttle area. "Don't wait up," Miranda yelled after her. "At least one of us is doing her job."

"I haven't the last two nights. Why should tonight be any different." Although she barely arrived, her quick response told onlookers she had been part of the festival from the start. Her legs burned as she trudged up the steep steps to a circular drive filled with yellow school buses. "Which bus heads to the hotels," she asked the teenager in the red staff shirt.

"I'm not sure," he answered. "Ask the drivers."

After three "no's," the fourth driver said to climb aboard. "I'll go back to the hotels, no problem." Alia slumped down into the first seat and closed her eyes.

The injured shoulder slammed against the wall as the bus jolted to a stop. A few exited while another twenty or so, loaded up with tents, backpacks, and cases of beer boarded. As more people squeezed on in the aisle, Alia saw her, the hotel person, as the only thing standing between the rest of the bus and the festival.

"You can drop me off at the end of the road."

"Are you sure?" she returned a nod.

The bus came to a graceless stop—a giant step over the person in the aisle. A quick squeeze by two others crouched near the driver finally delivered the space to exit the bus. Her left hand threw a dollar in the tip jar. At the same time, she yelled, "Thank you." Her left foot slipped off the bottom step.

"Are you okay?" the driver asked.

"Simply peachy," Alia responded with a wave. The bus jerked back in motion behind her.

The lobby lay quiet, not even a front desk person insight. Out in the courtyard, a couple guys sat on top of a picnic table, strumming acoustic guitars. About a dozen or so people milled around. Beyond the center courtyard, a tour bus' windows glowed.

"You are welcome to join us," a deep voice made her jump. "The boys are going to jam for another half hour or so."

Alia turned to look up to a hefty man with long gray hair and a matching beard. He took up most of the space around her. His eyes flickered as he spoke in a slow, southern drawl. "You can hang out with my wife. She's the pissed off looking beauty in the lounge chair." His finger pointed a bit beyond the group to a woman sitting off to the side, arms folded across her chest.

"Wouldn't she be more upset if you showed up with another woman?"

The man squinted his eyes before he moved his head to give a full-body appraisal. "Are you a groupie?"

"A what?" Alia put her hand over her heart with a touch of theatrics.

"A groupie. What else are they called, tour sluts. Bimbos."

Alia mimicked his wife's pose. "Ah – no."

"Good. She'll like you. Come on." The big, burly, bearded fellow took her arm to lead around the group of women in dresses so shear they might as well be naked, to stop at the chair next to his wife.

"I brought you a glass of water and a new friend. Can I go play now?" he handed her the glass. "This is…What's your name?"

Alia hesitated before she answered, "Althea."

"Althea, like the Dead song?"

"Yeah, parents are old hippies." Alia let out a nervous giggle as she pictured her ultra-conservative parents dressed in tie-dyed clothing, they wouldn't be caught dead in.

"Althea, this is my lovely wife, Zadie. Zadie darling, this is your new friend Althea."

"And I am sorry, you are?"

The big man's laughter bounced around the courtyard and off the building. "Ah – yes. I am Tiny – no joke." He leaned down to kiss his wife on the cheek. In one fluid motion, he turned to go join the other two musicians on the picnic table.

"He's something, alright." Zadie sighed.

"Yeah – about that. I was getting on the elevator…"

"Were you at the festival?" Zadie pointed towards the lament that bounced out in front of her breasts.

"Yes. All-day. Actually, I kind of need to…" Alia's chin nodded towards the door.

"No excuses needed. How is the scene? Any good bands?"

Alia rested one bent knee on the chair next to Zadie. "Scene is okay. I think I overdid the dancing a bit…" She moved her right arm in a circular motion. Her eyes squeezed shut as her elbow extended behind.

"Happens to the best of us." Zadie surveyed a group of women in skimpy bikinis, all positioned within the sightlines of her husband and bandmates. Tiny and the others paid the woman zero attention. The soft sounds of multiple guitars, along with a subdued pluck of bass strings, echoed off the hotel's cement walls. "You here alone?"

"No, I am here with my sister, Miranda."

"Where is she now?"

"Probably on a tour bus." Zadie flinched. "No, no, it's not what you think. She's a journalist."

"A journalist, you say." Zadie took a long sip off the water bottle she kept along her side. She rolled up onto one hip. Her entire form now focused on Alia.

"Yes. Miranda writes for different magazines. Maybe you've heard of her, Miranda Stone?' Zadie spits the water out. Bits of spray splattered dark spots on her dress.

"Miranda Stone is actually your sister?" Alia nodded. "Holy crap! Does Tiny have any idea about this?" Alia shook her head no. As Zadie clapped her hands, shook her head, and cackled, Alia wondered if she should have used a different connection.

She opened her mouth to speak at the same moment, Zadie blurted, "And what do you do?"

"Oh, nothing. I'm here because I ran away from home. Miranda is sharing her space while I figure my life out." As Alia stood, her right hand extended in Zadie's direction. "It was nice to meet you."

"And you," Zadie took a stronghold on her hand. "Where are you going?"

"I need to… anyway. Good night." Alia turned to disappear through the closest door. Zadie walked over and mumbled something in Tiny's ear before heading in the direction of the old dark blue tour bus.

Once inside the building, Alia climbed the staircase to the second floor. "My floor." She pushed open the metal door. The booming sounds knocked her back a bit. The hallway shrunk with people.

"Excuse me," she pushed past the twirling bodies that mounted each other against the wall. Everywhere her gaze fell, boobs and naked butts jumped into her sight. She zipped and zagged, releasing the occasional "excuse me." Simultaneously, hands grazed along her body, some getting too close to her lady parts for comfort. "I wish I had my gun," Alia mumbled, "or at least some pepper spray." She slapped a hand away as it tried to reach under her shirt.

Two hairy hands moved to lift her skirt up. She raised her fist and slammed her knuckles into a naked chest. The hairy body faltered back into the crowd. Her last view of a fellow in a dark blue tie against a white naked torso disappeared into various colors of human flesh. The next group divided as she pushed her way through. This gave a narrow path, yet Alai could see the bright, red exit sign, above the mayhem, in the short distance.

Muscle bounced off tissue. Her heartbeat pounded above the trembling base. The next figure received a hard shove to the side. A small woman stared wide-eyed back at her as she flew into the vanishing route. "I'm sorry," Alia shouted back over the din.

The smoke watered her vision, an immoveable object blocked her escape. A shaved-headed beast turned his entire physique in her direction. With a toothless smile, he reached for her. Alia took a step back into another body.

"Darlin'," a voice emerged, yet she couldn't tell from where. The giant stepped aside to reveal a skeleton in a tank top and skinny jeans. A body that only served as a hanger for clothes. Black eyeliner circled his blue eyes.

"Captain Sparrow?" Alia whispered. She closed her eyes and shook her head to make a feeble attempt to clear the image. "I'm not high. I don't drink…" His boney arms reached around her.

"I have been waiting for you all night."

Alia dove out of his grasp to bounce off the breasts of a well-endowed white blonde. "I'm so sorry," she mumbled as she bobbed and weaved back into the crowd. The exit lay in her sight, a hard grip pulled back on her upper arm. She fought the force as her body fell back into the mix, into the pirate's waiting arms.

"I've missed you," he shouted. His breath reeked of onion and stale beer. Alia covered her nose with one hand as she pushed back with the other. "Come on darlin', everybody loves—"

"Tristin!" The smile froze on the pirate's face. He turned his head around yet kept a tight grip on Alia's bicep.

"Tiny, I am surprised to see you here," the pirate said. "Did Zadie let go of your leash?"

Alia let out the breath she held. She strained to raise her head above Tristan's to lock eyes with Tiny. Tiny slipped in between her and the pirate and gave her a quick wink. "My fair lady," he bowed to Alia, "you shan't wander off like that. We have been searching for you."

Another man she recognized from the picnic table stood to Tiny's left. An acoustic guitar rested in one hand. Tristin, the pirate, attempted to circle around. Tiny stopped his movement with one hand while he wagged his index finger on the other. "Go play over there," he pointed at the naked blonde.

"But I—

"Tristan," Tiny held Tristan's gaze and pointed again. The pirate let out a growl, turned, grabbed the closest blonde. Both vanish into the forest of people.

"I'm not high. I don't drink," Alia mumbled.

"Excuse me?" She turned towards the man with the guitar.

"Something I say when I think I am hallucinating."

His laughter sprung above the crowd. He gave a slight push in the direction of the exit sign. As soon as they walked around the corner, the commotion faded.

"What the hell were you thinking?" Tiny asked.

"I was attempting to avoid walking back by you all," Alia answered.

"How that work out for you?" Tiny ran his hand over his face. "You are lucky Zadie called me over. Said her gut was acting up—

"Never doubt the gut," the other guy added.

"Not where your sister is concern," Tiny turned back towards Alia, "She said I had to go find you because you went in the wrong door."

"Say what?" Alia stopped a few feet past her room.

"Zadie's got this sense," Tiny continued, "Keeps us out of trouble."

"Most of the time," the other guy interrupted.

"What do you mean by sense?" Alia's curiosity spiked.

"Well, Zadie told us not to play at Watkins Glen…"

"Disaster," the other man shook his head.

"So, we didn't. And look, life worked out fine for us."

Alia couldn't hide her surprise, "So your sister wife—

"His sister, my wife, though she wasn't at the time..."

"Tells you not to play one of the biggest festivals—

"That ended up a total disaster—"

"And now you listen to her?"

"More than listen," Tiny's lips turned upwards, "we made her our manager."

"Zadie, is your boss?" The two men nodded. "Huh."

"She also told us not to hire Tristan—

"But the fella's voice—

"And as if on cue, he turned out to be a pain in the arse."

"Huh." Alia's head started to bob. "Thank you for..."

"Before I forget, Zadie was wondering if you are going to the show tomorrow?"

"Yes - though I am not sure when."

Tiny replied, "I will let her know." The two disappear around the opposite corner from where they came. With a quick slip of her plastic key, the door opened to silence. Once inside, Alia bolted the door shut and pushed the desk chair up against it to add to the lock.

On the bed lay a scribbled note from Miranda. *Hold down the fort. I am camping with Dopamine Factory and fans. Interviewing the band manana. Sleep is overrated.* Alia shook her head.

She remembered Alister's comments about Miranda playing her part a little too well.

The note stayed on the counter as a morning reminder. Chair against the door, she put the safety bar down on the slider before brushing her teeth. Alia crawled into the king-sized bed closest to the bathroom. Within minutes her breathing deepened—her final deliberation of what a dopamine camp would look like faded into her dream.

The black Mercedes sped along I-84. The goal was to put as much distance as possible between the occupants and the investigators back in Hartford. The driver's eyes volleyed between the police detector app on the front screen and the bright spot where the headlights met the road. Except for the occasional tractor-trailer, the lone car appeared to be the only movement on the throughway.

In the back seat, Harlot Grace's head lay across Yarok Yarokov's lap. Her quiet coos, the only indication of the life within her body. Hopped up on several types of pain killers, she slept soundly, even as the glow from Yarok's cellphone brightened the back wall. His left hand rested on Harlot's shoulder while his thumb absentmindedly caressed her flesh.

On the screen, a dark knight flipped off a court jester. The jester then blew up into a thousand tiny pixels. "Pobeda," Yarok whispered the word victory in his native tongue. Within seconds another jester popped into the center of the screen. This time the character dressed in a bright pink unitard while rainbow long hair sprang around its head. Yarok rolled his eyes up to the ceiling. "When will you give me a competitive foe?" he typed into the crawler.

The jester danced around the screen then bent over to wiggle his rear end at Yarok. The words, *kiss my pink ass,* rolled across the crawler. Yarok responded *I thought we were having a dual of intelligence? You seem to be unarmed.* The jester turned to face forward. The animation brought a hand up to rub its chin. The eyes became uncharacteristically greater, peered out of the screen, and turned black.

*We have a bit of candy floss here, do we?* The jester responded. *Or do we have a notable coward, an infinite and endless liar, and the owner of not one good quality?* A wicked laugh came out of his phone.

Yarok muttered, "Idiot! If you are going to quote Shakespeare, include the whole passage." He thought for a moment, then typed, *Ugh, more of your conversation shall infect my brain (Coriolanus). You poisonous bunch-back toad! (Richard lll)* And that is how you quote William," he chuckled. He waited for a response with his fingers perched over the keyboard screen. "Come on, you loot, type something!"

Harlot stirred. She stretched her arms over her head, her hand missing the phone perched above. He smiled down at her as she pushed up to a sitting position. The car rocked before her.

"Hello, darling," Yarok said. "How are we feeling?"

Harlot forced a smile. "A little queasy," she answered. Yarok's smile faded. "But I am okay," she added. "I will be fine." Yarok nodded and went back to concentrate on his screen. The car swayed with the wind's movement outside. The little actions rocked what was left inside Harlot's stomach, inviting the bile to rise into her throat.

She shut her eyes and rested the top of her forehead against the cold glass as she tried to force the rising tides of vomit back into her stomach. The *Welcome to Pennsylvania* sign blurred by.

Alia awoke, showered, and dressed. She stood up straight and tall in the center of the room, eyes closed. Through her nose, she inhaled to the count of ten, waited for a beat, then exhaled to the same count. Her hands rested in a prayer position near her heart.

With one motion, her hands reached to stretch towards the ceiling. Her body folded at the hips. The blood flowed into her head. "Ten, nine, eight, seven…"

A knock stopped her count. A deep breath brought her body back to an upright standing position. Her arms floated up over her head as the knocking continued. The sound got louder as a woman's and a man's voice argued.

"Dagnabit," Alia blinked her eyes a few times. She opened the door to a smiling Zadie extending a paper cup.

"Brought you a coffee," Zadie said.

"Thanks, but I don't drink coffee…"

"Yeah, you seem like the tea type. Tiny will be back up in a minute with a cup." Alia nodded. "Mind if I come in?"

Zadie walked past her towards the couch. A small section cleared the piles of wrinkled clothes to fall into a new pile on the floor with a single swipe of the hand. "Sorry about the mess," Alia scooped up the clothing. With a hard toss, the mess moved to a table on the opposite side of the room. "Miranda basically uses this as a dumping point. I am surprised she hasn't been back today…"

Zadie didn't comment. Alia shoved the skirts, tops, panties, and blankets that fell off the table to the yellow counter of a standard hotel room kitchen. The stranglers got piled on a second fake wood table in the corner. "Are you going to the show today?" Zadie took a long sip of her coffee. Another knock on the door had Alia dash to answer.

"Tea," Tiny said as he extended another paper cup in her direction.

"Thank you," Alia replied to his back. Tiny disappeared around the corner. "He left."

"Yeah. The boys are getting ready to go to the show. I stopped by to see if you wanted a lift?"

"I can take the shuttle. Thanks." Alia took a sip of her tea. She cringed as her face twisted away from Zadie,

"Too much sugar?"

"Yes, I am sorry. This is so kind of you both to think of me."

Zadie waved her hand, "No worries. Full disclosure, I am hoping you would come on the bus to keep me company. The boys will do their set. After Tiny and Chords—

"Your brother?"

"Yeah, you met him last night, are going to do a guest set with - wait, I can't tell you that." She took a sip of her coffee. "Anyway, I will be hanging…"

"Why can't you tell me?" Zadie rolled her eyes. "Miranda. I understand. I won't see her probably—not the point?" Alia waited for a beat before adding, "I really don't want to inconvenience—

"You're not. After last night—

"Thank you, by the way."

"No worries. I figured you would like someone to hang around with. It's cool." Zadie rose to move towards the door.

"How much time do I have?"

"Could you be out by the bus in fifteen?"

"Will the imbecile be on the bus?"

Zadie snorted. "If you mean Tristan, no. He takes a limo over with his people." She used air quotes to emphasize the word people. "Tristan will do our set. He will promptly disappear until we play Denver in a few weeks." Alia stared at the carpet. "Althea, Tristan is nothing more than a bad hiring decision that will hopefully end sooner than later."

"Oh."

"That statement is not for publication."

"I'm not the writer, remember…"

"Yeah. So, you say. Will we see you on the bus?"

"Give me ten."

The door shut behind Zadie. Alia reached for a knee-length wrap-around skirt. She tied the floral garment over her yoga shorts, threw a long-sleeved denim shirt into her oversized purple bag. Alia took inventory of the rest of the contents. "Sunscreen, money, room key, notepad, pen, cellphone…" She moved her new laptop into one of the kitchen cabinets before placing the *Do Not Disturb* sign on the door.

She left via the breakfast buffet adding an orange, apple, and a granola bar to her bag along with a stainless-steel bottle filled with citrus-infused water, tipped upside-down for a leak check. After a quick preparation of plain green tea in a paper cup, she headed out the front door towards the busses.

Alia stopped short after rounding the corner of the building. The number of busses had multiplied overnight. "Damn." She walked in the general direction of the rear parking area.

The furthest bus away, purple and gold, had a stringy, long-haired human with skin covered in bright colors, combining bodily fluids with a small blonde while a well-endowed redhead looked on.

"Not the purple and gold," Alia said to no one. Although no memory of the coloring from last evening, she did recall the busses parked lacked the smiling skeleton or the covered wagon art of the two parked off to the side. Now the choice is reduced to blue and turquoise or dark purple and gray.

Both had open doors, yet no activity.

A ponytailed man emerged from the dark purple and gray bus. He stretched his arms over his head to bring his hands and gaze up to the sky. From there, his hands sank downward to touch the earth before his body bent back to a standing position. He did the same movements two more times.

He moved his head from side to side. His focus stopped where Alia stood. Both stared at each other until Tiny's deep voice broke the spell. "Althea, over here," he waved from blue and turquoise. It took a minute for Alia to realize he meant her.

Alia gave the other man a small smile. "Runaway with me." She turned to see an empty space next to the bus.

Zadie waited by the door. "Are you okay?"

"Fine," Alia replied. "Why do you ask?"

"You have a funny look."

"That is my face," Alia said, adding, "Thanks for the lift," as she climbed aboard.

Alia sat on the sofa in the front portion of the luxury vehicle. While she sat engulfed in the crisp air condition, Zadie stood outside in discussion with a gray-haired gentleman sporting a festival t-shirt. She pointed at the bus before hands gestured towards the stage. He returned her gestures with a nod, followed by a palms-up shrug.

The other buses from the hotel lot idled behind. Tiny, Chords, and Joe, without a nickname, exited the bus upon arrival with guitar cases, drumsticks, and Calzone briefcases in hand. They disappeared amongst the mayhem.

"Should I get out here?" Alia stood next to the driver.

He jumped in his seat. "I forgot you were still here," he said. "I'd wait a minute or two. I think Zadie is trying to find you one of our passes.

"Oh, I'll be fine," Alia grabbed her laminin out of the bag. "I still have this from yesterday." Without waiting, she stepped out the door. "Thanks for the ride," she added with a wave. The man with Zadie yelled something about credentials as Alia passed by the guard at the gate. Immediately the crowd carried her up the path towards the pavilion.

She walked down the aisle towards the front of the stage, counted eight rows back to find an empty end seat.

"Good morning, sunshine," Kevin, one of the security guards, greeted.

"Back at ya, moonbeam," Alia answered.

"You can move up a few more rows. We are doing fifth and back this morning."

"Nah, I like this spot. Have you seen my sister today?"

"Not this morning. Let me see, how do I put this nicely," Kevin tapped his index finger against his lips before smiling, "I did see her tripping balls at the late set. I would bet she won't be around until the third band today, at the earliest. She left with—" Alia held her hand up to stop him.

"The less you tell me, the better."

"Understood." He waited for a beat before walking over to greet another group with the same genuine smile. Alia reached into her bag to remove her journal and a pen. *Miranda is late for our connection, again. To keep up this façade, I am writing this stupid column again.* She scribbled in all caps *OFF THE RECORD.*

On stage, Tiny stood behind the first band's set up with Chords. He pointed at something out of view while Chords nodded. Alia checked the line-up for the day. Tiny and company were scheduled in the second spot. Blame The Dog, the first band, noodled guitars, pounded a few times on the drums, and made strange vocal chants into the microphones. Another man joined in, carrying a trumpet.

Alia made a quick note of the time and the crowd size. She slipped earplugs in as the trumpet player counted down from three. "If you ever… change your mind…" a soulful sound of four voices blended into one to silence the morning crowd. "Bring it on home to me… yeah… me… yeah… me…" A burst of a reggae beat melted into a sweet jam Alia would later describe as an innovative blend of genres.

Since it was her job to assimilate, her body jumped, head shook, and hips shifted with the rhythm. A small group of women had assembled next to the railing below the lead singer/trumpet player. In what disappeared like a long breath, the band exited the stage. Alia made notes to look up the lead singer's background and a few facts about the group.

A quick survey of the crowd, along with positions of the promoter's security, and a group of men in suits, had her hand moved swiftly across the page. In the corner, a primitive sketch of the positioning of suits. Alia moved across the aisle towards a couple of college-age guys. "Hey man, a great set."

"Yeah, they are pretty good," he handed her a joint, which she declined with a smile and a wave.

"Tell me about the band. Where are they from?" She glanced back at the suits. On the opposite side of the stage, one pointed up towards the lawn. She moved closer to the guys to get a clear sightline.

"They are from Colorado, I think." He elbowed the kid next to him, "Dude, where are *Blame The Dog* from?" The other kid shrugged. "Yeah, I think they are from Colorado."

"Yeah, that's what I thought." He handed the joint to Alia, who declined again. "I saw them last week in St. Louis. They did a free show in some park."

"No way, man," his friend answered. The two's comparison of setlists of the band's last few appearances faded into the background. Alia followed the man's finger up to the fence running between the concert grounds and the woods. A few people mingled up in the area, yet Alia observed nothing out of the ordinary. She turned back to the kid, who took a breather to inhale another hit.

"Thanks, dude," she gave a quick high-five before turning back to her seat. Alia noted that the suited guys had disappeared from the stage.

In the forest, two men in camouflage suits sat on the rocky earth. Music weaved through the loom of trees, the sound traveling up far beyond their perch. One listened to an earpiece while the other observed a substantial, iron pavilion in the distance.

"Brendan Curry's bus left late last night," the first man said.

"Did the tracker work?"

"I repeat, Curry's bus left." A slight head shake told his companion questions are not welcome. "The bus is heading west on I-80. Our people are following."

"Is our mission complete here?"

Again, the slight head shake. "Someone reported seeing the missing woman last night at one of the hotels."

"Alia Price?"

"If that is her real name. She was in a hallway during a party." He squinted his eyes to clear some of the pollen floating in the air.

"Frank added this is not confirmed because of our guy—"

"Slockered?"

"I believe he used compromised." Both men's laugh echoed. "I guess our boy plays his part a little too well. Anyway, he said to sit tight until it gets dark. Walk around the festival and see if we see anything out of place."

He leaned back on both elbows. The sleeves of his shirt rose to reveal a wristband for the festival. "We can hang here for a bit or head back to the base camp and change."

"Yeah, did you notice that camo at a hippie festival makes people nervous? I can't understand why." The man rose to help his partner up. "You realize we are literally searching for a thread."

"A thread of gold. If we can bring in this woman, or get to Curry even, to Yarok." He rubbed his hands together. "Brother, our lives will be set. I mean set!" The other man nodded. He trudged in the opposite direction of the sound.

"Hey, speaking of threads of gold, I thought I saw your brother's old tour bus last night."

"Jimmy's?" The man stood to squint in the direction of the pavilion. "Haven't heard from him in a while, though he gave up on the music thing and was living off his government pension. I'll be damned if he is here," he said, adding, "That wouldn't be good for either of us."

"I am not worried about your post-rock star vigilante brother," Deal leaned back on his elbows.

"My brother was the reason I went into the military in the first place and met you."

"He's also the reason you did time for drug trafficking and got kicked out." Fred pondered this idea.

"How was I supposed to know that customs would search a private jet. Who would have thought that?" Fred sat back down on the hard ground. "Did I mention I hate camping?"

"Camping is a small sacrifice for where we are going to be in a few months. The Army may not have trained us for a suit and tie job, but they did train us how to hunt."

The other man stood a few feet ahead. He moved his hand around his neck as if to loosen a tie. "Stepping stone," he reminded himself. "This is only a stepping stone."

Zadie sat off to the side of the stage. She followed Alia's gaze to the men in suits. From there, her focus followed up to the expansive lawn dotted in every color of the rainbow. Nothing out of the usual in her world, yet what did Alia see that she missed.

Around her, the stage crew moved amplifiers, drum sets and switch out microphones. They rolled out an Indian printed rug, adding the duct tape in the corners. Alia went back to scribbling in her notebook. On the front of the stage, Zadie caught her attention to wave her over.

Instead of putting the journal away, Alia moved her fingers to a dogeared page as she strolled towards Zadie. "Sorry I couldn't get one of our band all-access passes," Zadie's eyes went straight to the book.

Alia gave her shrug. "Look what I've been working on," she opened the journal to reveal a very primitive sketch of the stage. "Not bad for the first thing in the morning." Zadie exhaled at the sight. "Are you okay?"

"I'm fine, why?" came back a little too quick. Zadie caught Alia staring. "I merely had something pop into my head. But now it's gone," she gave a weak smile.

"All good. Sometimes when that happens to me, I remind myself that whatever it is, is not my circus."

Zadie erupted with laughter. "Yeah, Chords told me about your chants."

"I don't chant, I," Alia's face grew red. "Oh, forget it!"

"Forgotten. By the way, we are up next." Zadie brought her attention back to the setup. Three stools were added to the center of the stage. "Tiny and I will be hanging around for *Kung Fu*. I think they go on at six. Are you staying for the headliners?"

"I have to check my energy level. The body dictates…" Zadie nodded, yet her facial expression read confusion. "Thanks again for the lift."

"Yep. We will be by the pool." A ripping guitar sound brought Alia's attention back to the stage. Chords stood in front of one of the stools. Eyes closed as he fingered a fast Hendrix-Esque jam with one hand, the other waved thumbs up.

"He wants more monitor," Zadie explained.

Tiny's body overpowered the small drum kit of bass, snare, and high-hat. Joe stood next to the counter stool, bass in hand. Zadie followed his gaze to the two NFL size gym rats who had accompanied Tristan earlier.

"Shit," Zadie muttered. "I'll be right back." She sidestepped those who had migrated to the front before disappearing around the gate. In a matter of seconds, she reappeared in the back of Tiny. A quick kiss and a short conversation followed.

Alia almost missed Tristan. Journalists would describe the man as a quarterback in the middle of his linebackers. Alia wrote the phrase *in the crack of the ass Tristan developed into.* She snickered at the same time she filled in similar observations made about the first band. The more massive crowd grew silent with a strum on Chord's guitar.

"One, two, three," Tiny counted off a soft beat. Chords and Joe joined in to produce an almost jazz-like jam. The music was built upon itself. A sprinkle of a guitar riff. The boom of a bass note. Tiny's steady beat starting to develop into something more. The crowd began to nod and sway with the rhythm.

A body bounced off her left side. Zadie smiled. She leaned in to say something as another force slammed both her and Alia from the right. The smile vanished. The pungent smell of an unwashed body caught both off guard. Miranda stood, eyes half-closed, in the same clothes from the previous day. A sliver of drool escaped from her lips.

"Yo," she managed to mumble. Zadie said something then hurried away in the opposite direction. When Alia turned her attention back, Miranda had her filthy dirt-covered hands inside the purple bag. "I need food," she whined.

"What the hell!" With one move, Alia brought the bag out of her reach. "Listen, Miranda, I don't know a lot about you, yet I think you are playing your part way too well." Miranda folded her arms under her breasts, scrunched her nose, and stuck her tongue out.

"Screw you," her lips rose to a toothless grin. A high-pitched howl shifted the crowd's attention from the band to her. Without dropping her stare, she stated, "I need food." Alia handed the orange and apple from the breakfast buffet over. "Real food," Miranda pushed the offending fruit away. "And cash. You have the petty cash from our expense account. Alister cut off my freakin' funding."

"This is what I have for food. Take it or leave it." Miranda grabbed for both, "As far as Alister goes," she lowered her voice, "that is between you and our boss." Tristan's jarring screams cut through the tension. "Great. Now I missed his entrance."

"He walked on stage, sneered at the audience, and screamed into the microphone, exactly like the rest of the prima donna's. You missed nothing. Besides, you are not a real—" Alia took the apple from her hand to shove into her mouth. Tristan, dressed all in black with several red scarves draped around his neck, pranced, posed, and screamed his way around the stage.

Someone had moved the stools to the side.

When Tristan came closer to her area, Alia noted he wore black eyeliner. Last night might have been childishness and raging hormones, yet today his ego took center stage. *Des Nutz* started into their first hit, a remake of the old blues song Back Door Man, by the great Howlin' Wolf.

The noise level from the crowd tripled. Tristan strutted, sulked, and slithered around the stage. Joe, Chords, and Tiny faded, like the Wrangler jeans they wore, into a back-up band roll. Tristan jumped on top of the monitors to thrust and pose. The half-naked twenty-somethings below pierced the air with their high-pitched appreciation.

A flash behind the band caught Alia's attention. The men in suits were back. Today they had added additional people dressed head to toe in black. "F.B.I.," escaped her lips.

"This guy thinks he's Jagger," Kevin shouted. He stood in the walkway, arms crossed, shaking his head. "Except that dude is no Mick Jagger." He sniffed the air a couple times.

"There are definitely issues there," Alia answered. She grabbed his arm as he started to wander. "Hey, what are the Feds doing here?" Kevin followed her gaze to the side of the stage.

"How can you tell they are feds?" His face remained calm, yet the corner of his left eye twitched.

"Dressed in black. Arms folded. I watch a lot of television." Kevin laughed. "So, come on and tell me, what's the scoop?"

"Can't tell you much," he said. "They got here yesterday. And I am not in that pay grade if you get what I mean." He gave a smile and a finger wave before shuffling towards the stage. Alia took a casual glance over her shoulder to where the agents had gathered. The spot is now occupied by two longhairs dressed in similar clothing as Chords, Tiny, and Joe.

A slight turn in the audience's direction, recognition struck—the man from the turquoise and blue bus from this morning. Arms folded in front, he followed Tristan's antics without any expression. Tristan skipped to the opposite side. The stranger chatted with one of *Des Nutz*'s crew.

He stopped to look over the audience, pausing to smile directly at Alia. She fell back into her chair.

"Who's that?" Miranda's finger pointed up, passed the band.

"I don't know."

"Well, he sure knows you." Alia shrugged. "I have been around bands for a long time. His energy-focused here," she pointed to Alia's chest, "and knocked you over." Miranda took a giant bite of the apple then proceeded to chew with her mouth open.

"Energy." Alia laughed.

"Yeah, but it's gone now," Miranda said in between chomps. Both stared at the empty spot backstage. "He'll be back. By the way, what's the deal with you and the witch lady?"

"Witch lady?" Miranda pointed to Zadie now on the side of the stage. "I should ask you the same."

"Met in the lobby of that festival upstate. What was the name of the fest? Oh wait, that was before you were outed." She smacked her hand into her forehead.

"Outed?"

Miranda pretended like she didn't hear her. "The guitarist up there, he was talking me up—"

"That's her brother—"

"Explains a lot. Then that singer there asked if I wanted to party. We hung out—"

"And he tried to accost you?"

"More like the other way around." Miranda's laugh exploded. "Obviously didn't work out for either of us. I left the party. The end."

"So, we didn't write anything about the band, and there was nothing more to your query?"

"I can't remember if we wrote anything. Did we? And I can't remember if I filed a report. It was over a week ago."

"Huh."

"Yeah. Huh, back at you." A softer, soulful voice interrupted. Tristan leaned on the side of a speaker, to the front of his bandmates, yet still in full view for the audience. Zadie swayed next to the monitor board.

The voice belonged to her baby brother, Chords. With it, he brought the audience to silent awe.

*"She's a witch, oh so evil, she's like a queen yet more mean. She broke my heart, and I let her. Bring her back. I can't forget her."* Alia could hear those around her softly singing along. Chords dropped his head away from the microphone as he directed the song to an electrifying end.

The audience erupted in screams and applause.

Tristan bounced back to the front and center. "Let's hear it for my bandmates," he shouted. "Now, back to the rock and roll!"

Alia made a note to ask Chords about the witch song later. She also jotted down a few band dynamics observations.

"Thanks for the food," Miranda interrupted her thoughts. Alia had forgotten she was there, although the stench should have reminded her.

"Where can I contact you? And what do you grasp about my situation?" Miranda shrugged. Alia pursed her lips before adding, "And no offense, shower!"

"Hey, I got to play the part." The crowd split as she passed. Miranda's laugh rose above the music as if the wicked witch of the west flew above. A few even pinched their nose. Unfortunately, her scent lingered. Alia made a few quick notes. She held her phone covered by her bag as she typed, *She's out of control. We have friends here. Any advice?*

"I'm not drunk. I'm not high. This is real." She chanted barely loud enough for anyone to hear. Something was off. Her stomach had a bocce game going on inside as she volleyed her focus between the crowd and the stage. Kevin was nowhere in sight. No suits or feds, yet somewhere in that massive crowd—

Alia made the conscious choice to focus on Zadie. She stood backstage, pointing, and directing. The stools came back out in front. A stagehand replaced Tristan's microphone. He brought it to Zadie, who gave a thumb gesture towards the busses. Tiny and Chords stood off to the left, both with acoustic guitars in hand. They are joined by two others, although Alia couldn't see who, all backs and shoulders. One carried a third acoustic.

Kevin drifted back. "How's it going?" Alia started to answer at the same time he lifted his finger. "Get Jerry involved and keep me in the loop on his directive." He brought his attention back. "That was a fun set." He sniffed the air again.

"Not me. Miranda—"

"Yeah, I smelled the stench when I came by earlier. Say no more."

"They were interesting. We are staying at the same hotel. Most of the band is really cool."

"That will change to 100% in a minute." He wiggled his eyebrows. Zadie slipped into the seat next to her.

"What is that smell!" She waved her hand in front of her face. "Doesn't matter. I need to talk to Miranda." The notebook clutched in Alia's hand. "Or possibly I should talk to you. And before you start, I saw Miranda here, and Miranda is a hot mess who can't string a complete sentence together, never mind a paragraph. My sources tell me that she is never, how do I put this, coherent enough to comprehend where she is, never mind to review entertainment. You may want to check into that, by the way. My sources don't know who, but it is not her who writes the column. One theory is that perhaps someone feeds information to whoever writes it?"

"I don't know what to say." One of the suits was back on stage. This time he scanned the crowd with binoculars.

"I will make you a deal. You share yours, and I'll share mine." She took a swig off a water bottle before adding, "And mine is huge!" A flash took away her attention. The man in the suit lowered his binoculars. A smile sparked across his face as he disappeared behind the speakers.

A few guitar chords broke her concentration. Zadie wore a massive grin as she chin nodded towards the stage. "Pay attention."

Tiny and Chords sat up front, strumming on acoustic guitars. Joe had one butt cheek on the stool and one foot on the stage in balance. His bass rested against his chest. Alia didn't recognize the drummer, though he could have been any of the senior's son.

They strummed, noodled, and floated sound around the crowd. A few women made their way to the front of the stage, yet most sat and nodded. Another man, this one a bit shorter sporting a glittery purple t-shirt and jeans, entered from the side. He turned to strum a deep purple, almost matching, guitar, sending a wave of energy throughout the crowd.

The man faced forward to scan the audience. His attention stopped on Alia. He lifted his lips up into a grin and winked.

"So, what do you say?" Zadie broke the spell. "Do we have a deal?"

Alia extended her right hand. "I believe we do," she said. "My gut tells me, yes."

Zadie laughed as she took her hand to shake. "I have one of those too. Hence why I am here," she swept her hand in a circle, "versus there," she pointed to the stage.

"Full disclosure," Alia now shouted into her ear, "I will tell you as much as I am able. Some parts about me you don't want to have knowledge of."

"And I shall do the same, yet if I feel you are holding back to hold back…"

Alia brought their attention back to the performers. "Are Tiny and Chords doing a pop-up set with these guys?"

"Nice change of subject. Tiny, Chords, and Joe," Zadie waited for a beat, "oh heck, the puppy's out of the bag anyway. Now watch and see."

The entire band spun into a jazz type jam similar to the way *Des Nutz* started their set. Alia observed the crowd, who had migrated from sitting, to standing, now swaying. The half-naked females made their path back to the space in front of the mystery man. She couldn't see his eyes behind mirrored sunglasses, yet the gals climbed over each other, vying for his awareness.

A flash came from behind the drums. Tristan's gym rat stood at attention with arms folded. The flash, combined with a spotlight on his glasses, gave away his position.

"Is he supposed to be there?" Zadie followed Alia's finger.

"Oh shit." Zadie grabbed Kevin as he passed. Alia could only hear Kevin's "Ah-ha's" as Zadie yelled in his ear and pointed to the stage. Kevin said something into his two-way, he held up one finger. Another man appeared to escort Tristan's guy off the stage.

"Thank you," Zadie said as she shook Kevin's hand. He gave her a quick salute before shuffling down the walkway. "He's the best," she shouted in Alia's direction. She brought her attention back to the stage. Zadie glowed, her lips curved into a massive smile, she swayed in her seat. "When will these guys simply trust my gut."

Fred, the older of the two, stood in front of a mirror hung off the trunk of an old oak tree. The struggle to fit a wig over his balding head continued. His few gray hairs peeked out. He squirted gel on his natural hair to slick it back into a paste against his head. The wig slid around to rest with little showing. "It will be fine in the dark," his partner, Deal, barked from behind. "Every move doesn't have to be perfect."

"Or does it?" Fred positioned the wig a little more forward. The long hair tickled the end of his shoulder blades. He reached around to combine the strands back into a low hanging ponytail.

"All that work to tie it all back?"

"Says she likes rock stars with long hair. I doubt if one is wandering around in the crowd, he would be so recognizable."

"We are betting on that, no?" Both laughed.

Deal rubbed a little dirt into the festival shirt he bought earlier. He opted for a baseball cap instead of a wig.

As Fred struggled to put on a ripped tie-dye shirt, Deal let out a low laugh. "We look like a couple of those light rock stars," he said. "I bet if we weren't working, we could bag as many of the Loose Lucy's as they do."

"You would need to get a little hairier, my friend." Fred tossed his ponytail side to side. "The ladies do love the rock stars."

"You mean the light ones," Deal placed a small taser, some chewing gum, a couple twenty's, and an I.D. card in a side pack. He rifled through the front pocket, "I can't find my-" to pull out a laminate that resembled an all-access pass, "ah, here it is."

Fred's moves mirrored. As the shadows became less visible, he checked his watch. "It's time." He did one more inventory before he began to descend the hill. "We bring both back here, correct?" Deal nodded.

"Preferably alive."

"Gotcha."

An assemble of young women, all dressed in white mid-drift tanks and cut off jean shorts, pushed their way to the front of the stage. The half-naked forced to the side. Together the barefooted congregation moved in unison with the mystery man. They lifted their arms higher at the same moment his guitar screamed louder.

The mystery man smiled down at the ladies.

"Where did you get the dancers?"

"Imported, you mean," Zadie said. "They follow him around."

"Why?"

"Well, he is gorgeous—"

"That is not a reason."

Zadie held up one finger. "And he used to play with *Petrified Rock*."

"*Petrified Rock*? Wait! That's not—"

"In the flesh." Zadie smiles ran across her face.

"But I thought he walked away from music. Something about the lifestyle not being conducive to his sanity, yet I had heard it was a drug bust?" asked Alia.

"Conducive to sanity sounds like him. Drug bust sounds more like his idiot brother."

"How?"

Zadie explained, "He's a childhood friend of Tiny and Chords. We all grew up in the same neighborhood. Jimmy was back in town—"

"Jimmy?"

"That's his real name. He went by Win Scout on stage for a while."

"Huh."

"Jimmy was visiting his parents, and he bumped into Chords and Dandy, Chord's wife. They started talking and," she gestured towards the stage, "Wha-la!"

"Wow."

"Yep. We decided to debut the new band here." Alia stared at the stage.

"New band?"

"Yep, new band. Too bad Miranda isn't sober enough or here to get the scoop." Zadie's smug smile said it all. That part played bocce in her gut as Alia rubbed her unsettled stomach.

"You just saw the last performance of *Des Nutz.*"

"Seriously?" Alia absentmindedly opened her journal and made a note. Zadie did not move.

"I swear on my mother-in-law's grave."

"Tiny's mother is dead?"

"Not exactly, but the announcement will be made officially tomorrow when they do the noon acoustic set." Zadie's smug smile radiated.

"They are the T.B.A." Alia jotted this next to the last performance note.

"Exactly."

"What about the rest of the tour?"

Zadie leaned in closer. "Most of our venues wanted the new band and the few who canceled, well let's say they were pains in the ass and leave it at that."

"Tristan?"

"Relieved of his duties."

"Was he told before the show?"

"Huh. You ask a lot of questions."

"I am a curious human."

"He found out right before the show and didn't handle the news very well."

"I noticed." The area around row eight began to thicken with bodies. People climbed over seats to get a closer look at the stage.

Kevin took note of new arrivals as he zipped up and down the walkway.

Alia turned her full attention to Zadie. "Are you trying to give me a scoop?"

The other woman slapped her knee and pointed to Alia's notes. "I knew it! I told Chords last night that Miranda can't formulate a sentence, never mind write a paragraph." Alia cringed at the accurate description. "Besides, I noticed that articles appeared from concerts she never attended."

"Please don't tell anyone. Not even Tiny—"

"Oh, my dear, Tiny figured this all-out last night. He may be big, but he is not dumb." Zadie leaned in a bit closer. "So, why the illusion?"

"Not here." Alia did a quick crowd scan. "I'm done after these guys. Can we talk back at the hotel?"

"I thought you were staying for *Kung Fu?*"

"Crap. Yes, I am staying for their set. I will head back as soon as they are done."

"Poolside rehearsal at seven, with the full band. Toes crossed that the prima donna and his goons are long gone."

One of Tristan's gym rats stood side stage. He turned towards each area of the audience. His head nodded up and down. His angle lingered a beat longer when he lined up with the two women. Alia said, "I wouldn't count on it."

Alister made his way up to two flights of stairs. For a man of his age, who smoked and drank like he was still in the early Watergate days, he moved with grace. Light radiated from the door to the top floor. His boss would be waiting.

He took a smoke out of his breast pocket, while his other hand searched his pants pockets for a light. He strolled past several empty desks, straight into the conference room on the opposite end of the stairwell. He didn't recognize two men seated along one side of the sizable, oval, oak table. He tucked the cigarette away back behind his left ear.

"Gentlemen," Alister greeted the group with a head nod. The two strangers extended hands, which he gave each a firm handshake in return. His boss, Morris Webb, sat at the table's head, fingers rested in a pyramid shape in front. Alister took the seat on Morris' right. The two strangers moved to position themselves as one, on the opposite side.

"Alister, I would like you to meet Attorney General Curry and Captain Louis Pilsner of the Connecticut State Police." Alister again recognized each with a nod. "Might as well get right into it - Alister, we have a problem."

"We do?" Alister noted both men nodded.

"Yes." A.G. Curry jumped in, "my boy is missing."

"Pardon me?" Alister said. The unlit cigarette rolled in between his fingers.

"My boy, Brendan, has gone missing." Attorney Curry waited for some type of response, then continued, "He was out on tour," Alister noted air quotes the father put around the word tour, "and now they can't find him."

"Who is they, sir?" Alister asked.

"His band, *The damn Flying Monkeys,*" Morris interrupted. "It seems that A.G. Curry here hired his own security. The band left Pennsylvania yesterday for a performance in Ohio. The equipment trailer, along with one bus, arrived. The other bus, with Brendan and that crazy bass player, are missing."

"It hasn't been 24 hours—" Alister noted.

"I can tell time! My wife called him and nothing. He's not answering. Security isn't answering. Nobody. I'm in the middle of—" Attorney Curry ran both hands through the little hair left on his head.

"Sir, we are aware of your situation—" Morris Webb responded.

The man ran his hands over his face. "I am told by Morris here that you have someone on-site in PA. They might have seen something. Someone. Anything. Can you please help?" Curry's gaze bounced between the two men.

Morris scrutinized Alister, who continued to watch the A.G. The state cop didn't utter a sound. Allister wondered if his function went beyond the driver. "Could he have left with a woman? He is in a band after all," Alister said.

"Possible yet not probable." Curry gave the cop a glance, the continued. "Because of my situation, we, meaning my wife and I, fully funded Brendan's tour. We paid for the busses, vented the drivers, and hired a security team. My colleague here made the recommendations for most. The deal was that if he does this our way when the case is closed, I would retire and give him a normal life."

"He agreed to that?" Alister asked. Curry nodded in response. Alister turned his attention to the state cop. "And you vetted all participants?" He received a confirmation nod back, then continued, "What about his bandmates?"

"All childhood friends except the bassist," Curry answered. "And before you get all suspicious about Marvin. He and Brendan were college roommates. My son taught the boy how to play bass so he could be part of the group."

"The roommate checked out," the cop interjected.

"Have you received any more threats, sir?" Webb asked.

"No. The trial starts next week. My office has all the evidence needed to convict Salvi of drug manufacturing and distribution, thanks to your team. We got the others on tax evasion charges too. The jury is under the sequester. It would be a bonus if Salvi would turn in state evidence, yet I don't see that happening at this time. That boy is keeping his mouth shut tight. There isn't much more that I can do." Curry shrugged.

"I thought Salvi already admitted to masterminding the lab?" Webb jumped in.

"He did at first, but lately," A.G. Curry glanced at his escort who waved his hand in the air. "Salvi doesn't matter. What about my boy?"

"I can have someone ask around," Alister said. He stood to leave at the same time the other two rose. Morris remained seated. "I will send an update as soon as I have something." The two men shook hands then disappeared from view down the hall.

Alister reached behind his ear to retrieve a smoke. "You were quiet," he said before lighting up. Morris nodded.

"What's coming in from the festival?" Webb asked.

"Miranda Stone is officially out of contact. I have an itch that she is playing the part a little too well— " Alister lit the cigarette and took a long inhale.

"And the other?" Webb moved around the few papers that lay on the table.

"Alia sends dailies. She had said that Curry had a guard, someone named Wally when they were on site. We obtained a background on Walter H Whiting, a former Seal. I instructed her to back off and see what else she could find. If you remember, Alia manages to find out secrets."

"Have you heard from her today?" Morris asked. Alister responded with a quick head shake. "Bring her up to speed and get a status on Stone. If we need to pull her, let's do it sooner than later. I also want the tracker on the Curry kid's phone. Conceivably we can get a location."

Alister moved to leave. He paused in the doorway. "Sir, don't you think the state police?" Morris's hand raised to halt the conversation. "You will hear from me soon." Alister left the other half of his cigarette burning in the ashtray.

Alia made her way up the steep incline towards the lodge and second stage. Her legs pulsed as she pushed forward. Her stomach joined the agony with a release of loud growls. Two longhairs smiled and said, "Good one," as they passed. The smell of sesame noodles motivated her up the last twenty-five feet.

She waited in line for over a half-hour. Behind the makeshift tent, the group of five struggled to keep up with the crowd's demand. While one boiled the noodles, two other chopped vegetables, a fourth commanded the metal frying pans floated above the blue flames. The fifth stood off to the side. The choppers overfilled containers to hand to the waiting mass.

This was almost the opposite of the fancy coffee shop Alia liked to visit. One worked while four stood around to watch. This line moved. At last, she held an overflowing container of broccoli, something green, and sesame noodles. The sauce dripped off the side onto her hands.

Alia found an empty chair along the lazy river, a man-made pool that stretched out as a fake current propelled people on blow-up rafts around its shape. She shoved the noodles into her mouth fast enough to barely feel the slight burn of cayenne pepper as the flakes descended into her stomach. She picked at a few broccoli pieces before closing the lid on a still full container of food.

The smaller stage played to the hillside, where people dotted the landscape like the lawn area below. Halfway up, Miranda sat on a blow-up plastic purple couch. Her gold bikini flickered in the sunshine. Next to her sat a guy with his arm around her. As Alia got closer, she noted he wore a dirty festival t-shirt. Yet, the size of his biceps indicated he must lift something.

He was a clone of Miranda's last.

Alia forced a smile as she handed over her leftovers to Miranda. "Eat this," she instructed.

Miranda turned to his companion, "See what I mean? I said to the universe, give me food, and wha-la, food!" Her new friend nodded. His face hid behind sunglasses and a baseball cap. When he turned, Alia noted the neat ponytail along with dark hair.

"Who's your friend?" the stranger asked.

"Oh, Alia—" Bits of food flew from her mouth as she answered.

"Althea," Alia corrected.

"Althea," Miranda rolled the name on her tongue, "This is my new friend, the lead singer of *Twisted Wristband*."

"Does your new friend have a name?" Alia (Althea) asked.

"Fred," the stranger extended his hand. Alia (Althea) took his hand to shake as he dragged one finger around the inside of her palm. She did a quick release before wiping both hands down her skirt.

"Miranda, we need to talk." Alia (Althea) instructed. In between bites, Miranda produced incoherent words while bits of food flew in the air. "Seriously."

"Hey, man, be cool," Fred said. "Why don't you hang with us. My buddy went to get a couple beers…"

Alia's stomach flopped. "Thanks, but no. Miranda, why don't you—"

"I can meet you at the big stage for the headliner. Say 6-ish?" Miranda swallowed. Alia started to say no. Miranda turned her attention back to Joe as she pressed a forkful of dripping noodles into his mouth.

Alia recoiled. Without a word, she walked down the hill. The band on stage started a downbeat funky jam as the flock engulfed her to the center of the crowd. She became surrounded by moving bodies.

She turned back up the hill. Miranda sat alone on the couch. She skimmed the area to find Fred in conversation with another guy. He pointed towards the crowd then back at Miranda. Her stomach flipped.

The band morphed into the Buddy Holly song, *Not Fade Away*. Alia bopped and weaved more into the crowd cover. The louder the band jammed; the more uninhabited people danced. Hands, arms, hair, torsos swerved around her, back up the hill. Fred's gestures had become more frantic. His arms flew as his fingers pointed in her direction. The other man threw his hands up in the air.

He pointed back at Miranda. Time had expired.

Flip and flop.

Miranda stumbled along the path. Fred led the way, and his friend followed close behind. They passed signs warning they were about to leave the festival grounds.

"I'm not sure we should—"

"Don't worry, baby," Fred said as he slid his body next to hers. "The whole band is camping up the hill. It will be a party."

"Okay." Miranda's head spun. Her feet tripped on the exposed roots along the trail. The lights from the concert faded. *Alia would come to look for me.* Fred had her leave a message to meet in the back of the lawn. *That wasn't the spot,* she thought. Her head ducked under branches as her brain tried to remember the path back.

Behind her footsteps, crackled.

"Hey Fred," Miranda stopped under a massive pine tree. "I need to…" She heard a crack. Her legs buckled and fell.

"What the hell?" Fred's voice carried.

"We need to go get the other one. This one is not the prize." Deal fiddled with something inside his pack. "She can stay here, and we can pick her up on the way back." He flicked the outside of a plastic syringe, held the needle to the light, and inserted it into Miranda's arm. As he pressed against the top, the cloudy liquid disappeared into her body.

He left the needle hanging out of her flesh. "New batch," Deal smiled. "Hitting the market soon."

"That's not cool—" Fred pointed at the hanging syringe.

"No, Fred. What is not cool is you letting the other one go. You should have made her stay and wait. We could be long gone by now." Fred turned away from Miranda's slumped over body. He reached to take the needle out of her arm. Deal slapped his hand away. Fred stood full height and clenched his fists.

"How? How could I have made her stay?"

Deal moved to an inch from Fred's face. "Don't ask me. I wasn't there. But if we had her too, I absolutely know we would be miles away from here, wealthy men, instead of dealing with this bullshit—"

"This bullshit? Really!" Fred paced in a circle around the tree trunk. He turned to see Deal working another syringe. "Be aware of what you put in there. They want this one alive," Fred's voice calm, yet the muscles in his neck bulged.

"Ready," Deal focused his attention on Fred. "Stop staring at her. See the dollar signs instead of the flesh."

The two descended back down the hill, to disappear back into the crowd.

*Kung Fu* brought the audience into a synchronized jumping session as they banged the final notes of Stevie Wonders *Superstitious.* Kevin started to clear the rows. "Sorry, man, people paid for that seat," he said as he guided folks up the walkway. "Come back tomorrow around noon, and you can sit upfront."

Alia walked sideways until she hit the wall, closets to the bathrooms. She wandered down to the last open stall. Muffled sobbing sounds floated under from the next one over.

"Are you okay?" Alia asked as she finished her business and flushed. The sobbing turned to quick breaths. "Hey, open the door. I can help…" A mascara covered face of a teenage girl greeted her. Alia handed the woman balled up the toilet paper, which she accepted with a nod. "Why are you crying?"

The woman didn't say anything. She stretched her neck around Alia to look at the empty gray hallway. "Hey, I asked you a question. Are you okay?" Alia asked.

"Yes, and sort of," the teenager's voice came out barely above a whisper. Alia offered her a granola bar, which she waved off. "I'm not hungry. I left my car on the side of route 81."

"Okay..."

"It was on fire," she started sniffling again.

"Your car is on fire?" Alia's eyes went wide open.

"Was. This guy stopped and put it out. He said he was coming to the festival and since I already had a ticket..." the teenager shrugged.

"You can go to the festival with him," Alia finished the sentence.

"I wasn't thinking. Well, I was, kind of thinking, get to the show, and life would be okay. Except now this is getting—"

"Weird?"

The teenager shook her head. "Creepy. The dude is old and clingy, and I should have totally stayed with the car and been, you know..."

"Responsible?" Alia said at the same time she glanced down at her watch. Miranda should be at the meeting location. "Where is he now?"

"He was on the lawn. He tried to, you know, so I ran in here. I don't know…" The teenager's eyes opened wide. Again, she extended her neck to look beyond Alia.

Alia squeezed her eyes shut. "Follow me—"

"What if he—" she pushed off the ground.

"I said, follow me." Alia took the girl by the hand over to the handicap entrance. They waited for Miranda well into *Saturn*'s set. The electronic overdubs started a different type of bocci game in Alia's stomach. Her new friend jumped at every passerby. "I don't drink. I don't do drugs. This is reality," Alia murmured while speedo wearing, glitter-covered men and their topless, nipple painted women glided pass. A human-sized marijuana plant started to fill their space with smoke.

There was still no sign of Miranda.

The music pounded into Alia's head. "Come on," she tightened her grip on the girl's hand to lead away from the noise, towards the shuttles. "We can call the state police about your car. Is there someone you can call for a lift?"

"I can Uber to the train station downtown," the teenager said. "I'll some need cash. I left my backpack on the hill."

"Of course, you did." Alia walked over to the police trailer. She explained the situation to a young woman in uniform who took notes and nodded. "This officer is going to help you." Alia shook the young girl's hand. The clock on the wall read 7:15.

Alia sprinted back to the handicap entrance. No Miranda. The nausea in her stomach started to rise. With a quick skim of the audience, Alia shrugged. She turned to run to the shuttle drop off and caught the last one leaving.

The driver said, "I'm not a hotel shuttle, but I can take you there." Alia pulled a five dollar bill out of her bag and placed it in his tip jar. The driver nodded a thanks.

Zadie greeted her with, "I thought you were a no show."

"Yeah, well, I had a situation with a bathroom crier, and then I tried to find Miranda before I left. She was really weird this afternoon."

"Miranda, weird? Really?" Zadie said. Alia returned with an overexaggerated eye roll.

"Look, Miranda may not be the most responsible person, but she still is that." Alia responded. Zadie tilted her head to one side. "Human. She still is human," Alia practically yelled.

She jingled her car keys. "What's with the keys?" Zadie chin nodded towards Alia's hand.

"I need a cookie. The shuttle passed a bakery flooded with lights. Want to take a ride?"

Zadie's smile vanished. "You are not going to kill me and dump my body, are you?"

"Nope," Alia shook her head, "I simply need a cookie."

The bakery had a small café in the back. Alia spent a good ten minutes looking at each pastry in the case. She stared and studied the rocky road cannoli, drooled a little over the tollhouse cookie pie. Around the bend, the tiramisu, mint chocolate torte, and banana crème pie all flirted in the near proximity.

She took a seat at the glass-topped iron table next to Zadie and sighed. "I want them all." Zadie laughed. Alia ordered a warm salted caramel chocolate chip cookie along with a decaf chai tea. Zadie declined anything. Alia added, "She will have the chocolate whoopie pie and a decaf coffee."

"I can't have a whoopie pie. I will do the crème one," Zadie pointed towards the case.

"No, whoopie pie?" Alia raised an eyebrow.

"Too many cases of whoopie pie regret."

Alia nodded. She confirmed the changed order. The cookie arrived with a slab of vanilla ice cream on the side. Alia forked a mouthful, sat back, and closed her eyes.

"You really like your sweets," Zadie said. Alia held up one finger and shushed her. The pie sat untouched.

After a long moment, Alia opened her eyes. "I don't drink. I don't smoke…"

"I get it. But isn't sugar?"

Again, with one finger raised, Alia repeated, "I don't drink. I don't smoke…" This time, she added a huge grin. "Yet, I did have a giant pot plant stand next to me before I left."

"Watching you eat that thing that I believe." Zadie adjusted herself in her chair, took a long sip of coffee. "So, what is your story?"

"My story?" Alia swallowed another mouthful. "I am a sugar addict. You?"

"I am a road manager for my husband's band. Now that we've established the obvious…"

Alia signaled for the check and handed the waitress a credit card upon arrival. She pointed to the unfinished desserts. "Can I get a couple to-go containers, please?"

Zadie observed when the slip came back, she signed Miranda's name and left a hefty tip. Inside the car, she noted, "That Miranda is an excellent tipper."

"Yep- she is the best." Alia parked the car near the bus area. She opened the to-go container and started in on the remainders of her dessert. "We should talk."

"I agree. Let me start with Miranda isn't a reporter," Zadie stated. When Alia shook her head no, she added, "you are?" Zadie raised an eyebrow.

"Not really," Alia said. She shoveled another bite of caramel sauce into her mouth.

"If you are not a reporter, then what are you? I ask because I need someone to break the news about the new band that I can trust to not twist the story." Zadie crossed her arms over her stomach.

"I understand. I may be able to help you there," Alia answered in between bites.

Zadie blew out a breath. "I will ask again, what is your story?"

The empty cardboard container didn't even have a few crumbs to lick. Alia let out a big sigh. As if she didn't hear Zadie, Alia continued, "I can get a freelance piece into one of the small mags. Based on the significance of this announcement, it should have legs from there."

"You are avoiding my question." Zadie leaned against the passenger door; one hand rested on the door handle. Her face void of expression.

"My life is complicated. I can tell you that I am here looking for someone—" Alia started to explain.

"Old boyfriend, jilted lover, who?"

"I wish my presence was that simple. I am not sure." Alia barely got the words out as Zadie let out a howl.

"Not sure," Zadie practically shouted. "How can you not be sure who you are looking for?"

"That is part of my problem. I am kind of hiding out at a rock festival." Alia let go of a nervous laugh. "I am not joking. But I really can help you get the word out about your new band. I need to drop off some stuff in my room. I'll meet you at the lounges in ten?"

Zadie looked directly at Alia, who met her eye. Neither woman wavered. With trepidation, Zadie answered, "Okay, but don't be late."

Alia noticed the *Do Not Disturb* sign was missing from her door handle. The hallway appeared empty in both directions as she slipped her plastic key into the pad. The door buzzed open. Nothing seemed out of place.

The bed was made. Fresh towels stacked high in the bath. The garbage, dirty towels, and takeout containers were all gone. She pulled her laptop out of the kitchen cabinet. A whoosh of air escaped from her mouth. Immediately she ran around the room, opening closet doors, peeking under the bed, then pulling back the long curtains. The entrance to the slider's security bar was still lodged in place.

She let out a second breath. At the same time, her fingers moved rapidly over her cellphone keyboard. She waited for Alister's response. The phone buzzed on que.

"We have a problem," both said at once, followed by "you first."

Alia broke the silence. "Miranda Stone."

"What about her?"

"She is incompetent, inconsiderate, or playing her role way too well. I am not sure of which, yet I am aware of the fact that she failed to check in this evening," Alia said.

"When is the last time you saw her?" In the background, Alister took notes. The clicking sound of a typewriter rapped in the background.

"Today, mid-afternoon. Stone was sitting at the upper stage with some guy from *Twisted Wristband,*" Alia responded.

"What the hell is *Twisted Wristband*?" Alister barked back.

"A band."

"Did you check to see when they are on the bill?"

Alia mouthed, "duh," as she opened the program on the table. "Crap!"

"Now what?" Alister said.

"There isn't a band called *Twisted Wristband* playing." She gave Alister a brief description of the person last seen with Miranda, adding, "He had a friend. Same build, no hair."

"Got it. My problem is a bit bigger. Brendan Curry is missing." Alister gave pause to allow the thought to sink in.

"What do you mean by missing?" Alia pulled the journal notebook from her purple bag and began to write.

"One of his buses and an equipment trailer made it to the festival in Ohio, the other is—"

"Missing—" Alia wrote *one plus trailer in Ohio* on a blank sheet of paper towards the back. She dog-eared the page then, with care, ripped the triangle off.

"The missing bus's passengers include Brendan and the kid playing bass on it," Alister read.

"Marv?" Alia added *Marv missing, too,* to her list.

"How do you know, Marvin? Where is his last name?" The sound of moving paper filled her speaker.

"His last name doesn't matter. I met Marvelous, as he told me his name, backstage today during the Flying Monkey's set. Strange dude, yet I think he is harmless," and clueless, she thought.

"Marvin doesn't matter. Curry and his bus are missing," stated Alister. "The Curry kid is our top priority."

"Does the second bus have a trailer, too?" Alia asked. More paper rustling came over the phone.

"Yes. Though it doesn't say here what was in it."

"What about the muscle?"

"Missing. I need you to travel the route to Buckeye Music Center yesterday."

She wrote *muscle missing* and then circled it three times. "I will fire up the old-time machine…" Alia gave a mock salute towards the phone.

"Alia, you are not humorous, and this is significant. The same people who would want Brandan also want you," reminded Alister.

"Huh. Maybe this would be a great time to have, say, a gun or some sort of weapon on me." Alia waited for some sort of response.

Alister ignored her comment. "You need to be discreet with how you get to Ohio."

"I can't fly? Or drive Miranda's car?" Alia stood to pace the room.

"Flying is a definite no, and if possible, leave the car. They probably have seen Miranda's car. Wait a minute, could you catch a train?"

Alia blow out a hard breath. "Alister, how is catching a train getting there yesterday?"

Alister spoke slow and deliberate. "We cannot bring attention to you or to the situation. I have a team arriving at your current location first thing in the morning."

"What about the ones that are here now. Could any of them help?" Alia thought back to those hanging back stage in full black clothing that sported the agency logo. Ticking noises from the phone speaker hung in the room. One leg bounced by her side as she waited on Alister. "Undercover, huh! You do understand that, Alister, the Feds have been visible all day. I asked one of the security guys about them, and all I got was something about them being above his pay grade."

"Are you certain they are government employees?" inquired Alister.

"All in black. F.B.I. in white letters on their shirts. The ones I couldn't identify were the black suit guys. They seem to have all access and have been here since yesterday."

"Huh, I think that would be important for me to be aware of." More paper movement. "Alia, at least one member of Yarokov's organization is on the premises and spotted by another undercover agent—"

"Um, Alister, not to be disrespectful, don't you think that we could have covered this better if we knew the others on our team?" Silence followed.

"Under the circumstances, we thought we could get more done in pairs. Alia, look up the train or bus schedule. Uber to the station and get out of town, tomorrow at the latest."

Alia gave a mock salute before she disconnected. She found the next train to be on was a 9:30 train to Pittsburgh. The clock on the wall read 8:45. The train wasn't happening tonight.

Outside her slider, the twangs of guitar strings being tuned caught her attention. "Crap. Zadie." Alia grabbed her notebook to follow the echo.

Four men sat to face each other inside a black Mercedes SUV while an over dented gray Chevy Malibu idled next to one of the shuttle bus stops. From their view, too many blurry-eyed concert goers waited in the dirt-covered lot, most almost half asleep.

Fred and Deal staked out the area soon after the headliner took the stage. They had split up to cover the entire pavilion area yet failed to locate Alia. The two men who faced them spoke in soft voices. Fred caught every other word. Even with his limited language skills, the conversation did not go in their favor.

"We need to get out of here," his voice barely audible.

Deal gave a slight nod. "Not until we get paid."

"I am not sure that is an option." Both men smiled in the direction of the voice. Deal's hand went to his side. His fingers closed around the cold metal object hidden from view.

"That wouldn't be a wise choice." One of the men nodded towards Deal's belt. His grip tightened.

"Look, all we want to do is get paid, at least for the Stone woman." Deal's voice did not waver.

"The Stone woman is not the primary target. Plus, she would have been more useful if she was alive and could tell us something," the man on the left said. "We need Price."

"Price just disappeared."

"No one disappears." Both men let out a hearty chuckle. "They are always somewhere." The man on the right pointed at Fred while he whispered in the other's ear. Fred moved his hand to the door handle. A loud click echoed.

The man reached behind Fred's shoulder for the bottle of Jack Daniels on the bar. "Clean yourselves up and take advantage of these," he threw two laminated passes on their laps. "She is somewhere. Our intelligence suggests Price is still at the festival. Make certain to find and bring her to us alive. We will be in there." The two men followed his finger across the parking lot to a faded grey tour bus.

"Do what you have to do," the other said. A loud click was followed by the door on Fred's side, swinging open. "Until tomorrow."

The divider between the occupants and the driver's area lowered as the two exited. Yarok Yarokov's accented voice broke the silence. "They are incompetent." His hand rested on his driver's upper thigh.

"We give them one more chance, tomorrow, and then…" came from the backseat.

Yarok gave a slight nod. "What about the next batch? Are we ready?"

"The new batch of Harlot will be on the street at the fish festival."

"Fish festival? What the hell is a fish festival?" barked Yarok.

"Some electronic music festival in Florida next week. The new lab is producing samples as we speak."

"Watch those idiots," Yarok instructed. He pressed the button to unlock the back doors. "Eliminate all waste." The two men nodded then exited the car. Yarok brought his attention to his driver.

"I can't believe you named this batch after my last cover," the women murmured.

"Oh, my Tianna, I did this as a tribute to you." She glowed as his hand moved further up into her lady area. "Are you feeling better?"

"Yes," she lied. "The pain is almost gone."

"Tianna, I can remove him even in jail."

"Oh Yarok, Salvi is a fool. Let him rot. That will bring him and his family more shame."

Yarok jerked his hand to her face. He brushed his knuckles against her soft cheek. His lucky charm sat still.

Alia slid into the lounge chair next to Zadie at the same time the boys started to jam. Off to the side of the pool, a group of twenty-somethings in nothing left to the imagination bathing suits stop their revelries to listen. The group moved as one closer as the band solidified their sound.

"Well, that's a good sign—" Zadie chin nodded towards the group.

"What?" Alia looked across the pool.

Zadie chin nodded again in the bikini-clad females' direction. "Tour sluts are taking notice."

"That doesn't bother you?"

Zadie let out a loud snort. "Hell, no. These guys are beyond the Barbies. Besides, I am always here."

"You on tour definitely has its advantages," said Alia.

"Damn straight." The crowd grew as others migrated towards the sweet guitar melodies. Pretty soon, the courtyard filled up with swaying bodies. The circle of women around the band started to close. Tiny stood on the picnic table. He waved both hands above his head in their direction. "There's my sign."

Zadie made her way through the bodies. She tapped, gently pushed, and finally shoved people out of her way. She divided the mass from the lounge chairs to the band. Tiny lowered his mouth to hers. She gave a glaring stare to one of the well-endowed topless dancers, turned away towards the door. All four men followed her through to the hotel on the other side.

A couple of the women in bikinis tried to follow. Zadie smiled and wiggled her finger. They hung their heads and moved back in the other direction. Some filtered out to move towards the busses. Alia couldn't see how many now docked behind the hotel.

A cold ripple passed up her back. She spun around. No familiarities. "I'm not drunk. I'm not high," she began to chant. Another jolt prompted movement. Alia started towards the closest door, turned in the opposite direction, and entered the hotel through the lobby.

Behind the tour busses, a Mercedes SUV idled. The car's occupants scan the crowd with night vision goggles.

People milled about. Some sat in the breakfast area talking, others argued with the front desk. None of the faces brought recognition. She slipped out of sight, back to her room. Once inside, she checked all closets, under the bed, behind the curtains, the slider's bar. She moved the desk chair against the door.

The light on the desk phone violently blinked. Alia took a paper towel sprayed with Lysol to the handle. She pressed the speaker to play. Alister's voice filled the space.

"Alia, we have a problem," he hesitated a beat. "You need to contact me as soon as possible. That is A.S.A.P., we have a problem." He repeated the same sentence two more times. Alia pressed seven to erase. She dug her phone out of the purple bag. Alister answered on the first ring.

"Are you alone?"

Instinctively, she scanned around the room before answering, "Yes."

"Good. You need to leave now."

Alia asked, "Now? Can you tell me why?"

"Why? Are you getting involved in that scene too?" The chill visited again. This time it rested on her neck for a beat.

"Not at all, Alister. As always, I am doing what I am trained to do. My job." The statement came out void of any emotion. "You, of all people, should recognize that by now."

He ignored the jab and continued, "Good. That is what I need to hear. I want you to follow up on the Curry situation. Get to that festival in Ohio. Drive if you are able."

"Alister, I have the skills to drive. I am certified—"

"That is not what I mean. Procure a vehicle and hit the road." Alister tapped on something against his desk. "I suggest you wait until daybreak to be able to see more…"

"Alister, make up your mind. Do you want me to leave now or in the morning?" Her query was met with silence. "Alister, what is going on?"

"Your presence at the festival," his voice cut out, "terribly compromised."

Alia wanted answers. "In what way?"

"Anyone ever told you that you ask a lot of questions?" Her laugh caught him off guard.

"Seriously, Alister…"

"We need to focus on finding the Curry kid. You will need a good night's sleep. I am waiting for news from my contacts and will have more information for you in the morning," he instructed.

The phone clicked silent. "Typical Alister tells me everything yet nothing." Alia let out a long sigh.

Brendan Curry stretched out on the king-size bed. He kicked the covers off. Sweat clung to his body. He placed one hand against the still wall. No generator vibrations. No road bump jolts.

He pulled on the pair of jeans from the floor. The door to the bedroom hesitated to open. Although he lacked in the gym, Brendan played football in high school. He hit against the door with a bit of force, driving his shoulder against the surface.

It moved about an inch.

"Yo, anybody here?" he said. Brendan backed up a few steps to rush the barrier. "Damn." His shoulder popped on contact. The door moved only another few inches. He peeked out into an empty room. The front curtain, left up, a pine forest spread out through the windshield.

Wherever they were, the bus was off-road and parked.

Brendan brought his hands up to the door and his feet against the base of the bed. He pushed off to squeeze his entire body against the door. The wood swung open to slam against the opposite wall as his face hit the carpet.

Outside the front window, Wally dragged something substantial on a green, mud-covered tarp into the trees. It created a path in the pine needles as it moved. His heart sped up.

"What the—" He took a minute to look out the back and side windows, all the while keeping one eye on the front. Trees surrounded the perimeter. He could not see a road or even a path. His driver and Marv were nowhere in sight, nor were any of the cellphones connected to the front counter's charging deck.

Wally emerged out of trees. Brendan slid across the floor. He shut the bedroom door with his foot. From an outside view, nothing appeared out of place.

Alia woke as the sun started to peek through her drapes. She took a quick shower, packed up all her belongings, sat to wait for Alister's instructions. The quiet brought heartburn instead of peace. She jumped up at the sound of a shoe hitting her door.

She walked across the carpet without sound to bring her eye to the peephole. A grinning Zadie stood outside, a paper cup in each hand. "Bout time you answered," Zadie handed her a cup. "Green tea. No sugar," she said, still with the grin. Zadie walked past, stopped beside the packed bags. "Going somewhere?"

"Um, yeah," Alia took a generous sip of the hot liquid. "Possible family emergency. I am waiting—"

"Possible?" Zadie lifted an eyebrow.

"—on a call from my, um, uncle." She took another gulp

"Anything I can do to help?" Zadie's face softened to show genuine concern.

"Not at this point. I am waiting on—" The phone vibrated against her purse. "Excuse me," Alia reached into her bag. "Hello. Affirmative." She turned towards Zadie. "I need a bit of privacy," Alia pointed towards the door."

"Oh, hey, no problem." Zadie rubbed her hand along Alia's arm. "Let me know if we can help in any way." Alia gave a small smile before she closed the door.

A couple beats of silence passed. "Are you alone?"

"Yes," she answered.

"Alia, you need to get out of there," Alister said.

"When and how?"

"As soon as you can and as untraceable as possible. Brendan Curry's bus is still missing. None of the trackers are functioning. The last time we had a visual was at a rest stop along I-80 outside of Harrisburg last night," said Alister.

"Do we have a time?"

He replied, "Between two and three a.m."

"I will see about getting a lift along that route. Is there anything else I need to be aware of?" Alia peered into the bathroom and checked the cabinets as they spoke.

"Yes." Alister's silence brought slight shudders up and down her back. Her stomach flipped.

"Alister?"

"Miranda Stone's body was found in the woods this morning," he said void of emotion.

"I knew there was something weird about that guy she was with yesterday."

"Alia, the coroner ruled her death overdose."

"No, Alister. That doesn't fit." Alia pulled out her journal and started to flip through her notes. "Alcohol poisoning, maybe mushrooms, Ecstasy is a possibility, but not, no. I would have seen the signs."

"You said that she played her part a bit too well. All circumstances indicate—"

"No, Alister. Call this intuition. Call it spidey sense. Heck, call it pure crazy; I don't care. Miranda Stone did not overdose. Have them check again, specifically for whatever substance killed her," Alia's voice rose as she spoke.

"Alia, I can see you are upset—"

"Please do not appease me. I am telling you that whatever happened to Miranda, it wasn't self-inflicted. Look for bruises. Look at toxin levels," she said, adding, "Look for—"

Alister interrupted. "First things first. Get out of there and do your best to locate Curry. Do not give information to anyone except me. And for God's sake, turn the damn locator on your phone on."

"Got it."

"And Alia," Alister added, "good luck."
She hit the end before going to the settings on her phone. She turned the "Locator" set to on and placed the phone on the table. With quick movements, she piled Miranda's clothes, suitcase, and purse onto the couch. She pored over every item from Miranda's bag: lipstick, an empty notepad, several pens, her work I.D., and car keys.

Alia removed the I.D. and shoved it in her pocket. She pointed the key fob out the window and pressed unlock twice. In the distance, two beeps responded. She returned the keys to the cushion next to the purse then rushed outside to the unlocked car.

The trunk contained the usual spare tire and tools, nothing out of the ordinary. The back-seat floor lacked visibility as empty Wendy's bags and to-go containers piled up even with the seat. Alia reached under to feel something wet and sticky. She pulled her hand back, covered with red goo. She took a quick sniff. "Exploding ketchup packets. After a quick clean with fast food napkins, Alia made a few quick notes in her journal.

*The car contains old fast food. Exploded ketchup packets. Last time here?*

She left the mess in the back. Inside the front under the passenger's seat, she pulled a stuck, hefty file size envelope off the carpet. After a quick examination, the envelope disappeared into her bag along with the spare change in the cupholder. Satisfied, she had what she needed; Alia glanced around the empty parking lot. She re-locked the vehicle and sprinted back towards the lobby.

Every few minutes, flashes of light bounced off the side of the mountain like giant fireflies joining in on the tribal drumming sounds coming from the stage. Most people didn't notice when a series of jeeps turned out of the lower campground's backlot onto one of the many ski trails used in the winter.

Fred walked through the sea of people. For him to keep balance on the sloping lawn, he stopped every few feet to adjust. Dressed in his ponytailed wig, tie-dyed t-shirt, and patched up shorts, he disappeared between the rest sitting, dancing, and charting the lawn. While the guy next to him swayed to the right in the beer line, Fred counted the flashes of lights above.

While the girl in front of him squinted at the landscape looking for friends, Fred studied each face as he searched for a stranger among friends. The lights on the hill became his timer—the more dominant the flash, the less time for him to complete his task.

Deal walked up and down the aisle inside the pavilion. He dressed in all black. The bright, fake all-access pass stood out in front of his chest. His tall stance, short hair, and look of disdain kept most of the crowd at bay.

Lack of light, along with most of the crowd standing, made his job more difficult. He repulsed at any query, frequently pointing an usher. A member of the security team overheard him tell a young woman, "That's not my job," at the same time, he pointed towards the usher—the latter blocked entry to the lower seats.

"What exactly is your job?" the security guard appeared by his side.

"Same as yours, buddy." Deal started to put distance between them.

The guard grabbed Deal's arm. He asked, "Who do you work for?"

"What's it to you?" Deal accentuated his height by stretching his neck up and shoulders down, then turned to sneer down at the twenty-something dressed the same except for the promoter's logo on the shirt. Deal's lips twisted down into a frown, He barked, "I asked you a question, boy."

The young kid turned away to mumble something into his shoulder walkie-talkie. Neither man moved. "I'm only joking," Deal explained as he attempted a smile. "Merely taking in the crowd's reaction to the new song. Sorry if I caused a commotion."

Deal hurried to get lost into the crowd before the young man could stop him. From the opposite side, his new friend gestured and pointed. Deal let out a laugh.

"What's so funny partner?" Fred bumped him from the opposite side. "I hope you have better news than me."

"I got nothing but a small hassle." Deal pointed his chin in the direction of a group of men, all in the same outfit as Deal, yet all sported the promoter's logo on their shirts.

"I got nothing, and we've got company." He turned back towards the hill.

"I'll be damned. I thought it would take the feds longer," Deal watched the lights bounce in between the trees.

"I don't know what to tell ya." Fred started to walk away from the stage. "I do know we need to get out of here."

"Not yet," Deal grabbed Fred's arm. "One more day. I got an idea of how to find her in the morning."

"Bad idea, bro," Fred shook off the grip. "I am telling you—"

"Just listen. I have a plan. We are going to find that bitch and cash in!" Deal raised his fist in the air.

"Okay, so what do we do until then?" Fred glanced around at the ebb and flow of people.

"Get some new clothes. I could go for some grub." The crowd thinned as they moved towards the upper lot and lodge. "Probably get out of here for a bit."

Both men nodded. "As long as we have a plan," Fred sighed.

Alister's words twisted around her brain and in her stomach. *You need to disappear and find young Curry.* She knew how to do both. Alia followed orders, yet the locator button usage bothered her. Someone in her office gave away her last cover. She flicked the tab to the off position.

A car, plane, bus, or train were all trackable. The most viable option was a car, yet with identification requirements, E-Z passes, and gas receipts, even cars made it hard for someone to disappear today. The half dozen or so tour busses glistened in the morning sunlight. Rock stars and families alike both drove along the highways in these enormous vehicles as incognito as those zipping passed in cars or trucks.

She noted that few outer panels featured any identifiable markings. Most sported a solid color or two. Many appeared a decade or so old. "In plain sight," she whispered, followed by, "I am not high. I am not drunk. This is my reality."

She walked around the perimeter of the giant beasts. Tiny sat out in front of Zadie's bus, acoustic guitar in hand. "Good morning, my lady," he greeted with a slight bow. "You movin' in?" He nodded towards the bags.

"Only if you'll let me," she let out a nervous laugh.

Zadie shouted, "Who's moving in now?" She came around the side of the bus. "Oh, it's you. Everything okay?"

"Yes and no. You got a minute?" Alia nodded towards the entrance. Zadie led up the stairs into the living room area. She gestured to sit on one of the long couches and sat across in a recliner. Alai glanced at her surroundings. "This is a styling way to travel."

"It works for us. We have two of these. The other one is already at the festival with our equipment. I should probably be there too…"

"Yeah. About that." Alia scanned around. "Are we alone?" Her voice dropped. Zadie leaned forward in the chair. She gestured with a nod to continue. "Okay, so between you and me," she peeked over her shoulder again, "something bad happened to Miranda, and I need to get out of here. But…"

"Oh man, I hate the butts…" Zadie interrupted.

"Me too. I can't do anything that requires an I.D.—"

"Because—" Zadie now sat on the edge of her chair.

"Because I can't, but I will tell you that this is nothing illegal." Alia waved her hands in front.

"Okay."

"Where are you guys heading next?" Alia asked.

"Buckeye Music Center in Ohio," Tiny's voice made both women jump. "What is going on here?"

"My new friend is in a bit of trouble," Zadie said as she chin-nodded to Alia.

"What kind of trouble?" Tiny's attention volleyed between the two.

"Not illegal," both said in unison.

Zadie turned to Alia, "What do you need? A ride?"

"Yes. I need a ride," Alia blurted out.

"And once we are on the road, you'll tell us why?" Tiny asked. Alia nodded. "Put your stuff in the closet on the left. Instruments go on the right," he pointed. "Now, can we go? Otherwise, we debut without you or me."

"I will get you a pass—"

"No pass. No one can see that I am here," Alia answered as Tiny and Zadie exchanged a glance. "I realize that this sounds crazy, but no one can know. Please."

Zadie gave her husband the slightest, little nod at the same moment their driver, Smoky, started up the bus.

Zadie shrugged, pointed, and glanced back at the bus while a different guy from yesterday nodded. This one was a bit older and not as expressive with his hands. He mirrored her shrugs before his hands leaped into the stop position. The two shook hands to split in opposite directions. Zadie's lips turned up into a toothless grin as she entered the bus.

"Sometimes, I amaze myself," she said as her body fell against the long sofa. "I definitely missed my calling."

"What did you do?" Smoky asked from the driver's seat.

"If anyone asks you, though they shouldn't, we had minor bus trouble this morning," replied Zadie.

"Minor bus trouble," Smoky repeated.

"Why minor bus trouble?" Alia asked.

"Because anything less gets us fined for being late." She shifted towards Smoky. "I told him we may need to keep this baby going, and if need be, we'll back up towards the hill."

"Fair enough."

Outside the window, men and women in black T's with white letters on the back that read CREW, move roadie cases around like a giant three-dimensional puzzle. One band's name stenciled on the side of faded blue containers; the black boxes had a different one. The window aligned with the horizon of the stage. Up there, stacks of cases are divided by stencils and colors, lined along with the interior.

Joe, Tiny, and Chords stood in a circle off to the side, out of the way. Legs moved to the beat while all three strummed. Alia couldn't hear what they placed, yet she could see genuine smiles spread across each face.

Smoky lowered a shade across the front windshield. "It's not totally blind to those outsides. You have outlines of folks on the bus if you stand in the doorway. In the backroom, you would be totally invisible if that's what you are looking for," he instructed.

"I will hang out here for a bit. We are on in about twenty. After we finish, we pack up and should be out of here by two," Zadie added. She turned towards Smoky. "Nobody, and I mean nobody, outside of us, gets on this bus without a warrant."

Smoky nodded, and asked, "Are you going to share—"

"Later." Zadie grabbed a stack of lanyards from a hook against the far wall. She flipped through to find what she needed, "I need to be out there chasin' checks and balances. Don't do anything…"

"You left out the stupid," Alia filled in the blank.

"Don't do anything smart or stupid." Zadie went out the door to follow a case with Tiny's name on it up the ramp. Stopped at the top, she held her pass out to disappear within the maze.

"Listen, I don't want to be a bother. I can stay out of sight…" Alia's eyes got a little glossy.

"I really don't care what is going on," Smoky said. "I am going to do my job. That includes whatever Zadie says." Smoky gave a quick wink. "Now, don't you worry. I am very good at my job."

Outside, a sharp note blasted out the front. A small roar followed. "I'm going to watch the boys from the side over there." He pointed to a spot next to a monitor board. "I'll keep an eye on you too. Now stay out of the shaft of light."

"I will." Alia heard a few beeps, followed by a loud click. Smoky had left the driver's side window open about an inch. She could hear a muffled version of Dylan's *Tangled Up In Blue* in the distance. She observed both men and women walk around the bus, up the ramp towards the performance.

"What is this bus running? That smell is disgusting!"

"If you didn't find her attractive, then why were you flirting?"

"Listening, honey, I realize this is your job, but I need to get the kids home, and I am tired of living out of that bus for the summer…"

"Is that who I think it is playing?"

Snippets of conversations passed her by. Most people walked by on the door side. Their conversations muted by the glass.

With the vibration from the engine, Alia's eyelids became heavy. Her breaths matched the beat of the drums. The cushions of the couch formed to her curves. Off in the distance, Joe's voice announced the new band. Applause. Screams of joy. More applause. Lights dimmed. Noise vanished.

Behind the band bus, Deal and Fred sat on the picnic table, the same one that Alia had hidden on days prior. Deal smoked a hand-rolled cigarette. He stared at Fred's back. "We think she's on one of the tour busses here," he heard him say. "Not one hundred percent but at least ninety."

A loud sigh escaped behind him. "Whatever you say, boss," replied Fred. He shook his head, turned, hands-on-hips.

Deal replied, "They want us to grab her. They said that there is a man in place to take her as soon as we do. They already have the Curry kid somewhere and need this finished yesterday."

"What if we don't?" Fred asked. Sparks dropped to the ground; Deal's work boot crushed the fading glow into the dirt.

"He didn't say." Both brought their attention to the running bus.

"I think we should let this one go," said Fred.

"We don't get paid, and we have—" Deal's voice grew louder.

"I understand. We should—" Fred pleaded.

"Let's take a peek inside that bus. I have a feeling." Deal put on a dust-covered cowboy hat. "I believe my lost love is inside."

"And if she's not?"

"If she isn't, we drive highway eighty until we find wherever she went," answered Deal.

Fred tapped the metal wall as he walked along the driver's side. Deal did the same on the passengers. Inside, Alia started to wake from her state. She stood at an angle barely out of view to see a male by the driver's side window. She moved into the center shadows.

The man hid his face under a baseball cap. Alia saw only a plain blue cap, everyday blue jeans, a faded blue shirt. She watched as he walked to the back of the stage to leaned on the edge.

Clicks and scrapings sounded next to the passenger door. With a slow movement, she backed down the hall. The sound stopped. "Can I help you there?" Smoky's snarled voice came through over the din.

"Not sure, buddy. Have you seen this woman?" Deal held out a polaroid. Smoky took a photo of between two fingers. In the center of a crowd shot stood Alia.

"Not sure. But this looks like this was taken up the hill a way." Smoky pointed just beyond the stage. The upper stage stood in the background of the photograph. Faces around her blurred out. Deal took the photo back. "Breaking into a tour bus is a sure way of getting arrested or worst."

"This is my wife," Deal said. He brought his eyes up to Smoky's. "She disappeared a few days ago. The kids and I are worried, sick."

"A few days ago, you say?" Smoky folded his arms across his massive chest as he spoke.

Fred noted the exchange. He gazed up into the front windshield. Deal caught his chin nod.

"She was last seen with someone on this bus. If I can take—" Deal tried to push past at the same moment Smoky blocked the door. "Look, I am sure you understand. This woman, no matter how messed up this looks, is the love of my life. Four kids need their mama."

"I wish I could help you, buddy. We have a crew guy sleeping on board, that's all. The only gal is Zadie, our manager. I can try to get her over…" Smoky offered.

"Naw, that's okay. I just—" Deal brought his hands to cover his face and shook. He rubbed his eyes with his fists for teardrops to smudged against rough skin.

Automatically, Smoky put a hand on his shoulder. "Wish I knew where she was, buddy."

Deal brought his gaze up, eyes now red from his palms. "If you see her—"

"I will find you," Smoky assured him with a nod.

Deal walked toward the stage. He leaned on his elbows next to Fred. "Think he bought it?" Fred looked over Deal's shoulder at the stout man who hadn't moved since Deal walked away.

"He's still watching you, partner."

Wally disappeared into the woods again, this time with a cellphone in hand. "Marv?" Behind the curtains by the bunk beds, crumpled sheets spread on to the floor. Brendan reached between the mattress and the wall. He pulled out the small journal Marv carried everywhere.

He opened to pages of drawings surrounded by groups of rhyming sentences. Outside the windshield, Wally came back in view. Brendan squatted down, out of sight. Wally's part of the conversation came through clear. "Yeah, I got him here." The bus shifted. "Yes, of course, I turned off the locator. This isn't my first--" Brendan moved further in the shadows against the bunks. "To answer your question, one is disposed of. The whack job is missing, and the kid is in the back of the bus sleeping. Now, when can I get my check?"

"Good job, dad," Brendan swore under his breath.

The bus shifted again. Wally moved back out of his sight.

Brendan grabbed Marv's backpack. He began shoving items in: the journal, underwear, guitar strings, t-shirts. His hand gripped on to a plastic bag and stopped short of adding Marv's stash of candy canes. "Dumbass," Brendan mumbled. "These are almost a year old!"

A high-pitched note accompanied every intake of air. The small room started to spin. The backpack still in his hand, Brendan turned it upside down. The contents now spread across the threadbare carpet. The journal went back in first. He crawled around the living room area on hand and knees. One raised hand searched for the cellphones, rested on top of the empty charger.

He rose high enough to see out the windshield. Wally appeared and disappeared behind the leafless trunks. His right arm gesture as he paced. "What the hell was in that tarp?" His special Santa Cruz custom acoustic lay propped up in the corner, canvas gig bag on the floor. "Priorities," he muttered as he packed the guitar. As an afterthought, he transferred the journal into the front pocket of the soft case.

He stood inside the side door. Wally emerged from the forest. He walked around the blind side of the bus. Brendan tried to look out into the side mirrors to get an idea of his whereabouts. With a deep inhale, he slung the gig bag over his shoulders, backpack style. The dork's way of carrying a guitar, Marv would say. Some incoherent mutter escaped from his lips.

"Third time is a charm," Brendan said, at the same moment he lifted his foot to kick open the door with one swift motion. The metal door banged against the bus wall. Without hesitation, Brendan jumped down the stairs, and sprinted into the woods. In the wind, he could hear his name hollered from behind.

Without missing a step, Brendan crashed through a line of well-developed bushes. Vines ripped into his skin, while his breath strained, heart pump audible. His eyes moved in every direction.

"When in doubt," he voiced above a whisper. The guitar weighed on his shoulder. Something snapped behind him. He fell to the ground and rolled his body into the high grass. The only sound now a percussion solo of heart and breath.

Another twig snapped.

Brendan waited and willed his body to silence. The wood ticks crawl on his forearm, yet fear prevented his fingers from flicking the insects away. His eyes stung. His name continued in the wind.

Smoky put one finger to his lips at the same moment Alia opened her mouth to speak. He gave a slight nod no. She moved back into the shadows to watch him pick up his cellphone then sit on the front couch.

"That fella says that you're his wife," he said barely above a whisper before bellowing, "Darlin', it's me, yes me, the love of your life," His laugh filled the space. "I'm callin' to tell you we are heading south, back to Florida tonight."

"I thought—" he put his finger back to his lip.

"Yeah, I know. Zadie wants the new band to play Frog Fest in Jacksonville, so you get to see my handsome face." He smiled in Alia's direction. "I don't know if that is the dang name. Peach fest, Moe fest, Outlaw fest, Frog fest, what the heck's the difference! Darling, I will be in Jacksonville on Sunday, and then we can ride to Austin and Denver together."

He waited for a beat or two before adding, "Love you, darlin." He placed the phone on the table between the seats. Alia scribbled something on a piece of paper. She folded it in half, then into quarters, spreading the sides like wings. Alia cocked her arm back to send the small plane flying across the bus.

Smoky opened it up, said, "no shit, sherlock," and tossed it in the wastepaper basket. Both jumped as the side door opened. Zadie slammed the door behind her as she walked up the stairs.

Both sat wide eyed. "What is going on?" asked Zadie.

"That feller down there says that his wife is missing, and they have four kids together." Smoky jerked his thumb towards Alia.

Zadie turned to Alia. "Let me see your stomach."

"Say what?"

Zadie gestured towards Alia's mid-drift. "Your stomach. Let me see your stomach." Alia lifted her shirt up to her bra. Although not a six-pack, her stomach had a definition. Both Zadie and Smoky's eyes fell on an old scar from a lone bullet. Alia jerked her shorts a bit higher to cover it up. Zadie turned back to Smoky. "He is lying."

"How can you tell?"

"Because any woman who birthed a kid," she lifted her shirt, "never mind four, get these," Zadie pointed to puckered, off-color skin that lay across her stomach, "or something that makes our body different from before. Only the genetically privileged or surgically enhanced avoid them." She grabbed a Saratoga water out of the fridge. "And she don't look like the type to get the surgery, if you know what I mean."

As if the universe wanted to confirm Zadie's statement, a double D cupped overtly thin woman passed by the window." Zadie gestured outside in her direction. "As I said… Anyway, we leave as soon as Tiny gets back."

"What about the equipment?"

"Crap," Zadie responded. "The crew is normally fast here. They want us gone. If we move the trailer to Jimmy's rig…"

"We'll need to explain why…" interrupted Smoky.

"No, we don't, but we need his okay. If we do that…" Zadie tapped a pen against her top teeth as she plotted.

"It doesn't buy us much. Can we get her on Jimmy's bus?" Smoky suggested.

Zadie turned towards him. "That is a great idea… But how?"

"We can—"

Alia positioned herself in the middle of the two. "Hey guys, hold on a minute. I am putting you in too much—"

"Shush. Rock and roll were getting boring. This is actually kind of fun," Zadie's pace slowed. "If I remember right, Jimmy is going to the airport, and his bus is going to—"

"I can't let you do this," Alia said. "Listen, I will tell you this story down the road, but for now," she hiked her bag on her shoulder. Smoky blocked her path to the door.

"Look," said Zadie, "you brought us into this, whatever this is, and I said I would help you. Old Smoky here may not look like much, yet he was once one of the meanest bikers in the southeast. He does more than drive for us."

"Don't let the belly and the gray hair fool you," he smirked.

"I am not sure what you got yourself in to, yet I said it before, and I will repeat it, I am a good judge of people." She gave a small smile in Alia's direction. "We are going to get your ass out of here."

"Thank you, but—"

"No, buts," Zadie said, pointing at her rear. "However, tell us what you can so we grasp what we are up against."

Alia hesitated, "Can anyone hear us outside?"

Zadie pointed to the back of the bus. All three sat on the floor. Alia crawled closer.

"What I am going to tell you needs to stay between us. I have already been compromised somehow," she began. "The Russian mob is after me."

The two glanced at each other before spouting with laughter.

"No, I am sincere. See, there was this corruption case…" Although she left out a few key details, Alia told her circumstances.

Ten minutes later, silence. Smoky turned to Zadie, "What the hell did you get us into?"

"This is not what I expected—" Zadie responded. She sat back on her heels.

"Listen, I can leave. No one actually knows I am here," Alia crossed fingers behind her back. "I can put a hat on and—"

"You wouldn't make it passed the backstage gate." Zadie pointed to the floor.

"Stay in here. We will get you to Ohio, as promised. Smoky if you don't want to go—"

"Hell yeah, I want to go. This will be like the old days." Smoky gave Zadie a wink. "Only better, because I am much wiser now." Both erupted in laughter.

"Who are you?" Alia interrupted.

"You don't want that information. Zadie, there still is that feller out there who claims to be her husband," reminded Smoky.

"Show me." The two stood to leave.

Alia jumped in, "Those guys are dangerous. You can't—"

"Just watch us." The door whooshed open.

The sun started to stretch towards sleep, as it hovered just above the majestic pine trees. Off to one side, a battered building with outhouse-style toilets barely stood on its rotting foundation. Tacked onto its side, a beat-up highway map with condensation and mold growing in between the plastic. The *you are here* dot smudged above the brownish-green goo that ate away the rest of the location.

A pair of long arms stretched up from a faint outline of a human head and torso. Perched on the edge of a wooden picnic table, Marv blew out a deep breath, blinked his eyes open a few times, and let out a loud yawn. Unfazed by the surroundings, he made his way back into the outhouse. "This is where it all started," a chuckle bounced around the makeshift toilet. He raised his hands in an "I give up gesture" as his head rocked side to side. "I followed his directions. I remembered that

Wally said, never shit on the bus again. I tiptoed off the bus last night to relieve myself. Now, as far as I can see, I am here, yet my bus is missing." He cocked his head to one side. "Or perhaps I am missing?"

The walls swiveled, then righted themselves. Marv dropped his head into his hands. The world was still a bit dizzy. He scratched his head, smelled his shoulder, and smiled. "Barbies. I remember the Barbies."

Barbies, or lack thereof, still didn't explain how he was sitting on a toilet, in a run-down rest stop, somewhere in Pennsylvania, according to the wood sign on the front, alone. "Aliens. Aliens finally showed up to save me and to get me out of this crazy space. I wonder where the fellows went off to?"

Outside no one sat at the moss-covered tables. There were no family picnics with wood-paneled station wagons parked close so Grandma wouldn't have to walk too far. No voices combined into a gentle hullabaloo. No laughter or tears. The parking lot now more grass and weeds than the bright asphalt of years past.

Marv brought his hands to circle his ears, the constant ring more prevalent. He slowed down breath with a silent eight in, eight out, count. Now the only sounds in the air were birds, wind, and exhales. The multi-shades of green in the rolling hills to his right and the nowhere road to his left both refused to tell where he currently sat.

A flash of white light off in the sea of green caught his attention. "My people." He smiled. "I will go to my people." Marv started to move in the general direction of the light.

Alister stopped in the doorway of his office. The back of a shaved head occupied the seat across from his desk. He glanced back out. A few people remained at their units, his secretary's chair empty, as usual.

"You might as well come in. We need to talk."

Alister hesitated a beat before he moved around his desk to sit facing the state police officer. He folded his hands in front of his chest, visible to the person opposite. "Can I help you?" he asked.

"Pilsner. Captain Louis Pilsner," the cop repeated.

"How can I help you, Captain Pilsner," Alister said.

"I think we can help each other. I am aware of the Miranda Stone situation," Pilsner replied.

Alister smiled. "Who is Miranda Stone?"

"Are we going to play this game?"

In a swift motion, Alister dropped one hand to his lap. He grazed a small button below his desk. The recorder made a soft click sound that he attempted to cover with his smoker's cough.

"Okay, then," Alister said, "share with me why you are here?"

"My job," Captain Pilsner moved to mimick Alister's pose, "is to make certain that Attorney General Curry concentrates on that drug conviction that we all worked so hard to obtain." He then emphasized, "All of us."

"I took your silence during the meeting as your job is to guard the A.G." responded Alister.

"I have many jobs," Pilsner replied. "That is only part of what I do. I take Brendan's disappearance as personal as you take someone giving up one of your operatives." Before Alister could comment, he added, "A member of my on-site team found Stone's body. Whoever these people are, they are sick bastards. And for the record, it was not an overdose. Check the toxin report."

Alister swore under his breath. His tobacco-stained fingers flipped through the papers stacked haphazardly in the cardboard box with "in" scribbled in black magic marker on the side. He pulled an envelope near the top marked in red confidential. He muttered aloud as he read, "a lethal amalgam containing heroin, fentanyl, and what the hell?" Alister redirected his focus to the cop, "Carfentanil? Isn't that an animal tranquilizer?"

"You are knowledgeable about your drugs," the cop answered.

"I am aware of the ones that have been surfacing lately. This combination's name—"

"Is gray death—"

"Yes, yes," Alister continued as if he hadn't heard, "Gray death. Isn't this normally an inner-city preference?"

Pilsner leaned back in his chair. "There were a dozen deaths the week prior at the same location, and if I remember correctly, with a similar compound, in our area about a month ago."

Alister raised an eyebrow. "What were the circumstances in Pennsylvania last week?"

"Another music festival with a different type of crowd, mostly into harder stuff both musically and recreationally. Attendees were much edgier than the group this weekend, which we observe to be your standard marijuana, beer, and possibly mushroom indulgers." The cop waved his hand as he spoke, clearly enjoying his release of new information.

Alister threw the file across his desk. "Miranda Stone was no saint, but this," he pointed at the papers, "she did not deserve." He glared across into Pilsner's stare. "She was seen with a couple males earlier in the day, presumed performers. Turned out they used a fake band name. Due to Stone's past actions, the other operative on-site missed the clue when Stone missed her check-in…"

"Where is the other operative?" asked Pilsner.

"I am not sure," Alister's cellphone buzzed across his desk. Alia's name flashed on the screen, "that is necessary information at this time. Besides, she hasn't checked in as late."

Pilsner watched the phone buzz. "Are you going to answer that?"

"One of my kids. I will call back after you explain to me why you are really here."

The two emerge out the side door. The old guy punched in a code then leaned on the front grill, arms crossed on his chest. Fred noted the size of the guy's arms and the stance of the body. "This can't be good," he muttered.

Deal walked around, circulating the photograph among the road crews, musicians, and other drivers. He pointed back at the tour bus. "She's the love of my life," received more of, "I am sorry, buddy" than "Let's get you on that bus!"

"Hey there, buddy," another security guard approached. "Can I get a look at your pass? Some folks said you were asking around about a lady?" The guard's voice curved up as if he asked questions at the end of each sentence.

"Yes sir," Deal pouted the best he could, "the love of my li—. What the hell!" Two other members of security approached from behind. They turned Deal around to hold his arms up his back. Kevin came running over.

"We got one," he said into his side mic. "Where's your friend?" he directed the question towards Deal.

"I ain't got no friends," Deal said. "I just want—"

"Okay, buddy. Stick with that story." Kevin pointed towards the men in black, cutting through the growing crowd. "Turn him over to those guys," he pointed. Deal eyeballed over his shoulder. He elbowed the giant to his left in a feeble attempt to break free. "Not happening today, buddy."

"Hey, I have rights!" Deal shouted. Fred surveyed the commotion from a distance. As the feds ran by, he backed up towards the gate. When they reached Deal, he slipped around the corner, took off the backstage pass, and tossed it into a trash can. He moved away from the stage to dissolve into the crowd.

"What's your name son," one of the feds questioned as they pushed Deal towards the back gate.

"I ain't saying shit without a lawyer," he answered, surrounded by four, yet the only one who spoke walked aside to his right shoulder.

"Do you need a lawyer?"

"You tell me. I was grabbed backstage at a music festival by the feds—"

"What makes you think we are federal agents?" Deal got a chill. Off to the side of the gate, out of public view, the Mercedes idled. "I asked you a question, boy." He poked one finger into Deal's bicep. "Answer me."

"I, uh, where are you taking me?" Deal's eyes opened wider as they moved closer to the exit. Hot fluid dripped out along the side of his face.

"To that trailer over there," the man in charge chin-nodded in the direction of the last trailer before the gate. "We need to have a chat."

"About what?" A flash of white light brought his attention to the car. The driver's side window slid down an inch. "Can we have it here?" Sweat emptied down his face. His shirt soaked against his body. Deal stopped moving at the same moment pain ripped through his heart.

"No, we can't - hey wait!" Deal's limp body slumped to the ground. "Check out the woods over there," the one in charge pointed up the hill. "You go in that direction," he indicated towards the lower entrance to the festival. "Shit, we have over 30,000 people in there."

All scattered, guns were drawn. Deal's lifeless body lay in the gravel. Without notice by any, the Mercedes crept out of the lot.

Brendan lay still in the grass. The wood ticks crawled up and down his arms while other little insect feet scurried over the rest of his body. His guitar case covered most of his backside. Wally's voice wavered between "Get the fuck over here, boy" to "Brendan, your dad hired me to protect you. I am on your side."

Brendan still didn't have knowledge of who or what lay in the tarp. He twitched at every crack, scuffle, or movement. The hot winds of summer fluttered the tall grass. Brendan's clothes drenched in perspiration, attached to his body. Sweat dripped down his hairline to sting his eyes. Wally's voice faded as the crunch of the earth against footsteps grew more distant.

Brendan hesitated in the silence. When the illusion of hours passed, he pushed his frame into an upright position and stretched his hands forward over his legs. The guitar case bumped against the top of his head. He laid the case on the ground by his side. The cellphone in the front pocket had little battery and zero bars.

"Can you hear shit?" The locator indicator was off along with the GPS component. Brendan moved both to the on position. He held the phone in the air and turned in a steady 360 degrees pattern. No new bars appeared—field to trees to rocks to a cliff back to field and trees. His body's cuts started to form tight scabs, yet blood still dripped along with a few spots.

He wiped the sweat off his face with the back of his hand. Only the lowly wind broke through the silence. From this angle, he could see the rip in the grassy field that gave way to his entry. He picked up his case, turned to move in the opposite direction. His cellphone lay next to the folded outline of a guitar case in the grass.

Alia paced the length of the bus. Alister hadn't returned her call, and Zadie continued to yell outside for the crew to hurry up with their gear. "She's drawing too much attention," she muttered as her gait imbedded a trail in the carpeting.

"Damn!" and "Shit!" filled the air with an occasional "Fuck!" thrown in. Smoky spoke with a group of men in matching black t-shirts and jeans through the front windshield. He fluctuated his hand motion between the bus and the crowd. Kevin, the security guard, stood nearby. Alia noted that he turned away from the group to speak into a side mic several times during the exchange.

Her observation point granted her a precise evaluation of the interaction without hearing any parts. She rubbed her hands along her temples. If she could just hear the complete conversation, she could make an educated move. As is, she could only hypothesize.

Another tour bus backed up along the driver's side. Outside she could see the bright purple swirls, yet not the driver or passengers. Alia jumped at the pop of the door.

"You need to learn to relax," Smoky said. Her heartbeat, along with a few gasps, the only sounds. "Seriously," he broke in. Alia attempted to steady her breath with a silent count of eight on the inhale and ten on the ex. She wiped her moist palms on her shirt.

Smoky continued, "Sometimes Zadie amazes me," he walked by Alia into the long hallway. Smoky squatted down and pulled up a perfect square of carpet. "This here is what we call the angry husband escape hatch," he laughed. "Or the AHEH for short. With Zadie on board, we didn't have a use for it until…"

"Today?" Alia raised an eyebrow.

Smoky nodded. "Yeah. If this hatch could talk." Smoky let a small grin cross his face. "Anyway," he snapped back from his memory, "this gets you into the cargo area below. The fellers in the bus next to us," he nodded to the side, "are part of our crew."

"Do they—"

"Not that I know. Then again, I only get what the boss tells me." Both jumped as the door popped open again.

"You people need to relax," Zadie said, her voice slightly above a loud whisper. "Did you tell her the plan?" Smoky shook his head no. "Althea, here you have—"

"Angry husband escape hatch, yeah, I see." Zadie shot Smoky a glare.

"The trap door is actually another means to get into the cargo area. Sometimes it is easier to store guitars in their cases lined up here," Zadie pointed into the dark hole, "so the boys can get 'em when they want to practice without having to stop the bus."

"Also, as opposed to having the cases lay all over the damn place," Smoky added.

"The cargo holds of both busses line up. We loaded with an alley for you to slip out of this bus—"

"And onto the other," Alia finished. "If I didn't know better, I would think that you have done this before." Zadie and Smoky exchanged a knowing glance. "Guess what? I don't need to know. Can that bus get me to Ohio?"

"That bus—" Zadie began.

"And me—" Smoky interjected.

"And Smoky," Zadie nodded in his direction, "will take you anywhere you need to go."

"You going to tell her about Jimmy?" Smoky asked.

"I was getting there. Jeeze, Smoky."

"Uh, who is Jimmy?" Alia held both hands up.

"Remember the new guy, well, not really new..." Zadie and Smoky exchanged another silent communication. Zadie gestured with her right hand as she spoke, "You met him briefly, and he was part of the new group that played today with Tiny and company? The bus belongs to him. And—"

"Apparently Jimmy doesn't fly." Smoky jumped in.

"Excuse me, what?" asked Alia.

"I was getting there," Zadie stopped both mid-conversations. "Apparently, Jimmy stopped flying back in the '80s, something about altitude sickness and creativity..."

"I heard he freaked out on an airplane when he was traveling with—"

"Smoky, we agreed to never mention his former band or mates." Zadie took in a few deep breathes as she attempted to compose herself. "Jimmy will be on the bus, too," she said.

Alia looked back and forth between the two. "How much did you tell him?"

"You are my friend. You need a ride and want to take the scenic route. Nothing more," said Zadie. Alia's attention bounced between Zadie's pleading eyes and Smoky's stare out the window.

"I understand you want to help me, but I can't get more people involved," Alia's phone vibrated in her pocket. "If I may have a few minutes to think this through?" Both nodded as she disappeared into the bathroom.

"Were you really this bored?" Smoky turned to Zadie. "I mean really, woman; this is getting to be more like the old days than I care to remember or repeat. And don't forget about Jimmy's quirks."

Zadie listened for a moment in an attempt to hear Alia's conversation. "Ah, yes. The firework thing. No worries, we'll be gone long before that starts up." She bent her ear towards the bathroom door and tried to distinguish what the muffled voice said. "You still have a friend in the glove department?" Smoky nodded. "Not that I think you'll need it—"

"Being safer than sorry?" asked Smoky. "Whatever that one is in to; my gut says we are on the right side."

"Yeah, mine too," Zadie confirmed. Both considered the bathroom door.

Fred made his way back up the hill in the direction of the second stage. He boarded a ski lift next to the fake camps. The promotor charged the same as a nice hotel, so more polished folks could experience sleeping on a cot in a canvas tent in the middle of all the mayhem. The attendees waited in line for the chance.

"Suckers," he laughed. He had enough of cots and tents when he and Deal were in the military. The ski lift went high above to give a view of most of the festival. He could see the full second stage near the top of the hill, plus the crowd and waterslides. He had a limited view of the pavilion's backstage area off to his right.

Fred counted six busses. The one Deal tried to board still in the same spot. A light flashed closer to the backstage gate. Multiple blue lights along with a single red grouped together. Best, he could estimate the group consisted of numerous police with one emergency vehicle. He couldn't tell if the red lights were attached to an ambulance or firetruck from this distance.

The lift jerked his attention back. The sky peeked out from behind the metal wheel. Two adolescent males stood to the side. "Need help getting off, buddy?" the closest yelled as the other added, "Off the lift, he means."

"Okay, Beavis," Fred answered as he pushed his body off the chair and jumped to the right. The chair grazed his hip on the way by.

"Eh, eh, eh, he called you Beavis," the first boy pushed the other.

"That makes you, Butthead," the other pointed out.

"Hey," he turned to yell at Fred, yet the upper lift area had only grass and the hum of the wheel. "Where did he go?"

"Didn't see. Don't care. Not my job, man."

Fred walked down the worn path towards the glampers. Off to the hard right, the back-ridge road ran along the last row of tents. Behind the third from the end, he reached under the canvas to pull out a worn backpack. Inside he removed a clean gray t-shirt along with a logo-less matching hat. He pulled back a piece of Velcro cloth to reveal a second pocket.

He tucked a small pistol into his waistband before he added a jackknife to his lower pants pocket. Fred put his corporate golf shirt and hat inside the bag. He lobbed the bag over his right shoulder before he darted through the two tents to a center walkway empty of people. The bag slipped off his shoulder into a trash receptacle. He sauntered back into the woods.

English ivy wrapped around Marv's wrists as he plowed through the vegetation towards the flash. He repeated in his mind, "Brothers and sisters, I am here for you," hands back out in a surrender gesture. At the same time, he occasionally whispered the chant into the wind. His stomach cramped.

Marv placed one hand on his lower abdomen and the other on the tree to his left. He shook his finger in the air. "Last time I stopped," his lips formed a grin, "you left me. Yes, I must cleanse for our meeting, yet this time you must wait for me…" He pushed back several ferns to walk into a group of evergreens. The center tree's branches reached down onto the pine needle covered ground.

Marv made his way into the center to hang his naked butt over an out of place rock. He sweated and squeezed to release an occasional grunt in the mix.

Outside Marv's makeshift toilet, Wally walked along the path. He pushed back greens to look for any piece out of sorts. The broken ferns made a trail into the pine grove. With one hand resting on the lower branch, he started to pull the leaves out of the way.

The muffled grunt caught him off guard. When the sound rose in volume, Wally reversed direction to move back up the path in the same direction he arrived.

Alia squished into the combination toilet and shower towards the back of the bus. Her back against the toilet tank while her feet secured the door closed on the opposite wall. She ran the water from the faucet as an extra sound barrier.

"I can hardly hear you," Alister barked on the other end. Unfortunately for her, the water drowned out none of his hostility.

"And there are people outside who can hear me if I talk any louder," Alia stage whispered and typed into a text. A few breathes later, she received the text, *Then just listen.*

"I am not going to type this entire update," he said in his lecture voice. "The state cop assigned to A.G. Curry knew about Stone's death, and you were right, she didn't O.D... The cop is taking it personally that Curry's son disappeared. He put the eyes on the ground at the festival along with another attached to the kid's bus." Alia turned the water down to a drip as she adjusted the phone volume lower.

"Which bus?" Alia asked.

Alister ignored her interruption. "Another person, Otis "Deal" Dougherty, was shot and killed while in federal custody about 45 minutes ago. Preliminary information shows his background having a stint in the Middle East—"

"For us?" Alia interrupted.

"Not sure," Alister's raspy cough interrupted. He cleared his throat and hacked something out. Alia cringed. "Feds were walking him to their trailer for questioning. The next thing they knew, he clasped on the ground. Single-shot to the heart, most likely with a silencer. Before you ask, there are no arrests at this time, but agents are searching the area."

Alia gave an exaggerated eye roll. "My ass," she muttered.

"I am sending a photo of Dougherty in case you recognize him." The photo appeared on her screen as she let a small gasp escape.

"Alister, this guy flashed my picture backstage earlier this afternoon. Made up a sob story about me being his missing wife with four kids." Alister let out a loud laugh. He started to cough again. Alia ignored the interruption and continued, "Seriously, he tried to board this bus, but Smoky wouldn't let him."

"Who is Smoky?"

"Bus driver slash ninja," Alia started to explain. "Might be former military, definitely a teamster badass."

"Alia, does he know about you?" Alister's voice shifted to a quieter tone.

"Yes," whispered Alia.

"Alia, don't you understand that trusting strangers—"

"Probably kept me alive for the last 24 hours. Alister, with Dougherty gone, is it safe for me—"

"No. I still need you to find young Curry and escort him safely back here. Besides the father, his mother checked into a local hospital, apparently hysterical." Alister let out a small snort.

"Great."

"Now some good news," Alister said. "We have received a signal from Brendan Curry's locator around the same time all this went on at the festival. It came from a wooded area, fifty miles northwest of where you are currently located. Unfortunately, the signal disappeared about five minutes later."

"This is a lot of information to digest, Alister."

"Damn it, Alia! I don't want you to digest it. I want you to get to the location," Alister's voice started to rise. "I will text you and find that boy, hopefully alive. There are way too many moving parts to this scenario. The trial starts tomorrow."

"Alister," Alia tried to keep her voice as level as possible, "I am on a tour bus, at a festival where so far two people have died. The common point between the two people seems to be, well, me."

"And your point?" A flick of a lighter sounded, followed by a deep inhale.

"I have no weapons. No backup." Alia jumped at the sound of a knock on the door.

"Everything okay in there?" Zadie's voice came through the wall.

"Yes, give me a minute," Alia shouted back. She whispered, "I got to go," into the phone. "I will do my best."

"I will see what I can do to get you back-up. For now, do better than your best," Alister answered.

Alia pushed open the door. In the living room area, the entire band, plus Smoky, sat around the perimeter. They all focused on her. "Hey," Alia said as she stood in the doorway.

"Hey, yourself. Smoky said you didn't like the bus switch idea. You got a better one from your phone call?" Zadie asked.

Alia twitched then settled back. "My boss," she pointed to her cell. "I wasn't sure what he was going to tell me and needed a bit of privacy." She listened to hear no sounds below. "Are you guys ready to leave?"

"Yes," Each person gave a slight nod back as Zadie took note. "Althea, I like you, but this situation—"

"Another fella, the one who said he was your husband, got shot at the gate." When Alia didn't move, Smoky added, "But you already knew that, didn't you?"

She nodded, "I found out on that phone call."

"Doesn't matter," Zadie continued, "I like a good adventure, but this," she swept her hand around the room, "isn't what we signed up for. I can't—"

"I totally understand," said Alia. "Let me get—"

"But I can." All eyes turned to Jimmy.

"You can what?" asked Alia. An electric pulse ran up her back.

Jimmy started to say, “I can get you to where you need to be—”

Zadie interrupted, “Jimmy, we decided—”

“No, you decided. Look, you all see how I travel. Let me—”

“And me—” Smoky jumped in.

“Help the lady. We both,” Jimmy nodded in Smoky’s direction, “have been here before. And based on our experience, we need to move now, before—”

“I get it. No problem,” Zadie jumped in.

Nobody said a word. Alia scrunched her lips to the side of her mouth. She pondered the question that no one would ask, *who are these people?*

Brendan waited in the grass long after the footsteps silenced. A tick buried its head inside his arm yet he could not raise up his hand to flick the parasite away. After what seemed like forever, the shadows expanded across the grass.

He sat up and brushed his hands over his entire body along with his hair. His fingers found a few more wood ticks to pick off his skin. The trees stood tall on the edges of the field. The path not visible. He hiked up his guitar onto his shoulders to move in the opposite direction from Wally. The sun lowered over the hills in the distance, just shy of an expansive valley.

Brendan walked into the sunset. "The sun rises in the east and sets in the west," he remembered from his school days. The breaks in the vegetation lead to a well-worn trail. He moved into the undergrowth. His hands pushed back the branches while his feet shuffled to hit ruts along the way. The ground tilted forward at the same moment his knee hit something substantial. His palms scraped along the granite edges as his body fell towards the hard ground.

"Damn!" he shouted. His hands flew to his mouth as he brought his body towards the solid rock. His knee throbbed. "Shit!" escaped a bit quieter. Brendan took a moment to take in his surroundings. The trail lay behind, lush greenery to the left and right, and beyond the solid stone, his knee had met air.

He leaned onto his right hip to extend his torso over the edge. Sky and the valley stretched into the distance. Black dots swirled in front. With eyes squeezed shut his body slid back to the solid ground. Blood seeped through ripped jeans. A pushed off the earth brought a searing pain up into his hip. His body slammed back into the jagged edge.

With hands clutched in a prayer position, he righted himself to plead to the sky. He caressed the neck of his Santa Cruz custom and whispered, "Forgive me," as he removed the instrument from its case from the case. "The most expensive cane in the world," he said. The bag weighed nothing spread across his shoulders. One hand gripped the guitar neck hard to balance the lower bout on the ground. "I am so sorry." His voice came barely above a whisper as the ground grinded into the wood.

His steps deliberate, Brendan winced each time pressure hit his right leg. The strings gave off a slight shriek with each movement. The scraping of earth against the Adirondack spruce gnawed at his soul. The tears wept for the instrument as much as his pain.

Brendan backtracked to the worn-down path he had bypassed earlier. The forest stillness gave no clue of the direction he should follow, nor did any smells that lingered in the air. "Well, nothing so far went right," as he started down the path to his left.

Zadie directed both busses down a steep hill into the Gold lot. The Gold lot was the promoter's answer to the overflowed of late festival arrival RVers. Many are not happy about their off-site camping location as each site's tickets started in the two-thousand-dollar range.

Smoky pulled to the back of the lot and made the bus do a full turn to face the entrance. The second bus pulled in forward about two feet apart.

Both doors barely fit into space yet, when open, provided a shield to any onlookers. Zadie turned towards Alia, "You are switching here. Smoky will take you to Ohio on the other bus."

"I really—"

"Look, Althea, for better or worst, we are now involved. Out of all the busses backstage, the guy who was looking for you came over to ours. We need to get a distance." Smoky spoke soft, yet his intent came through clear. "Is there anything else we need to be aware of?"

"The trial is supposed to start on Tuesday. Brendan Curry and his crazy bass player are gone, and it is my job to stay near to the ground and find them."

"How do they expect you to do both?" Zadie asked. "Do you have any help?" Her face softened with motherly concern. "And what else are you not sharing?"

"Zadie, can I talk to you and Tiny on my rig?" Jimmy pointed towards the door. Alia observed as the two followed.

She turned her attention to Smoky and raised one eyebrow. "Damned if I know," he said, adding, "And stop doing that! It's creepy." Alia stretched her arms overhead. Her tank top shifted up to reveal the line of flesh punctuated by an old bullet wound.

Smoky's eyes drifted towards the scar.

Jimmy pulled the door shut behind the group. He pulled back bunk curtains, opened storage areas, and peeked inside the back room as he walked the entire length of his bus. Upon completion, he joined Zadie and Tiny in the front room.

"Still checking under the bed?" Zadie joked. When no one laughed, she continued, "You do your hotel room check on your bus too?" Jimmy nodded. "Huh."

"Huh, indeed." Tiny considered his old friend. "Why the dramatic exit?"

"That was dramatic?" Jimmy ran his hands through his hair. "And I thought I was cool." A nervous laugh broke the silence. "Look, you two remember the deal with Goober and my private plane, right?"

"Your brother Goober?"

"Is there any other?" Jimmy asked. Both confirmed with a nod. "Well, the part you might not have heard is I came off the road because the idiot got into a situation that put him along with our entire family in danger. I haven't seen the idiot in years, and as far as I knew, he disappeared into the military, and yeah, that was it—"

"Until," Zadie jumped in.

"I swear I saw Goober backstage today. He disappeared into the crowd as that other fella was getting take away," Jimmy stated. He looked back and forth between the two.

Tiny let out a long breath. "Do you know—"

"No. I am not even sure my brother is using his real name."

"What is his real name?" Zadie asked. "I mean, as your younger bro, we all remember him as the Goober." An uncomfortable laugh followed.

"Wilfred, though, I think he tried to go by Fred most of the time. He was embarrassed by our great-grandfather's name."

"You think?" Tiny asked.

"Hey, I was named after a great grandfather, too," said Jimmy.

"Your real name is Wilfred?" Tiny jest.

"No, dipshit, my formal name is Winston James, yet I dropped the first part when we played as kids. Plus, my daddy was Winston too."

Tiny and Zadie took a moment to take this all in. "Win Scout," said Tiny. "Your stage name makes a heck of a lot more sense."

"Tiny, as far as my brother goes, we grew up together. Yeah, but me and the Goob ain't close. Fred was always a bit off. He made terrible decisions. I can't explain it. Heck, I don't even know if it was him. But if it was…" Jimmy let the thought sink in.

"Awe crap. Do you think he's still—" Zadie couldn't finish the thought.

"The kid never made a good choice in his life," Tiny pointed out.

"Crap." Zadie stood to leave. "Is there anything else we need to be aware of?"

"I would feel a lot better if Smoky stayed with you all." Zadie opened her mouth to speak at the same time Jimmy continued, "Look, both he and I have had military training. My driver may carry, but when push comes to shove," he shrugged, "I want you all safe."

"So, do I," Tiny added. "Do we share this with Althea?"

"No!" Both Zadie and Jimmy yelled.

"Why not?"

Jimmy held up his hand as Zadie waved him off. "I got this one. The gal is holding back information. My gut tells me that yet," she patted her stomach, "I also trust her if that makes sense."

"Makes woman sense," Tiny responded.

"Either way, woman sense is better than no sense." She wrinkled her nose then stuck her tongue out at Tiny. "She won't go with Jimmy if she thinks there is a double-cross and Fred the Goober would be just that. I say we hold off telling her."

"I will drive the bus," Jimmy brought the focus back to their current task. "I am sending you a copy of our route. We should check in with each other every three hours—"

"Yes, Dad."

"Tiny, this isn't funny."

"No, it's not. And I feel responsible," Tiny said.

Zadie put her arm across the big man's shoulder. "Why in heavens would you be responsible?"

"Because I commandeered her at the elevators and introduced you two." Tiny looked up at his wife. She absentmindedly rubbed his shoulders as she took a minute the consider her husband's words. "She seemed so normal."

"Yes, you did. Yet what do I always say?" Zadie waited a minute for her husband to answer. When he only shrugged, she continued, "I always say everything happens for a reason."

"You do always say that," Tiny agreed.

"There is a reason why Althea is here. We have to figure it out," Zadie said. She now had both Tiny and Jimmy nodding in agreement. "I'll let Smoky know the drill although I still would feel better—"

Fred weaved through the crowd until he arrived at the top of the lawn. He leaned back against the wood fence that served as a boundary between paying customers and state forests. All around, people swayed, jumped, and stumbled, some to the current music waffling through the speakers, others due to their altered states' poor timing.

Either way, he made it into hell.

Behind the fence, ATV's and other four-wheel-drive vehicles vibrated the ground. A lull in the music brought the undecipherable sounds of human radio static. Twenty feet to his left, a libation line stretched to the port-o-potties forty feet away. Twenty feet to his right, a toned male, dressed in black kaki's, a black polo, and a black baseball hat scanned the crowd behind military issued aviators.

His eyes followed the fence to find two more.

"Why so sad?" Fred turned towards a small woman. She stared up at him, wide-eyed.

He noted the thin strip of blue around her irises. "You look so sad," she stated as she reached for his hand. "Did you lose your friends?" Fred nodded. "I can be your friend." She followed with a megawatt smile that stretched across her entire face.

"I'm not…" Fred's eyes drifted from her bright teeth down to the barely covered ample breasts, the girls on high alert behind well-worn gauze. He stopped there. "I am a little sad…"

"But *Elfin Taco* is playing. You can be sad when *Elfin Taco* plays. I mean, that's well, like, you know, sad." Contemplation lines form around her eyes. "Why don't you hang with us for a while." Fred's eyes automatically glanced at the girls on us. "We are hanging down there."

He followed her finger to a small group of women in front of a cabana tent. All wore the same orange swirled floppy hat that this one held in hand not attached to his.

"Can I wear your hat?"

She hesitated a brief second before she plopped the canvas on his head. Fred let go of her hand long enough to adjust the sides. She laughed. "Yes, that is perfect." Her smile widened.

"So, what's your name?" Fred asked as he re-attached his hand to hers.

"Names are so archaic, no?" Her shirt slid aside to reveal one nipple. "Let's only be festie friends, okay?" She dragged her top teeth over her lower lip then slid her tongue across. Fred glanced back at the fence. Three more men in black stood off to the side. They pointed to several locations across the lawn.

He brought his head down. "Names are so archaic. Let's only..." She pulled him next to her.

"Let's," she repeated. She cut through the crowd as if the maze belonged to her. Upon arrival, Fred noted three other women dressed the same. "Sisters, we have a new friend." The others circled Fred. One gazed at him from toes to the hat.

"He's wearing—"

"I know—"

"There are rules—"

"It was the only way—" Her eyes dropped to the ground as she reached up to remove the hat from his head.

"That's better," the one in charge said. "Please sit." She pointed in the cabana. Fred heard shouts of "don't do it, dude" and "lucky you" coming from all sides. As he crouched, the group of three had spread out and now moved through the crowd.

"Shit," he muttered. A slap came quick.

"No swearing, shouting, or releasing of fluids in the sacred tent." He rubbed his cheek.

"I was thinking about hitting the other stage…" he started to say. All four women nodded no. "I really like the band that goes on next."

The tall one pushed him back on the blankets simultaneously. The small one from the fence crawled over to his left. "This won't hurt a bit," the one in charge whispered. She ran her fingernails down his arm. "Festival friends," she said a bit louder at the same moment one of the others tied his ankles together. He swung his arms in the air only to be tackled and tied at the wrists.

Fred found it hard to believe that these women could be so strong until the one in charge removed his wig. Three pairs of eyes stared back into his. "Don't worry, this won't hurt," she said, "Ladies…" He swung his legs together to take out the central pole that held the cabana up. Another swoop of his torso pushed two of the females off. The final move brought his tied legs underneath his body. He rolled out of the tent onto another group's blanket.

Someone pulled out a knife to cut his leg ties. "Told you not to go in there," the boy commented. "Those girls are cute yet scary."

He gave a quick thanks and stumbled further into the crowd. He fought with the tie around his arms as he attempted to loosen its grip as he dunked and weaved away from another batch of festie foes.

Harlot stood in the shadows of a lighting rig on the side of the lawn. She observed the sweep of the lawn the federal agents now performed along with their current problem. Out from the cabana, only his legs appeared in sight, at least for now. Another band would start soon. People would get up and dance. Her vantage point would be lost.

Most a bit high or drunk, the lawn contained many characters, all only out to have a good time. Harlot chose those who held the idiot with care. Their goal appeared to collect "festie friends" each day. All males, the ladies, preened and posed to get males alone in the tent. Best Harlot could tell, three would jump on him while a fourth kept watching.

Some emerged with a happy grin while others could be heard muttering how "messed up those chicks are." Either way, a little boy bashing went a long way in Harlot's eyes.

When she approached the group, their ringleader invited her to join.

"Tempting," she said, "yet I have a favor to ask." The ringleader nodded while the others circled to listen. "See that guy up there," all four followed her long fingernail to Fred, "that is my brother, and I am so distraught about him."

"Because he looks so sad?" one had asked.

Harlot shook her head. "He is sad. And I worry because he is supposed to take his medicine every day, and then he comes to these things—"

"And he forgets?" another interrupted.

Again, Harlot nodded, "Yes, he forgets. If I say anything, he gets angry and says really mean things to me." She waited for the *like what.* The ladies twirled their hands to continue. "He calls me a whore and makes fun of my body because my boobs are crooked." All eight hands extended to touch her shoulders.

"I see you get guys to follow you, which can't be hard because you all are so beautiful." The women glowed with the compliment. "I get this is a lot to ask, but can you give my brother his medicine. I have it here." She held up a purple velvet pouch. "He needs an injection a day, or he'll…" She turned away to brush a non-existent tear away.

The women all spoke at once. "Of course, we can help. I mean, its life or death."

The ringleader peered directly into Harlot's gaze. "How about we hold him and you…"

"I guess. He does get mean." A blast of a trombone brought Harlot back to the present. Something had changed in the tent. The women pointed and frantically waved their hands in the air. Harlot focused on the area in time to see Fred disappear.

"Crap."

"I am so sorry," the ringleader exclaimed. "That ass wipe of your brother kicked my sister. She was knocked dizzy, so we all focused—" Harlot silenced the woman with a hand raise.

"Did you give him the medicine?" The purple pouch lay in her hand.

"We didn't get to that point in the ceremony." Harlot grabbed the pouch back. "We are sorry. I needed to attend…"

Harlot nodded as she stuffed the purse into her backpack. The woman waited for some sort of thanks, yet when none came, she added,

"Yeah, it was nice to meet you too." She hurried to help move the others away from the offensive area.

Harlot blew out a stream of frustration. She chewed on her thumb while the band on stage played a Led Zeppelin song on horns. *Bop, bop, Badda bop, boom, boom, bop, doo di dute, doo di dute, bop bop di ba….*

"It's time to get to the rendezvous location." She jumped at Yarok's voice. "Is our other problem taken care of?"

"No. but—"

"Doesn't matter. We need to go. It is time to meet the bus. I hope the young man will cooperate with us."

"At least we have him, right?" Harlot wore her best smile, yet her eyes showed pure fear. Her body jumped as Yarok raised his hand. He brought it under her hair to rest on her neck. Intuitively she leaned into him. His grip tightened.

"No, this is not alright," his voice hissed. "All you had to do was administer Harlot's juice. We named the drug after you for your killer instincts," Harlot let out a squeak as his hands tightened further, "or your lack of killer instincts, as we now see." His grip loosened a bit. "Harlot, my love," his eyes turned black, "to expand our empire, it is time to expel our witnesses."

Yarok slipped his hand into hers to move through the crowd. Harlot bit into her lower lip. To run means death. To stay might be death, too.

Alister's office walls lay covered with maps, charts, and a web of photographs, some with red lines across. He stood in the middle to concentrate on each area individually. The only pulse from Curry's tracker came from the area of Loyalstock and Tiadaghton state forests. Three hundred and thirty plus acres to track down a missing tour bus.

He brought his attention to the photographs. Not including the drug dealers and users, he had six suspects dead, one missing, along with several others unaccounted, two of which were Russians in the country illegally. "Screwing with our elections isn't enough for you people?"

"Excuse me?" Alister turned to see his sixteen-year-old technology genius standing in the doorway. Not for the first time, he wondered if junior owned any clothes besides well-worn pajama pants and oversized thermal shirts. The reusable mug from the trendy coffeeshop completed his look.

"Nothing. I am taking in the big picture," Alister said. The kid moved to his side. The elder man winced as a loud slurp escaped. "Can I help you?"

"No," the kid said. He stared at one of the photos. "That dude looks familiar. I think he plays in my Soul Crusher Two league."

Alister sucked in a breath. "Which one?" The kid pointed at Yarok Yarakov. Alister's heart skipped a beat. "And what is Soul Crusher Two?"

"Only the best online game ever. You have all these different levels, and instead of guns and tanks and stuff, you play mind games with the other participants until they get frustrated or cry or freak out. In the end, they all drop out." The kid took another loud slurp before adding, "I'm on level eight. Your friend here passed me to number nine. He did a nasty on someone."

"A nasty?"

"Yeah. Yarakov, is that his real name?" Alister nodded, "he made a girl cry, at least I think it was a girl." He laughs, "It was probably because she had to use a dictionary to understand what he said. He called her a plague sore and a fustylug and my favorite, a smelfungus. All from medieval literature. He was quite the hedge born." The kid laughed at his own joke.

"Is he playing the game still?" Alister asked. He gave The Kid his full attention.

"Oh yeah," The Kid Answered. "He was on this morning. He tried to take me down but retreated when I called him waggish. I lulled him into a false sense—"

"Can you trace where someone is located while they play?" Alister interrupted.

"Can a monkey lick his butt?" The Kid laughed at his own comment. Alister furrowed his brow. The Kid stood up a bit taller and righted his stance. "It might take a little time. I'll have to hack the back wall. It would ruin the game for me…" The kid gulped down the rest of his drink. "But what the zounds."

"Do what you have to do, and please get back to me, A.S.A.P." The last statement got Alister a mock salute as boy genius disappeared around the corner. Alister dialed Alia. "I've got news…" he began to explain Soul Crusher Two and the possible Yarok lead.

As the chirping melody of crickets increased, so did Marv's singing. "When the crickets song connects with mine, my alien friends can't be far behind. When the sky is clear smattered with stars, the aliens can find me from near or afar…" He skipped, twirled, and sang really loud as he pranced along the dirt trail. Alongside the sound of his constant chatter, his stomach growled to the rhythm.

With only nature's visual guides of the moon and stars, he made his way through the dense forest. "I miss my tour bus that rocks… I miss my icebox filled with food… I might even miss Wally blocking my…" His laughter repeated in the trees. "Okay, actually, I don't miss that."

The muted sound of guitar strings floated in the distance. He stopped with one foot hung in the air as the rest of his body suspended in balance. Hands rose to cup his ears. "I must be dreaming," he whispered in the wind. "The elves are playing with my current mental state." He shushed himself so his mind could concentrate on the quiet, distant melody. "That poor instrument is being tortured. Tormented by whoever is attempting to stroke the beast. I must save it..." His foot came down hard against the path as his body stumbled in the direction of the noise.

The lower ferns brushed against his legs. Marv fought his way through the prickled vines. Hands swatted in front to destroy the sticky silk of a well-built spider web in front of his path. He continued to rub his hair and neck long after the spiders were left behind. The on-going sensation of an eight-legged creatures crawling around his upper half brought on a continued slap against flesh rhythm. His hands moved in constant motion circulating across the chest and upper shoulders.

Mid-step, he stopped again, the opposite foot raised in the same pose as before. A scoop of hands bending the outside of both ears in the direction of the sound. He listened to the crickets' song. The light strumming of a guitar now gone silent. "Damn it!" Marv's voice cut through the forest's din. Back came a gasp, or was that his imagination? His longing for human or alien cronies. He wrapped the hands-on top of his head. "Damn it!" He repeated a bit louder than the last.

He waited. The faint sound of a popular swear word whispered back. He kicked both feet in the air before throwing his hands above his head the way a ref would award a touchdown. "Okay, my new friends from the forest. I am the Marvelous one that you seek, in the flesh, at least for now." He kept his voice steady, his volume at a typical setting. "I am a lost soul, missing from the great golden bus, yet I am here to serve you."

Marv folded his body in half with the word serve. He waited as blood rushed to his head.

The twang of a guitar in pain drew closer along with a few grunts. When he lifted his head, the notes stopped. "It is me, Marvelous of the golden bus," he repeated with a bit more spectacle. He lifted his arms overhead. His body re-folded with hands touching the dirt. "Okay, Marvelous of the golden bus…"

"Shut up, you moron!" Brendan's voice cut through Marv's chat.

"Moron. I did not have knowledge of aliens using such human words. Huh. This is a new event," Marv said. He remained hung in the forward fold. "What news! They must be assimilating into our world! Oh, this is huge." His voice got louder as he spoke, "I can help you with the other language of our land. I can teach you the ways of planet Earth."

Brendan balanced his hip on the guitar neck. He took each step, delicately towards his friend's voice. A wall of tight leaves and vines blocked the view. Marv's proclamation came from the other side. "Marv—" Brendan spoke.

"Oh my god! You know my name. Yes, I am Marv—"

Brendan brought his hand to his forehead. He shook his head back and forth and blew out an audible exhale. "Step through the wall of leaves…" Brendan instructed. "Take the step—"

Marv turned his head around. Upside down, a wall of leaves blocked his view and his progress. Out of sight, Brendan anchored his good foot on the ground. He winced as he brought all his weight to one side. With forced effort, he smashed the neck into leaves to thrust the guitar body through the foliage.

His body hit the earth at the same moment, a loud twang erupted. Marv jumped at the sound.

"Oh my god!" Marv yelled. "What kind of beast are you that you would kill this beautiful creature?" He lifted the instrument to caress the beautiful wooden body with his hands. "Why! Why would you take away this exceptional joy maker—"

"I am over here, you moron," Brendan sat upright on the ground. The guitar's fall produced a window between the two. "And I could use a little help…"

In one fluid bounce, Marv parked his body next to Brendan's. He stared wide-eyed at his friend. "Are you a clone? The real Brendan would not torture this—"

"Marv," Brendan kept his voice steady. "Thank god you are alive."

"Alive and ready to serve, your—"

"Marv cut the shit. It is me, Brendan. What the—"

Marv reached his hand to Brendan's face. He touched his cheek with his index finger. Brendan slapped it away.

"Dude!"

"Dude!" Marv replied. He put his arms around Brendan and squeezed. "You came back! You came back! I knew you would. I mean, who leaves a dude on the crapper in the middle of nowhere, right?" He leaned back on his elbows. "Got any food? And where's our golden bus?"

Brendan kept his voice steady. "Dude, we are neither saved or safe. Freakin' Wally—"

"Who left me on the shitter—" Marv pointed out.

"I think he killed the bus driver, and I'm not sure, but I don't think he works with my dad." Brendan let that last thought sink in. "Marv, Wally is out there." Both brought their gaze to the night sky. "He chased me. I ran so fast!" Brendan sucked in more air. "We need to get out of here. We need to find a phone and call my dad. Most important, we need to get far away from Wally…"

"Yes, away from Wally. Freakin' Wally tells me not to crap on the bus because my shit stinks, and then he leaves me in the middle of this." Marv waved his hands in the air. "Freakin' Wally."

A slight breeze brought a rustle in the near distance. "We need to get out of here," Brendan said as he fought gravity to stand back up. Marv handed him the guitar, which helped prop his body to a standing position. Brendan turned to see tears on Marv's cheeks. "We are going to be okay, bud. We need to move."

"Not us," Marv said. He pointed at the Santa Cruz. "She was so beautiful."

The cane is now dented and covered with deep scratches. "Don't worry, she'll be beautiful again." Brendan turned his face out of view. His free hand wiped away a single drop of hurt from his cheeks before Marv could see.

Wally stomped around the empty tour bus. He picked up and threw the toaster against the wall. Next came the blender and anything else not attached. The sun had disappeared below the mountain tops. Signs of Brendan Curry had vanished into the trees. Even the imaginary sounds of guitar strings had stopped.

His brother, Otis, hadn't got back to him in hours. Yarok could drive up any minute for his missing package. Wally blew out his breath. "How the hell did I get mixed up in this?" He threw glasses at the wall as he spoke.

This one definitely came back to kick him hard. He should never have boasted to his little brother about his latest job. Otis had an unnatural attraction to damaged situations since he's returned from the Middle East, a place he should never have gone to in the first place.

The youngest sibling turned cold over there. Otis' joy disappeared. He wouldn't tell anyone, not even the older brother he looked up to, why. Wally took this job to get some cash to help out his damaged brother. That idiot Fred, another Middle East castaway, came up with this current cluster.

Wally loved the idea of financial independence since he got screwed out of his government pension by the latest administration. An island paradise appealed in many ways too. His body couldn't handle the winters anymore, and any visit to his ex-wife brought about Arctic temperatures.

She was one cold bitch.

Wally shook his head, and like the old Etch-A-Sketch, the image of the willowy brunette he once loved vanished from view. He texted Otis, *what is the plan? I am missing the critical element. May be time to cut losses – advice about your situation.*

His thumb rested above the send button as he scrolled through his unanswered queries. "Awe, what the hell." He hit send.

The ping on the agency's tracker screen caught the attention of the young hacker. He took a screenshot, added the location, and sent the information to Alister. He also bcc'd Attorney Curry's office, who, without hesitation, passed the information on to all involved.

And all involved still included Wally.

Prior communications were not visible to the entire group, yet the latest flashed back with his location information. "Freakin' double-cross," exclaimed Wally. At the same time his foot kicked through one of the Formica cabinets. With a slight shift of body, his left leg to cock back to deliver another blow. Before swinging his leg around, eyes focused onto daypack behind the driver's seat.

A quick rummaged through the closets had the bag weighted down with a few boxes of bullets and his spare Glock from the bus freezer. A box of Kind bars tossed in, just in case Curry's brat circled back after he left. "Let the prince try to find his special order," Wally laughed. In one move, his work phone slipped into the charger at the front of the bus. He grabbed the old sleeping bag that hung over the driver's seat and headed out the door.

"I made it back from halfway around the world without anyone's help. For me to get out of these Pennsylvania woods and disappear for the rest of my life should be as easy as ordering a cold beer on Deval Street," Wally mumbled as he circled the bus. At the edge of the pine forest, he froze. His lips turned upward into a sly grin. In one move, all that he carried dropped onto the pine needle floor.

"Screw them all," Wally said as he jogged back to the bus. Once inside, he threw every piece of clothing into a significant pile outside, on the ground. As he walked passed, a slide of the hand turned all the knobs on the gas stove to high. "Let them find the burnt-out skeleton of their precious tour bus," he laughed at the same time he pushed the door shut.

He ran into the woods to gather sticks and branches. The pile on the side of the bus grew with each trip. Down on his hands and knees, he shimmied his body underneath the vehicle. With a swift kick, the small hatch on the underside came loose. Wally stretched back to drag an awkward branch by his side. He positioned the dried-out top inside the trap then slid out from underneath.

He formed the remaining branches into a trail that stretched from under the bus to about six feet away. Most of the kindling appeared cracked. On top of the dead branches, Wally filled in the trail with the clothing thrown from the bus. The spare gas can from the back deck unfastened with ease. The smell of gas soon replaced the fresh mountain air.

The first match he tossed into the brush flamed out. Wally muttered, "Crap!" under his breath.

The second match smoldered into tiny puffs of smoke yet didn't catch. "Third time is a—" Wally didn't get to finish his sentence as a bright yellow blaze spewed out from underneath.

He grabbed his daypack off the ground and sprinted into the trees. A silent countdown brought a ground rocking explosion at ten. Wally's smile grew. "So long suckers," he waved in the direction of the furious flames.

The ground under Brendan and Marv shook. A red fireball moved across the sky.

"They blew up the aliens," Marv cried out. He stared up into the sky as he stroked his chin. "Or it could be the aliens blew them up." His face lit up with the idea of aliens destroying bad people. Brendan started to walk in the opposite direction. "Where are you…"

"Away from that," he pointed towards the gray smoke now mixing with peeks of orange.

"But the—"

"I don't know about any aliens, but I do know for us that can't be good." He started to hobble again.

"What about—"

"Marv, we need to get help. Think about it - good help doesn't torch things." Brendan kept moving. "We can find the aliens later, or they should find us," Brendan said. "For now, please come with me."

Marv stared into the flames. His body swayed with each movement. Brendan reached out to the guitar neck to knock into his leg.

"Uh, what did you say?" Marv's stringy hair lifted with each shake of his head. He turned to focus on Brendan.

Brendan repeated, "I said we need to get help and out of here. Listen, whoever or whatever…"

"I get it." Marv started to follow. "I don't like it. But I comprehend. Let's rock and—"

"Please don't say it. I have done enough rolling for my lifetime," Brendan responded. The two moved in silence away from the glow. The stars and moonlight somewhat lit the path. Their energy faded as the flames in the distance.

Brendan heard a loud yawn from behind. He turned to see Marv leaning up against a tree trunk. Eyes closed; breath rhythmic.

"Dude, come on, we've got to—"

"Five minutes. That is all I need…" Marv mumbled.

Brendan walked back the ten feet between them. A faded marker appeared above

Marv's head that drew his attention. "What is that?" he pointed.

"Spider? Snake? Bird shit?" Marv jumped away from the tree. Hands slapped all over his body as he turned around in a crazy circle.

"Shush, you moron." Brendan hobbled closer. "Holy crap, a trail marker! Marv, we are on an actual trail!" Brendan jumped around to the other side then winced as his leg nailed the ground. "Yes, yes," his enthusiasm slipped around the trunk, although his body was invisible. "There are two markings, one blue and another yellow. Huh."

"This side appears only blue," Marv confirmed. "If I remember right from my boy scout days, the yellow and blue go in our direction, and if this side is only blue, then the yellow split somewhere close by."

"You were a boy scout?" Brendan's head appeared around the tree.

Marv shrugged. "Yeah, it was before my alien abduction." He helped Brendan back around the tree. "Yellow or blue, my friend?"

"We have blue in front of us," he said.

"The yellow should be easier to see," Marv walked in a circle. He stopped at each trunk to examine the side. His circle widened as his body left Brendan's sight. He arrived back to announce, "Blue it is," as he took the lead.

"No more yellow markers," Brendan's voice rose from behind him.

"Exactly," said Marv. He pointed to the trail.

Smoky drove along the old highway that paralleled I-80, enjoying the calm quiet. Behind him, the polite conversation ceased between Jimmy and Alia. Neither had given away anything of themselves. Both practiced the mastery of saying nothing. Perhaps they fell asleep in the process.

His stomach grumbled a bit. He reached into his stash of bus nuts, a spiced-up version of pecans and walnuts he kept for such an occasion. A handful would take off the edge until they could find an all-night diner. Alia's phone buzzed in the charger next to him. He thought to wake her then decided against it. Whatever the message, it could wait.

The bullet-shaped scar on Alia's stomach raised too many questions for him. She had tugged her shirt down at the same moment he averted his eyes. Neither spoke after.

An expansive valley spread out in front of the windshield. A clear night, bright white dots speckled above the horizon, while below a natural state of calm lay in the shadows. The only man-made light illuminated from his bus to light the pavement.

He let out a small sigh as he reached over to pop in his Allman Brother's Brothers and Sisters cassette. The soft notes of Jessica filled the silence. As Dicky Betts started in on his famous guitar solo, Smoky's foot slammed the break. He forced the bus into the narrow breakdown lane.

Alia's feet hit the wall of the bunk with force. "What the—" She heard Jimmy yell from the other bed.

"Smoky, are we okay?" A barrage of swears followed. Both jumped out at the same moment. Their collision brought another round of f-bombs. "Smoky?"

"What the hell is that?" Smoky's startled voice rose above the clatter. The two leaned over the driver's seat and followed his shaking finger.

In the middle of the valley, the glow of fire ranged. "It was so peaceful, and then this ball of flames rose—"

Jimmy leaned in closer at the same moment Alia grabbed her phone. "That ain't no bonfire gone astray," he noted.

"More like an explosion." Smoky lowered his voice, "Do you think…" Jimmy waved his hand below his chin. "Yeah, me too."

Alia turned back towards the men and held up one finger. Alister didn't answer. She called the number a second time. Two rings, her finger hit end. Alia counted to ten and pushed to dial again.

Alister picked up on the first ring. "Blazes," his voice sounded hoarse.

"Exactly," Alia said. "We are currently traveling along," she turned towards the front of the bus.

"The old highway that runs outside of Susquehannock State Forest runs alongside I-80," Smoky said.

"The old highway—"

"I can hear, Alia. What is the situation?" Alister snapped back into the receiver.

Alia stuck her tongue out at the phone. "About three miles," she got a nod back from Smoky, "into the state forest a few minutes ago a firebomb explosion appeared on the horizon.

From our view, it looks like a quick developing forest fire."

"Turn your damn locator on, Alia," Alister ordered. Alia slipped the blue button on and waited. She could hear shuffling on the other end, along with Jimmy and Smoky's hushed voices from the front. She paced while she waited.

"That there is not good," Jimmy's voice got a bit louder. "Smoky, how far?"

"About an hour by this route. Of course, that depends what the police shut down." Smoky edged the bus back on the road. "I'll follow the edge for now."

Jimmy nodded, and asked, "Any idea?"

"Got to be something decent size," Smoky pointed back to the flames. "Whatever it is, it went up quick."

"Drug lab?" asked Jimmy.

"Don't think so, the way the flame went up and those usually have a blue tinge in their fire from the chemicals," Smoky noted. "I'd say something much bigger."

"I am waiting for my boss," Alia pointed towards the phone. She moved further to the front and leaned her body onto the back of Smoky's seat. Swear words poured from her phone's speaker as Alister's voice grew in volume. "What do you think that was?"

Jimmy turned in his seat. "Something pretty big. Could it be a gas explosion? That would explain the spread." The fire moved up the hillside. Several fire trucks roared past along with five helicopters overhead.

"Alia!" Alister's call cut into the conversation. Alia held up one finger.

"I'm here, sir," answered Alia.

"Alia, there are emergency units on the way. We have a crew that should arrive within the hour. How far out are you?"

"Less than forty-five minutes," she looked over at Smoky, who nodded confirmation.

"Drive slow. Watch the side of the road. Find a base camp at the perimeter—"

"Alister, you do realize that per your orders, I do not have a team. I am currently on a tour bus, with civilians—" Alia reminded.

"I failed to recall you are undercover. Hum. That presents a problem. Your team did not make a connection with you yet?" Alister shuffled papers in the background. Alia nodded her head at the phone. "That is unusual. They should be there. I'll get back to you. Continue heading towards the area of interest." Alister's voice ceased.

Jimmy grabbed a hold of Alia's arm. "So, what did your boss—"

"He said to continue towards the area." The orange and gray colors now spread into the valley below.

Smoky coughed. "We need to go in this direction to get to Ohio. Let's keep our eyes open for anything weird." He gave a slight nod to Jimmy. Smoky blew out a breath and stated, "God, I hate this shit."

"Back at ya, partner," Jimmy answered as he sat back in the passenger's seat. The dark forest pass by on the side. Every few minutes, out of place orange flames captured their attention.

Harlot leaned over Yarok to look out at the blazing skyline. "That can't be good," she noted as Yarok's hand drifted up and down her thigh. He said something in Russian and scoffed at whatever response his driver gave back.

"That fire may complicate our cause," Yarok said in perfect English. He stared out the window. "Try to get a hold of the one on the bus," he instructed.

Harlot pressed send and disconnected serval times. The driver watched her in the rearview mirror. "Does the phone ring or go straight to voice mail?" he asked.

"Straight to voicemail, why?" Harlot met his eyes with a half blank, half bitch stare.

Yarok's laugh filled the vehicle. "Straight to voicemail means the phone is off. Ringing indicates that the phone could be destroyed," Yarok explained. The flames drew his attention, "or the owner turned it off."

Harlot sucked in a breath. "Do you think Wally double-crossed…" Yarok dug his finger further into her thigh. "Ouch," she screamed as she pushed his hand away. Red indents remained.

"A double-cross is a death sentence," Yarok stated. He reached around Harlot to remove a pistol from the side panel. "A death sentence for all." He dragged the barrel of the gun along her left breast, up her neck. "Darling."

Harlot pushed the gun away. She crossed her legs away from Yarok. "You are an idiot," she said in perfect Russian.

"And you are a whore," he answered in English. Up ahead, traffic slowed as blue lights flashed in the distance. "Keep going," Yarok instructed. He turned back to Harlot, "And you know, you are my whore and no one elses," he said as he placed his lips on her neck. She shifted towards the door yet kept within the range of Yarok's hands and mouth. "I need a distraction."

Her lips turned up as he righted himself in the seat. The glow from his cellphone highlighted a growing five o'clock shadow. With a press of a button, the gaming app came alive. Harlot yawned as a black knight appeared on his screen.

The car inched forward towards the lights.

Alister walked into his office at 4:39 a.m. The soft glow of a computer screen greeted him.

"Bit early, even for you," he noted. The Kid appeared like he hadn't moved in days. His stained white t-shirt and ever-present pajama pants let off a distinctive adolescent boy's body scent. He slumped down in Alister's green high back chair. His eyes focused on the giant screen on the opposite wall.

"I haven't left," he said. "Told my mom I had to work late." He reached under the desk to bring up a bottle of Mountain Dew. Alister observed his trash overflowed with empties. "I hope you don't mind. My screen is way too small, and since you weren't around…"

"How did you get in my office?" asked Alister.

"Yeah, about that. The scanner locks you guys use, probably want to reprogram the whole building…" The Kid's fingers banged on the keyboard. "I mean I got in, but you comprehend, that ain't saying—" He stared at the screen. "Bingo."

Alister walked around the desk for a better view of the screen. In the middle sat a court jester dressed in purple and green. The figure bounced around the perimeter and danced across the middle in circles. Unfamiliar phrases spewed from its mouth and appeared on a scroll on the bottom. The Kid giggled as he typed.

"Take that you fuddle bag of manure!" said The Kid.

Alister observed as a *fuddled bag of manure* ran across the crawler. A black knight rode in from the pine trees on the left.

"Holy space balls!" The Kid yelled. He began to frantically type as the knight approached the jester. "That's our guy," he pointed to the screen.

"Whose guy?"

"The dude you are looking for," The Kid pointed at the black knight. "He wants to battle me. Oh yeah. It's on!"

Alister asked, "Yarok?"

"If that's the dude's name on that photo you showed me earlier," The Kid said. He moved to the side as Alister leaned in closer, the reminded, "This is who I stayed up all night for."

"Can you get a physical location on him?" Alister ran one hand over his face. Both watch the knight raise his sword. The words *plague sore* sailed across the crawler.

"Oh man, I thought he was smarter than this. See, he already used plague sore with his last victim. I need something good…" said The Kid. He waved his hand in Alister's direction to cut off his speak. "No, no, let me think. I am actually good at this. I can't let him beat me."

"To hell with the game," Alister pointed to the blank screen. "We need a location—"

"I can't get a location if I don't keep him engaged in the game. I need time for the tracer cookie. Oh, here, let's try this one." The Kid brought up the other screen. The rhythm of hands on a keyboard filled the silence. Across the crawler of the game, the words *bull's pizzle* appeared. He switched back to the gaming screen to type a second code.

"Wait, he's leaving," Alister said. The knight climbed on his horse. The figure moved towards the forest.

"He's not giving up that easily," The Kid said. His breath now shallow. *giving up easily? I thought you were better than that* scrolled across the crawler. The knight stopped. He drew his sword high in the air. The horse did a 180. A light blue streak whizzed across the screen towards the kid's avatar. "Oh shit."

"Lang… oh, never mind. What is going on?" Alister leaned in closer.

The Kid's fingers tore across the keyboard. His breath shaky, liquid sweat radiated through his t-shirt.

"Damn it," The Kid yelled. He banged both hands down on the space bar. "Come on, baby, move!" The upper portion of the avatar shifted to the left. The light blue bolt blasted across to turn the entire screen bright white. The Kid typed, and a moment later, *asshole* drifted across the crawler, followed by *how pedestrian of you.* The Kid stared at the screen, arms folded across the front of his chest.

"What happened?" Alister asked. His focused moved between the screen and his computer expert.

The scene on the screen changed pixel by pixel from the forest to a bunch of neon-colored tubes. The kid's avatar sat on top of a bright purple platform in the upper right corner. The black night climb atop a yellow platform on the opposite side.

"Damn, androgynous colors," The Kid muttered. He pressed down to hold on to two keys. With his other hand, he opened a small laptop computer and typed in the URL on the second screen. He waited.

The laptop screen turned a shade of mud. A little yellow dot blinked in the bottom left corner. Again, like rapid-fire, he typed in various commands. The speck grew as the mud turned to dark green. "Come on, baby," The Kid coaxed as he swerved his index finger along the built-in mouse.

The screen fluttered and went blank.

Smoky maneuvered the bus along the backcountry road. A few cars scurried by in the opposite direction. All aware that this is just a matter of time before they reached a traffic back-up, police, or both. He continued to monitor the bus scanner via an earbud in his left. His right ear paid attention to the sounds of the night. The Allman Brothers returned to the proper cassette case on the floor.

Alia had gone in the back to think. Not much noise coming from there. Jimmy sat to his right, phone rested on his upper thigh, eyes closed. The hum of the engine interrupted by the buzz of Jimmy's phone.

He jumped in the seat to send the phone hard against the dashboard. Smoky turned down the scanner in his ear.

"What?" Jimmy yelled. "Seriously? Where the fuck are you?" Alia crawled closer to the front, still out of both sightlines. "Are you kidding me? Hang on a minute." Jimmy closed his eyes and said something unintelligible to the ceiling. He mouthed *Fred* to Smoky, who nodded back.

"You did what?" Jimmy barked while Smoky grinned. "Awe, Jesus. Smoky, where's the GPS?" Smoky handed a small box to Jimmy. "Okay, give me your location." A beep on the screen indicated a mile difference. "Hang tight. We'll be right there."

Jimmy leaned back in the seat before a wealth of swears escaped his lips. "Where are we heading, boss?" asked Smoky.

"In about ten minutes, there will be a right-hand turn that heads into the forest," Jimmy pointed into the night.

"I take it you want me to drive towards the flames?" Smoky's question is answered with a nod, "Can I ask why?"

"Guess," Jimmy threw his hands up.

"Are you going to share with Althea?"

"No," Jimmy answered.

Alia crawled back down the hall into the back room. She shifted her body on top of the couch at the same moment Jimmy entered. She pretended to sleep, although she could hear her heart beating over the engine. "Althea," Jimmy shook her shoulder.

She stretched her arms over her head. Her eyes opened to Jimmy too much in her space. All of her space. "Did we get close enough to the explosion?" she asked. Her voice raspy although she hadn't slept.

"Not yet. We are going to be turning off up yonder. I think we found a back way in," Jimmy said.

"I will text Alister, the local. He can have—"

Jimmy placed his hands on top of hers. "I would wait on that text. We think we have a trail. We aren't sure. The road on the map could be a real trail, or could be it is another old highway…" Jimmy rose. "I wanted to keep you updated in case the ride gets bumpy."

She waited for a twenty count before she texted the change to Alister then refreshed for a response. When none came, Alia added an additional layer of clothing to her t-shirt and shorts along with pulling on clean socks and shoes. The bus took a hard-right turn and promptly hit a pothole. Alia slammed her shoulder into the side.

"You alright back there," Smoky yelled.

"Just peachy," she said. Her shoulder is pulsed with pain. She got her shoulder as close to the wall as possible before she leaned back in the opposite direction. A slight stretch gave way, yet the pain still pulsed. Alia filled a small backpack with a couple bottles of water and some energy bars. She switched her locator on and off several times in hopes that Alister would notice.

The device went into the front pocket.

The bus bounced again. "Hey, Althea," Smoky yelled. "You may want to come up here where the seatbelts are." She pored over a place to ditch the bag, opting for between a bunk curtain and the bathroom. Hidden out of sight, Alia held on to both sides of the bus as she made her way to the front.

"Where the heck are we?" she asked as she took the seat directly behind Smoky.

"Old highway. Must be a fire road now," Smoky said. Tree branches scratched up against the sides of the windows.

Alia asked, "Ah, Smoky, are you going to be able to turn this baby around? Or back her up to the main road?"

"Not sure," Smoky said, "mister genius here says he knows what he's doing."

"Huh," Alia responded. She sat further back in the seat.

"Don't worry, we'll get you to Ohio," Jimmy said. The flames are now reflected in the windshield.

"You sure about that?" Alia started her mantra, "I am not drunk. I am not high. I don't drink or do drugs…"

"Stop that!" Smoky said. "Just so you know, I texted Tiny and Zadie with an update. We all are going to be okay."

Alia asked, "Where are they?"

"Almost in South Carolina. They will drive through the night home and then head out to Colorado in a few days. No worries there," Smoky replied.

"Look," Jimmy started to say, "Your boss man was the one who said to continue on this route, which is what we are doing."

Smoky glanced at Alia in the mirror. Her face might be relaxed, yet he noted her eyes narrowed back.

Attorney General Curry and Captain Louis Pilsner barged into Alister's office while his secretary yelled an apology. "To what do I owe this pleasure," Alister said at the same moment Curry barked, "Now I can see why my boy is still out there, Reed. What do you people do here, sit around and play videogames all day? My wife is going crazy…"

Alister opened his mouth to speak yet got interrupted by Captain Pilsner, "That isn't a game, sir. See the dot that's moving?" All three leaned over the kid to watch the blinking yellow dot. "What is that?"

"We believe that is Yarok," Alister said with all the confidence he could muster. The Kid opened his mouth. Alister waved his hand under his chin. The Kid closed his mouth.

"If that is Yarok, why isn't he under arrest?"

"Good question, Attorney General," answered Alister. He glanced over at The Kid, gave a slight head shake no, then continued,

"We are confirming that is him because if it is a decoy, and we pounce, we lost an opening. You, sir, understand the way this stuff works better than anyone."

"What about my boy? I heard about something blowing up in those woods. What blew up?" Attorney General Curry interrogated.

"We don't have that information as yet. I have someone on their way there now. Believe me, we are doing everything possible—"

"Don't give me that politically correct bullshit line, Alister. This is me you are talking to. We have worked together for decades." Attorney General Curry looked up at Alister, "Please, tell me, where is my son?"

Alister blew out a breath. "As I started to say, sir, we have one of my top agents in the area along with her back-up on route. I am waiting for a report from her as we speak." Alister glanced at the missed call on his screen. "I am not trying to appease you here. Please do not interpret my next action as such. However, how about you and Captain Pilsner go get a coffee. I am going to give Alia a call and get an update. I hope to have good news when you return."

The two men regarded each other and then back at Alister. "Fine," Attorney General Curry answered, "You better have something." He pointed his finger towards Alister's face, which remained neutral. "I mean it."

Alister waited for a beat after they left to mumble, "I really hate that guy." The Kid responded with a slight giggle. He grabbed his phone off the desk to read through Alia's text. Her last sentence brought his attention to Yarok's tracker.

"Was there any other activity on this map?" Alister asked as he turned his gaze on the kid.

"Yeah, I think that a blue dot blinked a bunch of times over there," The Kid pointed up at the screen.

Alister kicked the chair. He wiggled his finger in the air. "Over where?" he asked.

The Kid stood. He stretched his arms over his head as he took a step towards the map. A lingering body odor followed. "Man, I got to make this map clearer. We can't even get the route number on this dude," he mumbled. With a few quick hits to the space bar the satellite photo focused. "Yeah, there we go. The blue flashers came from here," The Kid pointed to a remote area to the west of where the yellow dot moved.

"Can you get a locator to show the other location, too?" Alister moved closer to scrutinize the map. "And, are you able to turn on some type of heat sensors to show the fire locations?" he added.

The Kid responded with a bored look. "Do you want to have the location of the helicopters you sent too?"

"That would be nice," Alister answered. A crimson tide rose up from his neck.

"No problem. But I have to tell you," The Kid watched Alister waved his hands in the air to continue, "I am not a hundred percent on the dude's position as yet. I need about ten minutes and some nasty Russian swear words."

"Try Hillary," Alister barked as he exited the room. Down the hall, Curry and Pilsner leaned against the white tiled counter in the break room. Neither changed position when Alister entered. "The kid is hacking a program to get a location on Yarok. What we have now is preliminary. My agent, Alia Price, is close by with a team," he reported.

"When can we expect confirmation and an arrest of Yarok?" Pilsner asked.

"My hope is within the hour we will have at least the first part and be in process of the second. The Kid—"

"That teenager is your tech expert?" Attorney General Curry's eyes opened wide.

"Yeah, The Kid is my tech guy because that kid hacked into our system for fun. He has talents that need to be cultivated for our team. You know, the whole good versus evil thing. In theory, he's playing some online game with Yarok."

Both men went slack jaw. "For real?" Pilsner asked.

"I jest you not. If that is Yarok, the trick is to keep him engaged long enough to bounce off the satellite without him catching on. Lucky for us, that kid is very competitive and wants to win."

Alister took a slow sip off his mug. "And the explosion?" Attorney General Curry inquired.

"The explosion is under investigation. There are cross department people on the scene. From what we gather, it looks like a recreational vehicle had a gas leak and blew. Again, I am waiting for confirmation," Alister stated.

"A recreation vehicle?" Curry repeated. "Like a tour bus?"

"We don't have the vehicle type as yet," Alister answered.

The attorney general's face turned bright white.

Alister continued, "Listen, I appreciate this must be difficult, yet if we could avoid jumping to conclusions—"

"That's my boy out there!" Attorney General Curry yelled.

"I understand, sir, yet we don't have…"

Captain Pilsner turned towards his care, "Attorney General Curry this sounds like we need to put our trust in Alister's team and, unfortunately for us, wait."

Attorney General Curry gave a simple head nod in return.

The grey fog rose in a circle to hug the lush green vegetation. The calm of night now lost to animal panic—screeches filled in the quiet. Chipmunks scurried about as shadows of vultures moved in between the tall branches.

Brendan leaned up against a boulder, hunched over, arms rested on his hacked-up guitar. His breath labored. Marv moved ahead in the near distance.

"Dude, I think if we go this way, we get away from the flames," Marv said. Behind him, his friend's head rested between his knees. Marv stomped back. "No way, brother. This is not happening. You and I have been through way too much together." He lifted Brendan by his armpits to hang his torso over Marv's boney shoulders.

"Just go—"

"No," Marv responded. "Think about it. If anything happens to you, your mother will blame me. Every week, when we were at Skidmore, she would tell me not to do anything stupid and to please take care of you. Every. Single. Week. I really like your mom, even though I get the feeling that she thinks I am a bad influence—"

"Why would you think that?"

Marv continued as if he didn't hear anything, "although I can't figure out why because I have always been over the top polite to her. And I am the one who usually dragged your ass away from the parties in a drunken mess or saved you from your harem of groupies." Marv tossed one hand in the air. The other remained with a tight grip on Brendan's wrist. "It doesn't matter anyway, no, I am not leaving you." He stopped to sniff the air. "We got to move, brother." He moved his body to bend over to a forty-five-degree angle—Brendan's full weight on top of his back. "Wait," he said as he reversed his tracks. "We can't leave the Santa…"

"Marv," Brendan fell into a coughing fit. Marv shifted the guitar to rest across the front of his body. Brendan's wrists wedged underneath. "Damn."

"Hang on. I am going to follow the animals. The creatures know how to save themselves. And the aliens will help us too"

Marv pushed back the brush with the guitar body. Brendan bounced into tree trunks and thorn bushes.

"Marv, you really don't have to…" his voice wavered.

"Talk later," Marv answered. A hawk dove into the bush on their right. The scream cut through the chatter. A wide-eyed rabbit emerged between the hawk's talons as the strong bird rose back up into the treetops. Marv's body gave an involuntary shudder.

Visibility vanished with each step. Marv's eyes started to tear. The pace quickened. A slight shift in the wind brought a short reprisal of semi-fresh air. Marv shifted his direction into the puff of air. Brendan let out an audible sigh into his ear.

"Hang in there, buddy," Marv shouted. "We just played before a thousand screaming fans at that festival. We can get out of this mess too."

Although he couldn't see, Brendan's lips turned upward as his mind wandered to a crowd of bikini-clad young women.

Alia braced her body as the bus bounced up and down an obviously not maintained road. Smoky slowed and swore at each pothole. Jimmy sat silently in the passenger seat. His focus shifted from the road to the cellphone that rested in his palm.

"I'm sorry to ask again yet," she said as she slammed against the couch for the fourth time, "where does this take us?" Outside, a slight fog started to surround the brush. Alia's arms prickled.

"Short cut," Jimmy said.

"To where?" Alia pushed.

Smoky pulled the bus into a run-down rest stop. A wooden shack on one side featured faded outlines of a man and woman's shapes. The remains of a trail sign stood off to the side.

"Here," Smoky answered. He turned his entire body towards Jimmy. "This is it, bro. I can't go further without knowing we have a place to turn around. The road is getting worst as we get further in, and," he pointed towards the vanishing landscape. "I don't like the looks of that."

"I get it." Jimmy turned away. "Let's sit tight for a minute or two."

Alia excused herself to the bathroom. She checked the door to make sure it closed tight. Her phone read *no service* in the upper left corner, yet she typed out a quick text to Alister along with hitting the locator button three times. She splashed water onto her face. In the mirror, her lips curved into a semi-smile. Alia mumbled to her reflection, "Don't worry sister, I got this." The door of the bus whooshed open.

She returned to a quiet cab. Smoky sat in the driver's seat, his attention focused on something outside.

"What's going on?" Alia asked. She had seen that face before when he heard her story. From what she knew about him, this was a full-alert position. She moved by his side to follow his focus.

Two men embraced over by the shack. One, evident to her, was Jimmy, and the other seemed familiar. Again, prickles rose on her arm.

"Who is that?" she asked.

"Simply an old lowlife who seems to come around at the worst times," Smoky replied. "I want to talk about that scar you have on your belly, but not--" He leaned forward. "This is—" He shot out of his chair. The other man's face appeared in the lights. Recognition kicked in immediately with a series of flashes. The man from the hill with Miranda. The one backstage leaning on the stairs. The guy who tried to break into the other bus.

Her stomach bubbled.

Smoky moved to stand in the open door, arms folded across his chest. The conversation was now audible.

"Fred, what the fuck have you got yourself into now? I thought I saw you backstage—"

"Your new band sounded pretty righteous, bro," Alia mouthed "Bro" to Smoky, who gave a slight affirmative nod back. "I can't believe you hooked up with the old neighborhood again. "

"No thanks to you. Fred, your foolishness cost me my job. Put me back in the trenches for ten freaking years. Almost got me killed. That stunt you pulled—"

Fred released a booming laugh. "Stunt? Bro-man, that stash was worth millions. Millions! I mean, come on, we could have bought an island and retired."

"Bought an island? Bought an island! Where do you get these shit ideas?" Jimmy said. He poked his finger into Fred's chest for emphasis. "I mean, seriously, what is wrong with you? First, you bring illegal narcotics onto my private jet. My private jet, you ass!"

Fred's arms flew in the air. "I was trying to make us rich! And you were the idiot in that situation. All you did was complain about being on the road, dealing with the people in your band, wasting your talents. Your poor, pathetic life—"

"That's what people do, you idiot! We complain! Are you that stupid? I swear mom dropped you on your head when you were a baby." Jimmy took a few steps towards the bus. He turned to shake his finger at Fred. "I love playing the guitar. What I didn't love was being forced back into government work to help right your wrong."

Smoky gave only a slight flinch when Alia's hand brushed his shoulder. She mouthed, "Government work?" Smoky held up one finger and gave a small nod back to the conversation.

"Well, how was I supposed to know that? I was trying to help— "

Jimmy's voice rose to full volume, "Help who? I had to sign away my songwriting credits to make your shit right with my bandmates. And then you get involved with freaking drug runners! Drug runners! Do you want to go through what I spent the last ten years doing to make that right?"

"Now that wasn't my fault. The little lady asked me for a favor," Fred smirked.

"The little lady asked you to bring two suitcases full of heroin on my freaking plane!" screamed Jimmy.

"Yeah? So?" Fred repositioned his stance, arms crossed over his puffed-out chest.

"Yeah. So, someone tipped off the authorities, and they wanted to search my private jet when we landed— " Jimmy paced.

"My bad," Fred answered and continued as if Jimmy hadn't spoke, "Anyway, why would the Feds search your jet? You were running a hustle for them in the first place."

"Fred, I was not running a freaking hustle, you ass." Jimmy turned back towards the bus. His eyes scanned the windows.

"No, dude, you don't understand. Deal said--" The crunch of bones echoed in the wind. Jimmy turned his back to Fred. He shook his left fist. His brother hunched over, both hands cupped his nose—crimson liquid leaked between his fingers.

"Oh shit," Smoky said as he reached into the glove compartment to pull out a small white pistol. Alia raised an eyebrow. "It's the misses," he added, as if that explained everything.

Fred stood, still with one hand holding his nose, gun in the other, aimed at Jimmy. "You bastard!" he screamed. "I came to you for help!"

"Goober, you came to me because you are desperate," Jimmy's voice returned to calm.

"DON'T CALL ME GOOBER!" screamed Fred. The gun shook in his hand.

"Put that thing away—" Jimmy took a step closer.

"I should have killed you when I had the chance. They told me to kill you, but I said no. I should have listened. I don't need this bullshit," Fred's hand shook as he spoke.

"I'm your brother, Goob." Jimmy took another step closer.

"Stop that," Fred answered, He steadied the barrel on Jimmy's face.

"Stop what, Goob?" On his third step, Jimmy brought his left leg around. His foot hit Fred's hand to send the gun flying. Fred tried to swing a punch with the other. Jimmy blocked the move. "Stop," Jimmy said. Fred blew out a breath at the same moment his brother's fist met his stomach.

His body buckled over.

Smoky joined to help Jimmy carry Fred's slumped body towards the bus. Alia grabbed her backpack and slipped into the angry husband hatch. The bus tilted as Jimmy and Smoky dragged the body inside. She counted to five and raised the outside hatch. Without hesitation, she jumped onto the gravel, sprinted across the parking lot, into the dark cover of the woods.

Alister walked back from the corner store. New pack of smokes in one hand. His breast pocket buldged with matchbooks. He turned into the alleyway to the side entrance to the building. After a scan of his I.D. and passcode, the door opened to voices in the stairwell above.

The door bounced against his shoe before a quiet click against the frame. Alister backed into the corner, out of sight, and waited. Conversations in stairwells are never meant to be overheard. Deep in his building, someone gave away their secrets. His mission had become to find the leak. At this point in the process, all communication had possibilities.

"What do you mean the last location was a bust? That is what the kid sent to me." Silence. "No, the kid thinks I am part of the team. I made sure he connected me to Reed." Alister removed his cellphone from his breast pocket and hit the record button. He reached around the corner to place the phone on the stairs.

"I sat in Reed's office. I gave him the new information that came out. What? Do you think I am incompetent?" Footsteps clanked a bit louder with each step. "No, I am going to pick up his highness now. When will I see a deposit?"

Alister pressed his back against the wall as his body moved towards the emergency exit that leads into the lobby. He swiped his I.D. and again entered his passcode. The click of the door handle stopped the conversation.

"What? No, I heard something. I got to go. I will see you soon." The footsteps beat grew louder and faster. The door slammed behind Alister as he made his way into the lobby.

"Commander Reed," an agent greeted him with a nod.

"Do you have your sidearm?" Alister asked, out of breath.

"Yes, sir," the agent moved his coat to reveal a standard-issue Sig Sauer P226.

"Arrest whoever walks out of that stairwell," Alister turned towards the lobby. "I need back-up over here!" Two more agents ran around the corner.

"Commander Reed."

"Arrest whoever walks out of that stairwell. Bring that person to my office stat." Four pairs of eyes examined the stairwell door, guns drawn. After five minutes, Alister opened the door. "What the hell?"

The quiet calm of the gray stairwell caught him by surprise. One of the agents opened the door to the alleyway. "Empty," he reported back. The others stood to wait for direction. The phone lay in the corner, where he had placed it, still on record.

"Huh," Alister said. Hands-on hips, he walked over and looked up the stairway. With one move, he slipped the phone into his side pocket.

"Do you want us to do a floor sweep?" one of the agents asked.

"No, no, that is okay. I will take care of this," Alister moved around the group. "Please go back to your duties, and thank you for your quick reaction."

"Commander Reed—" Alister waved him off. "Yes, sir." With quick salutes, the three walked back towards the lobby in silence.

The Mercedes slowed down against a back-up of red lights. No cars passed in the opposite direction as the taillights extended around the curve, off into the distance. Yarok rested one hand on Harlot's exposed thigh while the other typed frantically into his phone.

"Take this, you little loh," as *you scurvy companion* flashed across his screen.

"Must you address your opponent as a sucker, darling?" Harlot's voice barely above a whisper. "Ouch!" she screamed as his fingers dug in.

"My games are none of your business, darling." His eyes floated to hers for a mere second.

"You are correct, Yarok, yet you possess such a better vocabulary than to swear at this toad in Russian." Yarok leaned over to kiss her cheek. Satisfied, Harlot closed her eyes.

"Yes, my dear, yet this little svoloch just called me a plague sore."

"No need to refer to him, or her for that matter, as a bastard. Didn't you use that one in your last battle?" Harlot asked.

"Ah, you remember, my darling," Yarok stroked her cheek with his free hand. "I did," her body bounced against the window as the car seat moved with his excitement. "Thank you, my love. I think you have won me this round."

Harlot opened one eye, shook her head, and leaned back on the headrest.

With fast typing, Yarok wrote, *thou lump of foul deformity, I used that in the last battle. Prepare to meet your maker, you Alexander the second zasranets!* His laughter filled the air. "Don't mess with a pro," he mumbled as he bounced with glee.

Alister returned to his office to find The Kid pacing between his two computers. He shook his fists at the larger screen and mumbled something about using Tolstoyian references with a modern-day curse. At the smaller, he stopped. His little, boyish fingers flew over the keyboards.

His jester wobbled. The screen burst into a bright crimson. Drips of red plummeted like rain off a windowpane. The Kid ignored the visual. "God damn, his brain is ear wax," the rhythm of the keys matched the beat of his breaths. "Freakin' pedestrian insult takes me down. I thought better of you!"

Manic laughter filled the room as his grubby t-shirt dampened. Almost like a psychotic tennis match, Alister's head jolted back and forth to follow the young body's bounce around the room. "Um—" began Alister. A young hand flew up in the air to signal stop. Alister pursed his lips as he made his way to the smaller screen. "Is that—"

"Yes," The Kid scribbled numbers down on a piece of paper as he spoke, "he's in the middle of Pennsylvania, not even the Russian badass he claimed to be." A whistled breath replaced the negative energy. The snort of a generous intake off a prescription inhaler followed. The Kid slumped in Alister's chair to appear even younger than his actual age. His underdeveloped body gave away his real maturity.

Neither spoke.

"I had him," The Kid began to mumble. "I had him until that bald dude came in and disrupted my concentration." He balled his hands into small fists.

"What bald dude?" Alister asked. The Kid stared back wide-eyed.

"When did you get here?" he stared at a paper in Alister's hand.

"You gave this to me," Alister moved to the other side of the desk. His face softened. "Don't you remember?"

A weak smiled returned the question. "I live in the other world. It becomes my reality. There I am not a nerdy little kid that everyone picks on. There I am, the royal court jester, loved by all. I am in power over my situations. Not like here." He stopped to blow his nose. "My mom says I get too intense at times. She doesn't get—"

"You mentioned a bald dude," Alister brought the focus back.

"Yeah, the dude you were talking to the other day. He was here right before you got back, I think. Maybe." The Kid's hands flew around him to brush away objects; only the kid could see.

Alister placed one hand on The Kid's shoulder to freeze his position. "He was here?" Alister asked.

As if snapped out of a trance, The Kid replied, "Yeah, yesterday too. The dude said that you said that I should give him any information I had because we were all one big team. You weren't around, so I figured it must be okay, right?"

Alister cupped his hands over his face to hide his frustration. "I said that all information," the words came out slow and punctuated, "goes to me and—"

"Did I screw up? Oh man, I," a choking sound escaped from The Kid's throat. Pools of water formed around his eyes. "I'm really sorry," came out slightly above a whisper. The silence that followed filled the space as teenage boy agitation as his odor filled the corners of the room.

"I think you should go home," Alister said. His voice is now soft. "Get some rest. Perhaps take a shower."

"Are, are you firing me?" The Kid rubbed his palms into his eyes then smeared the tears over his face.

"No, I am not firing you. You have been here for three days, and quite frankly, you reek." Alister's comment brought a small in harmony laugh from both. "You should shower and change your clothes. Take a nap, and then come back."

The Kid sniffed. "I could shower here and help. That's where the dude is," he grinned. "I ended the battle with something about Hamlet not having eternal rest. I can look up the exact quote and give you a citation." Alister waved his hand.

Alister started to say, "I really think—"

The Kid kept talking. "Oh, and I put a lead in his internet access—"

"A lead—"

"Yeah, it's like a tracer yet undetectable unless the person is looking for it," The Kid explained. Alister followed his finger to the smaller screen. "The dot will move where ever he goes, unless—"

"He discovers the tracer," Alister finished the sentence, then added, "You are amazing."

"That is why you hired me. I could still sit here and watch where Yarok goes," both legs now carried a staccato bounce. The Kid's eyes meeting Alister's.

"That would be wonderful," Allister said. "But first, take a shower and burn those clothes."

"You sound like my mother." The Kid grabbed his backpack off the floor. "I'll use the shower downstairs and be back in a jiff." He disappeared out the door.

As soon as the office emptied, he lifted the phone. "Morris, we have a problem."

Yarok raised his fist to the roof of the car. Harlot jumped at the bang. "Victory!" his laughter filled the space. "I defeated the little svoloch with a Tolstoyian era phrase." He smiled down at Harlot. "Russian superiority strikes again."

Harlot smiled back yet didn't speak. Her eyes still half-closed from her fitful rest. Yarok's animated knight did the same flossing dance that little kids performed at halftime at basketball games on his screen. The knight strutted about with arms at ninety-degree angles, like the old Egyptian dance. Yarok poured himself two fingers of Stoli's Russian vodka.

He took a generous sip, leaned his head back on the rest, closed his eyes, and smiled. For a moment, her lover actually appeared content. His fingers gently brushed up against her calfs. Harlot allowed her lips to form a similar smile. A sigh escaped from her lips.

His phone lit. A note moved across the crawler. His knight sat on a boulder in the top right corner. The character scratched his head as he stared at the bottom of the screen. Harlot tried to get a look.

*Yes, you have won this battle, yet victory in the war will be mine.* "What the hell does that mean?" asked Harlot. She nudged Yarok's attention back to his phone. "Is he starting another round?"

"What are you babbling about, woman?" Yarok follow Harlot's finger to the screen. He mouth read the message on the crawler. "That looks like frustrated threats from a loser. He can't come back now unless he starts at phase one, probably from his mother's basement." Yarok's snickered. He looked back at the screen.

"Could he have another working his way up?"

In one gulp, Yarok finished the remaining alcohol. He typed *sore losers are never victorious.* His thumb hovered above send. After a beat, he erased the comment. "He was a challenge. I hope he can maneuver to my level again. Of course, I will win, yet I will have a little fun in the process."

The car moved a fraction. The glow off to the side had grown. The divider window buzzed open. "Boss, the map says there is an old highway up on the right here. Might be a faster route to where we are going."

"Go there," instructed Yarok. "We need to pick-up our prize and get out of here. Harlot's new version will be ready to go. I think we fixed the customer dying part." The driver snorted. He inched the car into the breakdown lane to move past the others. The turnoff led into a pothole-filled road and completed darkness.

The forest on the opposite side of the bus provided the best shelter from view. Thick with vines, Alia dived into the spiny vegetation. Animals chattered and scurried around her location. Birds squawked overhead. Most migrated in a direction that went towards the right front of the bus, a path she wanted to avoid.

No human voices called her name, yet based on experience, safety was temporary. The thick vegetation currently provided a necessary screen from view. Alia plowed through the vines and branches. Twigs ripped through her clothing and into her skin. The night sky clouded by gray smoke, with zero visible stars. Navigation would prove to be a challenge, yet she stepped forward, with purpose.

A dance with a tree trunk on the right. A sweep of her hand through a gathering of vines and leaves to the left. A bright, worn trail to in front of her. A human presence surfaced on the right.

"Alia, come back here," Jimmy's voice broke into nature's din. "This isn't what you think!"

"This is exactly what I think," she mumbled. Momentum moved her to create distance between the call. The path became clearer, and her footing stabled. Her body moved away from the aggressive sound. A blue trail marker tacked onto the tree in front, gave a clear direction to somewhere. Yet the marker posted a concern. If she could find this so could—

The steps quickened as soft, white ghosts swirled around the trees off in the distance. Soon they will rest in her lungs as the heat moved closer. She needed to follow the animals and avoid humans.

Helicopters thumped overhead. Firefighters or others, she suspected. Friends or foes. The slope inclined down towards the empty valley. Small rocks bounced ahead of each step. The trail turned fiercer between a substantial incline and multiple ruts. Her ankle slipped over one and rolled off to the side. "Crap," she gasped as her body met the ground.

Alia rested her hip on a boulder. She took a long sip off one of the water bottles. Jimmy's screams could barely be heard above the screech of animals. Progress. The ghosts moved closer.

The thump and movement of the bus stabilized as Fred's semi-lifeless body hit the couch. Smoky secured his hands to an attached bar while Jimmy walked to the back of the bus. "She's not here," he said.

"Angry husband hatch?" Smoky continued to tie Fred's legs together.

"Yep." Jimmy stared into the storage area underneath.

"You going after her?" Smoky stood back to admire his work. Fred's nose still had a trickle of blood, yet he lay there barely moving.

"Can you handle—"

"The Goob? Are you kidding me?" Smoky let out a chuckle. "This one here is hogtied and not going anywhere. Hell, I have dealt with worse." He handed Jimmy his gun. "It's the wife's," by explanation with a shrug.

"I wasn't aware that you carried."

"Think about it. I'm a driver for a rock and roll band from Florida. Of course, I carry." Smoky moved to the front of the bus. "You are the second person I had to explain that to today. Anyway, I think your lady ran out to the back."

"What makes you say that?"

"Well, if she went that away," Smoky pointed out the windshield, "we would have seen her go by." He handed Jimmy a mag light. "Be careful out there, brother."

Jimmy's voice carried back to the bus the moment Smoky lost sight of him. Smoky shook his head. There was no way that a lady would come back just because Jimmy called her name. He might be a rock star and a former spy, yet at times Smoky wondered about the intelligence of that boy.

Fred let out a little howl to bring attention back to his present situation. Smoky sat and waited for the new guy to come to so he could ask the list of questions formulating in his head. The first, and the most important, who is your new boss?

The yellow dot's pace quickened across the screen as it moved closer towards the solid blue. The Kid moved his mouse to bring the location view on the small area between the two. A red blaze icon popped up to indicate the forest fire's approximate start point in the upper left corner. The image grew as the fire spread.

"I'm going to get a Blaster next store. Do you want anything?" The Kid asked. Alister held out a five as he passed.

"No. Pick up what you want," Alister said. A quick thank you followed. Alister brought his attention back to the screen. He scribbled notes on a legal pad as the dots proceeded towards a collision course with each other and the fire. Alister blew out a breath then reached for his phone. He pressed the call button.

Two rings later, "Morris, we have a big problem." Alister continued to explain their current status. "I have the location to send additional personal. How fast can we get a team on-site?"

He half listened as his boss explained logistics. "Al, we are behind the eight ball here. This could take a half-day—"

"We don't have a half-day!" Alister's voice rose. "We need a team there yesterday."

Morris re-explained the same scenario, only a tad slower. "You need to contact Price," Morris instructed. "Get her to take over the onsite command. We need her in charge of this situation."

"Will do, Morris, thanks." Sulfur from a sparked match mingled with the white tobacco smoke trail that follows Alister across the room. Each step softer than the last, he walked out the door.

"I need some air," Alister quickened his pace.

"Yeah, me too," his admin answered. Her hand covered her nose as he passed. "Preferably filtered."

Alister headed into the stairwell. He took the steps two at a time before leaving out the side door. The alley appeared clear in both directions. To the left, the street beckoned. The midday motion of people brought a cloak of inconspicuousness as he mingled in with the lunchtime crowd. Three blocks over, he entered another nondescript brick building.

Unlike his office, the carpets here are worn, the desk's metal from a bygone era, as were the people behind each. Alister nodded as he passed several familiar faces. The office at the end, the last place he wanted to enter, became his only destination.

"Still smoking, I smell," the greeting always the same, the man behind the desk extended his hand. His old Army buddy, and brother-in-law, sat on the other side.

"Good to see you too," Alister answered. After a brief handshake, he took the seat opposite. "How's the family?"

"Good, as I know yours is too. Now that we got that out of the way—" Tiberius Josiah Waters a.k.a. Tippy, made an imposing presence behind the large metal desk. Daily workouts kept his shape from his active Seal days over a decade ago. His skin matched the custom-made black suit while the blue gray shade of his shirt magnified his eyes. An olive tie lay folded on the corner of his desk.

Alister nodded towards the tie. "Burger accident," Tippy answered. "Now I am sure that you are here for something other than my fantastic fashion sense."

"I needed a team in Pennsylvania yesterday. I have an agent in the area of Loyalstock and Tiadaghton state forests that needs back-up," Alister explained.

"What about your department?" Tippy's stare didn't falter.

Alister scoped the office as if there were others in the room. He took out his cellphone and played the recorded conversation from the stairwell. "This is why I am not sending my team. Morris gave a bunch of bullshit reasons for not giving assistance, then flat out refused. He said Alia Price could handle the situation. At this point I do not think she can," Alister blew out a breath.

"Do you know where Price is?"

Alister nodded, "I have an idea where agent Price is located, along with the possibility that Attorney Curry's missing son is with her. Here is a possible location." He slipped a piece of notepaper across the desk.

Tippy's fingers flew over the desktop keyboard. "There's a forest fire happening there," he read aloud. "Started with an explosion. Alister, where the hell are you sending my men?" One hand-typed while the other reached for the phone. "How soon can we get a team on the ground at," he squinted at the paper, "approximately Latitude: 41.5109092 Longitude: -76.7202323"

Alister rolled an unlit cigarette between his fingers. A series of "ah ha's" and "please do that's" followed. His brother-in-law eyed the cigarette and pointed towards the door. A quick wave followed.

"Yes, yes. Thank you, and keep me posted. Please add Alister Reed to all communications. Yes, I do realize that he is with another division. This is a new dual taskforce— Yes… exactly… Thank you." The receiver hit the phone with a bang. "I need a photo of agent Price. They leave in thirty, should be on the ground within the hour. Is there anything you are not telling me?"

Alister replied, "Nope, I think you have it all. Russian mob, a major drug distributor, a crooked cop, and the leak—"

"Possible crooked cop and leaked, you mean—" Tippy corrected.

"Yes, what you said. I also have a fifteen-year-old computer wiz that managed to track the people in the forest and give their location to criminals. Not sure how I manage that arrangement moving forward." Alister glanced over at the family photo taken at Disney a few years ago on the corner of Tippy's desk. "Lately, I have thought that I will retire after this. Maybe," he pointed, "hang out with the grandkids, do more of this."

"Al, you hated that trip," Tippy laughed. "The kids were amped up on sugar most of the time, and the wives bought them anything they pointed at. No, what you need is a change of scenery. Come over to internal affairs. Your good at—"

"No, I am not, Tippy, I am lucky. Very lucky." Alister stood to leave.

"What are you going to tell Morris?"

Alister tilted his head to one side. "I am planning on coming up with that on my walk back. I have no solid proof he is in cahoots with these guys—"

"Yet you have a hunch. I get that. Keep in mind that after this is over, we can challenge his decision-making skills." The rhythm of Tippy's tapping on his keyboard filled in the dead space. "Al, you did lose an agent out there. You know there has be an investigation."

"True, true," Alister nodded, "Thank you for your quick response."

"I could set up an office for you over here. Save the exercise between the two," Tippy waited for some response. When none came, he added, "I will keep you posted via text. And please do the same and let's keep this arrangement between you and me, for now."

"I wouldn't want it any other way." Alister gave a quick salute as he moved out of the door frame.

Gray ghosts swam around each other while circling the large trunks to float on through the collection of bushes. Trees turned into grave markers that foreshadowed the eminent destiny of when man versus nature. The dense air became more visible with each careful step. Without a clear sky, Alia had little clue of her direction. A hard cough escaped from her throat to bounce against the trees. She removed a purple bandana from her pack and tied it around her nose and mouth.

The fire spread its wings rapidly. The flames held back, yet the smoke-filled crevasses moved so even the animals and their homes vanished within. The chatter of the forest now silent. Overhead the roar of helicopters along with a sweep of a search light, passed into the night. Alia imagined the large beasts carried tanks of water to tame the blaze.

A trail split brought on another quick decision. To the left appeared more transparent yet contained a steep downgrade. To the right made more sense as the path would eventually connect back to the old road the bus had taken earlier. At least in Alia's theory.

The more maintained path lacked roots spread across the horizon or other hazards that could twist an ankle or trip a person. Alia quickened her pace to a light jog, wincing each time her right foot hit the packed surface. In the wind, her name called from behind. The rhythm of feet on ground increased. The low hanging tree branches brushed up against her right side. A slight incline of her body to the left, graze another.

She turned for a quick review of the near misses yet didn't slow down. Distance was the key to survival. Up ahead, a bench sat off to the side—a good sign of civilization. Park departments tended to put seats not very far in on a trail. If she remembered right, the benches were part of the Americans With Disabilities Act that probably once funded the maintenance of this area. Even those who can't walk should enjoy the forest, and currently, she had trouble doing simply that.

Her fist raised in a mock victory at the same time her body hit something substantial.

"What the—" Her body lay on top of another's. One hand rose to cover the source of the sound as her shoulder pressed the other human down. The hand slipped to a grizzly neck.

"Who are you?" her voice came barely above a whisper.

"Who the freak are you?" answered back. Alia focused on the face. Some familiarity hit.

"I know you," her hand slipped from his neck. She sat back to right her body. A few dizzy dots appeared, yet with a head shake, left towards the sky. "Oh my god! I do know you! You are that guy from backstage at the fest."

Marv gave her the head to toe stare down before his gaze got back to her eyes. "Did we—"

"No! We met… Wait… You are—"

"Marv—"

"As in marvelous. Yes, yes, we met at the festival. What are you doing—"

"Are you here to save us?" His eyes pleaded for a yes.

Alia glanced behind him for a second person. "Us? I only see you." Marv rose up. He extended his hand to assist Alia to her feet and pulled down her bandana for a quick look at her face.

"Not an alien," he sighed. "I hope you are here to help us, because well." Marv pulled back a bunch of branches. Brendan Curry sat on the ground; his body barely upheld by a giant pine tree. His eyes closed. The remains of a guitar positioned along his side.

"Oh, crap!" She dropped to his side to take his wrist between her fingers. He had a pulse. A whoosh escaped from her mouth. "He's alive."

"I knew that," Marv said. "Although many have tried to kill us."

"How many?" Alia brought her attention back to Marv.

"Readers Digest version, Wally, our imaginary guard, decided to dump me at a rest stop while I took a dump," he laughed, "then he took off with Brando here." The gray ghosts started to appear behind Alia. "I think he might have started a forest fire too, although we don't know that for sure."

"Okay, so that is one," plus Jimmy, "that is not so bad. We can handle him." Alia's hand wiped sweat drops from Curry's forehead. "Do you have a cellphone?"

"If I did, don't you think I would have—"

Alia held her hands in front. "Please, Marv," she said.

"Yes, but it doesn't work. We have been wandering out here for a while. Brando escaped from the tour bus from hell. I escaped from an old shitter. We met somehow. I am not sure where we are."

"That makes two of us. Can Curry walk?" Alia asked.

Marv responded with a nod. "Although I have been helping him."

"Good. This is good," Alia said as she threw a bottle of water to him. "Please share." She moved to push back the branches on the opposite side. A groomed path led to open space: a lucky and not so fortunate occurrence from their position.

Together, each took an armpit to lift Brendan up by his shoulders. Marv bent over to reach for the guitar.

"We should leave that," Alia pointed at the object.

"Are you aware that this is a custom-made Santa Cruz—"

"I don't care. It makes noise we can't afford. Leave it."

Marv scrunched his face then stuck his tongue out in her direction. "It works as a cane and can help both of us to balance Brando here," he demonstrated on his side of the body. "Plus, if we need to, we can smash it over Wally's head."

Alia liked the idea of smashing something over each double-crosser's heads yet wasn't sure a custom-built instrument would be their knight in shining armor apparatus.

After a trial and error of balance, the three moved down the brushed path. The dirt shifted to gravel as the view moved from pine trees to an open meadow. In the middle, another bench sat perched with a picture of what could be the valley. Smoke seeped up the sides yet had not arrived at this spot.

"Let's head to that bench," Alia pointed. "We can get a look at where we are." Marv nodded yet didn't speak. The gravel made it easy to maneuver. In minutes, both Brendan and Marv sat to face away from the trail. Alia moved towards the fenced-off area, along with what should be an expansive view. Flames danced between the shadows of treetops along the ridge where they had emerged.

Lights from several helicopters swept the areas. The illumination of black and deep red ghosts gave an indication of the severity of the situation.

"Are you going to tell me who you are?" Alia jumped at the sound of Marv's voice. "Because you have information all about us, and we don't know anything about you. You said we met at the festival," his lips curved into a smile, "so I am going to ask again, did we, possibly, hook up?"

"Ewe! No!" She pulled her bandana down under her chin. "I am a journalist—"

"No, you are not—" Marv stood to face her. Arms crossed over his chest and his lips in a no teeth smile.

"How do you know?" asked Alia.

"Because I may be in a band, have long hair, and am at the moment, unkempt, yet I am not stupid. A journalist might be back at the barricades, but she isn't going to be here, running for her life. Tell me who you are, or I start screaming," Marv said.

"Please don't scream," Alia held her hands up in front. "My name is Alia Price, and I am an undercover agent for the FBI."

"No, shit?" Marv repeated the complete body scan stare down.

"No, shit," Alia nodded.

"Are you here to find us, or should I say, Brando?"

"Yes," she answered.

"Alright. High five." The stench from Marv's armpits teared Alia's eyes. She hit her hand against his. "Groovy. Now, where is our new bus?"

"Ah – the bus. That is a story," she nodded as she spoke.

"I told you mine." Marv crossed his arms on his chest. His foot tapped.

"My bus got a little crazy, too," Alia shrugged. "We need to keep moving." She blew out her breath as she brushed past Marv. Brendan sat prompted up on the bench. His body hadn't moved from the original placement.

The path morphed into a paved track with painted arrows in opposite directions on each side of a faint yellow divider—much more civilized, yet much more exposure for the trio. Un-natural light blinked in their path. It disappeared as quick.

"Aliens," whispered Marv.

"Headlights," Alia corrected.

"No car noises." Marv was right. "There should have been some sort of engine noise."

"Let's move this way," she tugged their bulk off the track, through a group of bushes, back into the woods.

Alister returned to a quiet office. Computer screens all blank with zero humming sound. His secretary gone from her perch. A soft murmur from outside said other employees are working at their desks. He sat down in his desk chair to stare into the nothingness. An unusual sight, the wooden 'in' box's bottom stared back. Where were all his reports? Or The Kid, for that matter.

Fingers tapped to the rhythm of the wall clock. Automatically his hand reached for a pack of cigarettes. The green glass overfilled ashtray left on the desk now glimmered. There were other abnormalities. The top of the pencil drawer and the middle one on the side opened hardly enough to show someone had pried. The rest of the desk, only accessed with an old key, sat shut tight.

The Kid's backpack and personal computer both gone, along with the garbage can filled with the fancy drink cups and empty Mountain Dew cans. The cleaning crew usually did their job at night and never touched anything beyond the floor and the garbage pail.

Alister pushed back on his chair. The shelves behind him framed his silhouette with a multitude of stacked law books. Some of the books were signed copies from former clients, a few awards, and an allusion of a book series that served as a hidden wall safe. Inside the safe lay two standard-issue guns, half a dozen boxes of bullets, a stack of twenties, and a small briefcase.

He opened the briefcase on an empty portion of the shelf to reveal a standard toolkit. He took out a small mirror then moved to a position angled to peer under his desk. Nothing appeared out of place, yet something wasn't right. The repercussions if he was followed today would be quick and severe.

One of the guns, along with the ammunition and money, made its way into his personal briefcase. The other weapon, he tucked into his waistband. The light from the hallway shifted as a shadow blocked the door. Alister brought his head above the desk to see his boss' frame taking up space.

"To what do I owe the pleasure, Morris? You usually have me come up," Alister stated.

Morris scanned the room. His gaze stopped on the open safe along with each blank computer screen before he focused his full attention on Alister.

"Where's the kid?" he asked abruptly.

"That pungent stench inhabiting your nostrils is from him. I sent him to get cleaned up and to burn his clothes."

"Quite the explanation, Alister. A little lengthy from the guy who gives one-word answers most of the time," Morris noted.

"Yeah, I have been reading a lot of Shakespeare to relax. Why are you looking for the boy?"

"No reason. I haven't received a location update in a while. I wondered if our progress had stalled." Morris pointed up to the screens. "Yet, it looks like they stopped moving."

"I went out for a smoke, and the computers were off when I got back." Alister waited for a response. When none came, he asked, "Why are you here?"

"Now that is the Alister Reed I value and love," Morris stood to leave. "Get me updates as soon as they happen." He looked around the office, "And clean up this pigpen."

Alister muttered, "Thou devilish mark's rotting hog," at Morris's back.

"Good one," came out of the hallway along with, "it's elvish, not devilish, although your version is good too."

"Where have you been?" Alister barked, although a smile reached up to his crinkled eyes.

"Shower, remember? Then I went and got another frap blast and sat along the wall while the old dude was here," The Kid explained.

Alister started to ask, "Did Morris," he watched The Kid tilt his head to one side, and corrected himself, "old dude, see you?"

"I don't think so," The Kid stood still in the doorway. "He took out his phone the instant he walked out. Must be a busy guy."

"Yeah, busy..." Alister nodded. "Did you turn off the two computers?"

"Uh, no," The Kid moved over to the central console. "Turning these off erases all the work we, well actually, I did. Damn." He fired up the smaller of the two machines and waited for the dark blue screen to boot up. Alister moved to look over his shoulder. "Give me a minute to check out the damage. I guess I could log back on the game and do a re-trace.

Although we have the coordinates, you wrote them down, right?"

"I did," Alister surveyed the empty desk. "It seems the cleaning crew came through early."

"There were people in here the first time I came back—" The Kid interrupted.

"People?"

"Yeah, a whole bunch. Not sure what was going on. That's when I went for the frap blast…" The Kid's focused stayed on the screen as his fingers moved across the keyboard, making rhythms that blended with the clock's ticking and a hush of background conversations. "Okay, this might not be as bad as I thought. I think I should copy some of this to my laptop. That way—"

"Did they have uniforms on?" asked Alister.

"Who?"

"The people?" he blurted back.

The Kid look up at Alister. "I didn't notice, but I think that the dude you were talking to was there, but I'm not sure. I think it was the bald dude who keeps coming to see you." He moved his eyes back to bring full focus to the screen. "Please don't make me go and see him. The dude gives me the creeps. I get that total weird vibe."

That got a small smile from Alister. "Weird vibe?" he pressed.

"Yeah, like, got it!" The two dots appeared on the screen, almost adjacent. "Whoa. They moved a lot." The Kid reached into his backpack to pull out a ziplock with some sort of edible green mix inside. He stuck the bag to his nose then lifted a piece out to examine further.

"Mom's now making your healthy snacks?" Alister asked.

"No, bald dude said his wife made a batch and his kids eat it all the time. But I don't know." The Kid offers the bag to Alister, "does this smell funny to you?"

Alister lifted the baggie to his nose. "Bald dude gave this to you? When?"

"When I was heading to the showers, I guess—"

The baggies still in Alister's hand. "Did he offer a snack to anyone else?"

The Kid put his free hand under his chin and tilted his head to the left. "Not that I remember, but I was concentrating on getting to use the showers when no one else was in there," his face turned red. "I think he had more snacks, like a couple baggies for himself?"

He reached to take the baggie back as Alister moved it out of reach.

"Turn off that computer and grab your stuff—" Alister snapped a quick photo of the screen.

"But I—" The Kid pointed at the baggie.

"I'll buy you lunch."

"Cool, but what about—" The Kid watched Alister reach behind his desk to pull the plug out of the socket. The machine went blank. "That's not a good thing to do," The Kid added.

Alister smiled. "Cool." He shouted in the direction of his secretary, who had magically reappeared in her chair, "Going to lunch." With a wave, she acknowledged.

The loud pulse of multiple helicopters hovered above to drown out the sounds of the tortured forest creatures. The trees tops shook venomously while the stiff, angry breeze moved leaves, twigs, and pebbles from their ground resting place to batter against trunks and skin in their path.

Jimmy sat crouched among the ferns. Even with eyes squeezed shut and head covered by his arms, small rocks and debris carved into his skin. Through his forearms, the ferns brushed like spiders crawling up the flesh. Instead of his current reality, his mind tried to picture each plant as an oscillating crowd of people who appreciated good music.

A nearby branch cracked and fell to the ground close to his position. The audience vanished. The place now a jungle, somewhere in the east. The thump turned to explosions. The fragments of debris are now past lives attacking his soul. The release of breath changes into fast intakes and exhales, hyperventilation that follows an erratic heartbeat. The crackle of a two-way radio heard through the din. He folds his body into thirds to make himself invisible above the bush line.

All of his attention focused back on the breath. Inhales come slow and steady. Exhales are released with force. Close, boots on the ground. Or was this his mind playing tricks again? In auditable orders given through a speaker cuts through the prominent sounds of a beating chest. He moves one hand to wipe away the rows of sweat that run down his face. Salty tears sting both eyes.

Jimmy stretched out enough to crawl back alongside the worn path on his hands and knees. An old bandana wrapped around his entire face forced limited visibility to the trail underneath. The movement was still impeded by nature's constant strike of rocks, twigs, and imaginary voices. "Freaking sandstorms in Afghanistan, mudslides in Honduras and El Salvador, crazy coca farmers in Nicaragua, insects the size of my head in Malaysian, and now this shit," he stretched his neck towards the sky, "why won't you let me quit and live a normal life?"

His hand slipped on loose rocks. Imprints of the jagged rock edges formed craters onto his palm. Scrapes extended partway up on both forearms. The terrain had changed from a well-worn path into man-made gravel. He was now more exposed to the elements, and if the voices were real, the strangers in the area could see him too.

The eerie glow of his bus sat across an open space. As quick as the wind and noise started up, the world calmed into a peculiar silence. Jimmy pulled down the bandana and again, stretched his neck up. "Thank you," he whispered, hands in front in a prayer position.

He stood and scratched his head, then brought both hands to cup against his ears. The crackle of wood meeting fire, along with the pulse of distant fire-copters, brought his heart back to a regular pulse. He shortened the distance between him and the bus with a quick jog. He arrived to Smoky on the phone and Fred moaning on the couch.

"Can I shut him up?" Smoky head nodded towards the lump of a human.

"The usual way?" Jimmy countered, adding, "I couldn't find her."

"Not surprised. Althea's eyes got really bright right when this one turned towards the bus. She took one look at his face--"

"She thinks we double-crossed her," Jimmy pointed out. He watched as Smoky rummage around the glove department. "We really aren't going to fill the bus with marijuana smoke, so he'll pass out, right?"

"You got weed?" Smoky perked right up. "I thought you government types—"

"Ex-government. I am retired." Jimmy's declaration had Smoky choked back a laugh. "I got enough problems without getting back into that mess." He gave Fred a sideways glance. "How are we even from the same family?"

"Vulcan death grip should work," Smoky said as Fred let out a wail.

"Always a better alternative than weed, especially in good old Pennsylvania." Both men laughed.

Smoky asked, "What about our other problem?"

"Give me a few minutes, and I will go back out. I can try the other direction and walk along the road." Jimmy hesitated, then added, "Before you think I have gone crazy, I swear I heard static out there."

"Two-way?" Smoky asked. Jimmy affirmed with a quick nod. "I thought that chopper was a bit low. Do we have any other weapons besides my missus' gun?" When no answer came, Smoky reached up into the compartment above the driver's seat. Under a stack of maps, he pulled out three-buck knives. "Not much use against a fella with a gun but better than nothing."

"Thank you," Jimmy said as he tucked one of the knives in his waistband. He grabbed a roll of duct tape out of a drawer and taped another to his calf. "You sure you'll be okay?" Smoky shook his head up and down. "Okay. I am going to stay close to the woods yet along the road."

"If you find Althea, or whatever her name is, you might want to explain—" Smoky said.

"I will. And I will keep an eye out for that Curry kid too." Jimmy disappeared out the door.

Smoky looked over at Fred, now slumped in the seat. He picked up the other knife along with the festival program and headed into the bathroom.

Wally observed the interaction from the shadows as Jimmy exited the bus. The door remained open, and he could only Fred inside. The latter appeared in an intoxicated slump against the bench. The burly biker was somewhere out of view.

Wally slipped around to the front of the bus. Light spread about four feet into the gravel, then the path disintegrated into the dark. Lucky for him. The driver's side lit up the parking lot enough to expose movement, yet he noted that the storage hatch sat open.

All tour busses should have about the same layout, except for the back third. Wally learned that when he and Lou Pilsner looked at busses for the Curry kid. A quiet chuckle slipped past his lips. If he knew back then what he needed now, they would have shopped for one with a padded jail for a backroom instead of the queen size bed the prince slept on. At least Wally got to cock-blocked any hotties that wanted the that kid. He made sure the others got enough to brag and make Curry miserable in the process.

"Some tour experience he got," Wally mumbled. He pressed his body close to the driver's side of the bus, making sure to squat out of the mirror's view. Butt first, Wally brought his knees to his chest. He circled to bring his entire self into the pitch-black cargo hold. He took a penlight from his pocket and flashed the beam around the area.

The entire storage void of any items. No crates, guitar cases, suitcases, nothing stacked in any of the corners. Just a huge metal space.

He crawled to the middle. A single hatch broke up the solid space. Wally closed his eyes to see a layout of the bus above. The jut out of space on his right should be the bathroom. He opened one eye to look at the size before he shut it again. He added a bath and shower to his imaginary blueprint. A bedroom would be a third of the space, bunks, and head, another third, and the front area the last.

The complete bus layout came into his mind's eye. This hatch came up in the hall between the bunks, closer to the bedroom than the living area. Wally took out his penlight to flash from front to back. The hatch lay two-thirds towards the rear. If the hall is blocked, so would be his entrance. If not…

He raised his arms to push.

Armpit sweat leaked clear through to the waistline of The Kid's clean t-shirt. A faint wheeze escaped as feet shuffled to keep up with the bop and weave of the lunchtime crowd. Every ten steps or so, his boss stopped to look into a store window. Or he would turn to stare into the rest of the world as strangers fought their way passed to a quick lunch, dry cleaners drop off, and a trip to the bank or grocers.

The Kid wore his backpack on the front, both arms circled to hold the bag in place. The crowd stopped to put him in front of the hipster coffeehouse, where he got his fraps. He completed a three-sixty spin, yet Alister was nowhere in sight. The smell of cocoa waffled out of the jammed open door. The Kid peeked inside—no line where there always is one.

He stepped up to enter at the same moments a hand clamped on top of his shoulder and pulled him back onto the street. "What the hell," he did a one-eighty to come face to face with the state cop from Alister's office. "Old, bald dude," The Kid whispered. The cop jerked him into the crowd.

"That is officer Pilsner to you, son," his lips tried for a grin yet ended in a sneer.

"Officer Pilsner," The Kid repeated. He eyeballed to his left and right—no Alister.

The officer's shoulders slumped a bit as his face softened. "Heading somewhere?"

"Yeah," The Kid caught another whiff of cocoa, "I am getting a frap. Maybe hanging here for a bit…"

Pilsner nodded. "You are a terrible liar."

"Why would I lie about a frap? In case you haven't noticed, I tend to drink a few." He waited for a beat before adding, "Do you or Alister need something? I can go back…"

"No, no, that's okay," Pilsner back-peddled. The crowd had shifted. Alister was nowhere in sight. "Everybody gets a break, right?"

"Yeah, right. Anyway, Alister slipped me a ten spot if you want one too. He doesn't drink this crap. His words, not mine." The Kid held up a crisp ten-dollar bill.

"No, no," Pilsner waved him off, before he asked, "By the way, when did you last see Alister?"

"About ten minutes ago," The Kid answered. "He said he was taking me for lunch, and then he took off. I lost him in that," both followed his finger pointed down the street.

"Is that your laptop?" Pilsner took an interest in the backpack.

"Yeah, my gaming one. The one I use for work is in Alister's office. Can I tell you a secret?" Pilsner gestured for him to continue, "I think I am in trouble."

"Why would you think that?" Pilsner asked.

Both nodded towards up and down the street. "Because I was wrong," The Kid's voice came out barely audible.

"Wrong?"

"Wrong coordinates, wrong guy, wrong everything! I don't get it, but all of my information was…" The Kid grabbed onto the hair above his ears and squeezed. His face turned bright red. After a minute, he brought his attention back to Pilsner. "I do crossword puzzles in pen, do you understand?"

Pilsner gave a blank stare back then glanced down at his watch. "I got to go." He pulled a card from his pocket along with a twenty-dollar bill. "If you get a location in Pennsylvania or even one on Alister, I would appreciate it if you would call me first. And," he glanced over his shoulder, "can we keep this between you and me?"

The Kid snagged the twenty. "No prob. You sure you don't—" Pilsner started to walk back towards the building before he could finish. "Ha," The Kid stuffed the twenty in his pocket. He ordered his drink, still wondering why there wasn't a line, then took a seat in the corner by the restrooms. Another hand clamped on his shoulder.

"I think once a day is enough for this crap," The Kid tried to shrug his shoulder out of the grip.

"Did Pilsner leave?" He jumped at the sound of Alister's voice.

"Yeah, thanks for leaving me with that creep—"

"Take your stuff in the men's room," Alister instructed.

"Oh no, I have read about you, creepy old dudes," said The Kid. He placed the drink between the two. Alister blew out a burst of frustration.

"We are going out the back way before Pilsner's guy comes in to watch what you do," Alister said in a terse whisper. The Kid repacked his laptop. "Leave your drink to look like you are coming back."

"Leave my frap?"

"I will have someone come back to get you a replacement. Let's go." The Kid followed Alister out the back door down an alley covered in plastic coffee cups and fast-food white bags. His feet kicked the litter to the side as he broke into a jog to keep up. At the end, both squeezed through an opening in a chain-linked fence. On the other side of the wall, a bright cobblestone walk led back to the crowds walking along a busy street.

Alister stood, foot tapping against the stone, about halfway down. He knocked twice. A door opened as The Kid caught up. "Where are we?" he asked as he followed Alister in.

"New office."

"Am I being punished?" The Kid's eyes started to water.

"No," Alister turned. "Promoted."

Brendan Curry's lifeless shape took up too much of the space on the bench. His arms reached down towards the ground while his legs stretched off one end. Close to the end Marv squeezed onto, Curry's head turned upward. His mouth released a stream of drool down to puddle on a slot of wood.

At least he still had a pulse.

Marv squished his body into as little real estate as possible. Hands rested, folded in his lap—shoulders pinned to his ears. No parts came in contact with Curry or his drool. Brothers in the backseat of a station wagon made less attempt not to touch. The oldest spread out to take up the most space, while the youngest feared a punch for going over the imaginary borderline.

Or perhaps only Alia's siblings maintained both physical and emotional borders.

Through the trees, crows circled above, their faint muffled cacows came as the gray ghosts continued to circle like vultures, waiting for the kill. Alia shook her head. Thoughts of death and dying ran from her eyes to graze down her cheeks. Everyone needed to get out alive. Her job required that all were saved. No one is left behind.

The battered paved path appeared to be both a Godsend and a curse. Her sneaker hit roots that had expanded underneath to push the tar into ununified rows. Alia balanced as she began to fall forward onto the heels of her hands. From her crouched position, cracks within the asphalt allowed little green seedlings to sprout towards the sky. The offspring of the tall trees and brush that once provided ample cover come to rest at the edge of a pine forest that sported peek-a-boo spots into a more civilized world. The smaller stage at the festival had a similar view.

Alia let out a sigh. What she wouldn't give for sesame noodles and an ice-cold lemonade right now. Her stomach released an appreciative murmur. She rose to stand and pushed on. Food and sleep will have to wait.

The tour bus glowed at the opposite side of a spacious, beat-up parking lot. The hum of its generator broke over the screech of a few of the last of the panicked wildlife, too frantic to make their getaway. Now here she stands, full circle back to her point of escape, Alia shook her head, disgusted by her lapse in judgement. Jimmy and Smoky appeared nowhere in sight.

Her thoughts turned to Zadie and Tiny. "Please get them to where they need to be safe." As long as they traveled in another direction, all would be fine. Still, the question of *who are these people* brought an on-going tennis match in her mind. Jimmy's latest actions made her question her intuition. There still remained doubt that he double-crossed her. And did Tiny purposely seek her out?

Doubt or hoped, she couldn't decide. A ripple spread across her back. She fought her way under the English ivy on one side. Towards the bus, a small window within the layers of green leaves allowed a partial view. Not even a shadow moved within its lighted windows.

The slow crunch of movement on rocks caught her attention off on the left side. No light poured in from that direction, yet the sound became more apparent the longer she squatted. When the wind shifted, audible coughs floated. Alia wished Marv and Brendan had a bag of cough drops. She gave a small chuckle with that thought. She is thinking cough drops while they probably want a ten-course meal complete with a groupie or two at the end.

Her hand hit the side of her head to release the imagined picture. Those two had to be classier than Triston and his band of idiots. A slight movement over her left shoulder brought Alia's focus back. The crunching noise stopped.

She waited.

The Kid sat with his keyboard on his lap. Both feet flanked the twenty-four-inch screen on his own desk. He still couldn't believe that Alister gave him an actual office. "Here is your new space," Alister said as he opened the door. "Keep the door closed, don't talk to anyone, and don't bother with any person outside this door. I will be right back."

The Kid acknowledged the instructions with a nod. "So, when my mother gets pissed, she can't find me, you'll explain," he said to the closed door. In reality, this new place, compared to Alister's office, was a dump. The desk chair squeaked every time his body moved, and the computer base must have taken at least fifteen minutes to warm up. Thank heavens, the security walls in these places are easy for him to by-pass. With a few keystrokes, The Kid could track where Alister went. The dot moved around the building then stopped in the opposite corner. A few more inputs and he had an aerial view of the building.

Unfortunately, Google maps lacked any sort of identifier to his whereabouts. Satellite photos showed a simple, no-name office building, approximately fourteen stories high. He estimated his location to be on the fifth or sixth floor. Most of the buildings in this area were part of the government's vast real estate holdings or housed people whose incomes came from the government. He opened a second tab and punched in the URL he had memorized with the two Pennsylvania locations. The two dots now touched.

The avatar jester stretched his scrawny arms over his head and let out a bellowing yawn. The figure brought one eye close to the screen, then the other as if it wanted to see who else was in the room. The jester took a half bow and sprang into a pirouette. A split jump across the sizeable space, float up towards the un-natural blue sky and enter a perfect flip to land cross-legged on a boulder in the lower right corner. *LET'S GO* came across the crawler, bold in caps. "I guess it is time to have some fun."

The Kid typed in a series of codes then waited. His left foot bounced against the desk. "Come on, you are out there somewhere…" A knight in bright pink armor stretched out of the opposite corner. An audible sigh escaped his lips. *I have come to duel you yellow-bellied sapsucker,* appeared in the crawler. "Are you kidding me?" *I only dual with noteworthy contenders. You are nothing but an abomination that got lucky.*

The knight turned a shade of purple then burst into flames. "That was too easy," The Kid noted as the smoke turned black. A silver sword tip cut through the darkness, and onto the screen stepped his nemesis, now in a dark silver suit of armor. He bowed in the direction of the jester. *The amateur hour is over – time for you to go away permanently.*

*You seriously need an attitude adjustment, you rumbustious bull's pizzle!* The Kid giggled as he typed. The knight swayed on the screen,

*You little kozyol*[2]*. You stuffed coat bag of guts.* Yarok's grin grew as he typed.

*Seriously? The phrase is stuffed cloak-bag of guts. Review your Shakespeare peasant. Or better yet, thou lump of foul deformity.* The knight stagger again. His jester now waved arms in the air. The avatar turned his back to the screen and waved his butt from side to side. Victory appeared close.

---

[2] Goat in Russian. The ultimate insult.

*With you, sin is not an accident but a trade. You rampallian! You futilitarian! I'll tickle your catastrophe!* The jester stopped mid-dance. His laugh startled Harlot. The jester fell on its butt and sat with rested arms on knees. "Zho-pa!" Yarok screamed.

The car rested in tense silence as Yarok waited on a response. Harlot's hand drifted along his thigh. The car tilted with each rut and pothole along the old road. "I still have wi-fi, no?" Yarok shouted at his driver.

"Yes, Yarok. The car is equipped with satellite wire," the driver answered. Harlot's hand stopped moving.

"Satellite?" she questioned.

"Yes, like phones. We are never out of range," the driver spoke with confidence. Harlot's hand thrust hard into the driver's headrest. His head jerked forward at the same moment; his foot hit the brakes.

"Kokogo cherta[3]!" The driver screamed.

"Ty mudak[4]! If a satellite follows us, then we are traced!"

"My darling, you are, how they say, paranoid. This is a game. I used an address

---

[3] What the hell in Russian

[4] You moron, again in Russian

halfway across the world when I signed up," he felt her relax a little. "The car is leased. The satellite bounces. We are untraceable." He turned his attention back to the game. "Let me destroy this piece of, what do the American's say? Piece of dog crap, and then I will give you my undivided attention." He leaned in to kiss her cheek.

Harlot gave a faint smile back. She didn't want to argue or go to prison, again, especially in the United States, for that matter. The glow from Yarok's phone illuminated the back seat. Outside, trees passed along with the occasional, unreadable road sign.

*I will stick with the spirit of Henry IV.* The Kid's response dangled across the scroller. *You, sir or madam, are a vile standing tuck.* The knight wobbled a little then banished a middle finger towards the screen. "Even I am more mature than that." The Kid laughed at the absurdity of the knight's confidence. He flipped back to the other tab. Only one dot appeared on his screen. "Crap," he yelled. Hands up in the air, he ran out the door.

Smoky sat back to relax inside the small bathroom. One of the perks for driving a tour bus included no rest stop toilets. Jimmy's bus interior stayed sparkling clean by a weekly visit of groupies who scrubbed the bus in exchange for backstage passes and an occasional escape from letches that seemed to hang around the rock circuit.

Jimmy perfected the set-up long ago when he grew tired of the women who wanted him only for his fame. When he toured, the same group of women, always in white and barefoot, stood in front as he played. They created barriers between Jimmy and the status seekers that seemed to work their way backstage.

Smoky noted that none seemed to want a sexual or exclusive relationship with his friend. The girls would show up at backstage barbeques, eat, hang out with the other musicians, and then disappear, either into the bus for the weekly cleaning or towards the stage to hear music more clearly.

At times, Smoky wondered about his friend. His entourage displayed an inner beauty that could be captivating at times, yet Jimmy showed no attention to any of them. Then again, from what Smoky understood, Jimmy had a different group of people, mostly old friends and relatives, that took care of him back home.

Smoky flushed the toilet at the same moment, something shifted inside the bus. He pulled his pants up, grabbed the knife, and pushed the door open. Wally sat in the hatch. Gun pointed at Smoky's chest.

"We meet again, hombre," Wally smiled. Smoky slipped the knife into his back pocket and froze. Wally pushed himself out of the hatch. "Not sure what I have here… Maybe another bus to torch," he winked. "Two in twenty-four hours. This could be a new record for me." Wally pressed his body against the wall then waved the gun to indicate Smoky should move back to the front. He made a move from Wally's angle that he appeared to pull up his pants. From Wally's blindside, he slipped his shirt over the knife and crossed his fingers.

"Who do we have here," Wally lifted Fred's chin with his free hand. "Huh." He pointed at Smoky, "Walk him outside."

"What if I say no," Smoky crossed his arms crossed his chest.

"Then you both get blood all over this luxury vehicle," Wally spat back.

Smoky lifted Fred off the couch by his armpits. He moved down the stairs, the hidden knife cutting into his back. "Where do you want him?"

"Up against the bus," Wally waved his gun. "Yeah, there." Smoky let Fred fall to the ground. He took a step towards Wally, who moved his head from side to side. "No, you stay there too." Wally placed himself directly in front of Fred. "Why is he on this bus?"

"Who are you?" Smoky answered.

"No questions," Wally's voice rose, "I ask the questions! Now, why is he on this bus?"

"I took a wrong turn and was moving the rig to backtrack," Smoky started. Wally fired a shot in the air. The gun held about 15 rounds of ammo, based on Smoky's guess. Too many shots left for comfort. He started again, "This guy came out of the woods as I was turning the rig around. He said he got lost camping and there was a fire on the other side. That explained the smoke," Smoky shrugged. He opened his mouth to continue yet was cut off.

Wally put his face up against Fred's. "You lying sack of shit," he sputtered. "Why are you here? I thought that they killed you at that damn festival." Smoky's attention perked up. "You and that idiot brother of mine. One easy freakin' job," Wally's voice grew. He held out one finger. "One stinking job—" He pulled the trigger. The bullet shredded through Fred's leg. Fred screamed in pain.

"What the—" Smoky reached behind his back. He brought the knife around to drive with full force into Wally's shooting hand. The gun hit the weeds almost soundlessly. Wally whipped his opposite hand across his body to connect with Smoky's jaw.

The big guy stumbled back. With his bleeding hand held against his stomach. Wally jumped up, cocked his leg back to attempt a roundhouse kick. Smoky blocked the leg with his forearm. At the same moment, he ducked to the side and landed a hard punch into his ribs. Wally fell back on his ass.

"What is your damage, boy?" Smoky yelled as he brought his heavy leg down on Wally's shoulder.

"Stop, please, stop," Wally held both hands up, one dripped a pool of blood on the ground, "Just let me go and die. I promise—"

Smoky ripped a piece of his shirt. He tied the material around Wally's hand and stood back to look at his work. Already the fabric color changed to crimson red. This beggar in front of him would bleed out sooner than later.

"Go," he nodded towards the woods. Wally's gun now resting in his hand, "Don't come back."

"I did you a favor with that one," both looked over at Fred, slumped against the bus, uttering soft groans. "He and my brother are damaged goods, man." As Wally limped towards the woods, Smoky called him back. Wally shouted, "No! We are all dead if they find us." He disappeared into the brush.

Smoky ran inside and got a first aid kit along with another shirt. He tied the shirt above the wound and then poured alcohol where the bullet entered. Fred screamed.

"Look, dude," Smoky started to say, "You may lose your leg, but not your life." Wait here. Smoky went back on the bus to gather a bunch of blankets. He placed the pile on the couch then spread over the couch and a low coffee table. He went back outside to lift Fred up. He plopped Fred off the pile of linens, raising his leg onto the coffee table and adding a couple more blankets to raise the injury higher. On the adjacent table, he placed a bottle of Jack Daniels. "Drink."

Fred looked up in a daze. "Huh?"

"I said drink, boy. And once you are passed pain, you can tell me how deep the shit we are in goes." Smoky rubbed some hemp oil slaved on his arm and along his left jaw. On the table sat the gun Wally had left, a newer Sig Sauer, military-grade. Smoky looked in the chamber to see he now had nine rounds of ammo.

And the level of shit just moved past his level of tolerance.

Jimmy moved along the road with the occasional stop to listen. Pops from the forest fire raging close by along with screeches filled the air. Now in the distance, the view of the bus slowly vanished in the trees. Imaginary voices became distant figments of his imagination. The crackle of a two-way radio now merely a noise from his past life.

The road quieted as his footsteps became the only prominent noise. "Where the hell did she go?" he muttered. His hand swiped at the vines and branches that succeeded to block in what lay behind. A few thorns caught to cut into his flesh, yet the burn of the ripped skin dulled.

The path would not clear for sightlines.

A worn, asphalt walkway appeared on the opposite side. Jimmy moved down the path with careful, calculated steps. What once might have been a break from a long drive, now weaved in between overgrown roots and vines. The surface now pushing upward, releasing the occasional pebble from its grasp.

With a mixture of smoke and pine, the trail brought senses of urgency and calm together. The smoke bouquet now the dominating force. The rule, perhaps it should be his rule since his employers never cared either way, was to leave no one behind. Everyone gets out safe had been a mantra.

His bus now peeked back within the trunks. Thoughts went to saving the few since saving them all is proving fruitless and, if he had to admit, frustrating. He ran his hands over his hair, squinted his eyes closed, and considered his options.

In his mind's eye, Alia’s face appeared. The wrinkles around her eyes. The hard stare of trying to get a read on him. Finally, her look of determination not to put him or Smoky in the position they were currently in.

“Damn,” he said to the breeze. Jimmy stepped out onto the road the same moment a light swept across the bend. He ducked back into the shadows, crouched below the vines, and waited for the next problem to present itself.

The Mercedes driver cut his lights shy of the clearing and tried to drive as slow as possible to make the least racket. On the opposite side, the purple and blue tour bus appeared in the gray mist. "I think we have found something, comrade," the driver announced. Harlot stretched her neck to see around the headrest that blocked the view.

"I saw that bus at the festival. It was parked behind the big stage today." Yarok continued to stare at his phone. "Yarok! Do you not see the bus?" He typed *LATER* into the crawler. His lips turned upward. "Did you hear—"

"Yes, my dorogoy[5], of course, I see the bus." He leaned forward into the front seat. "Yes, yes, that machine was behind the big stage. What do you think they took a wrong

[5] Darling in Russian

turn?" The two men in front laughed. "Though we have knowledge that is not Curry's bus."

"Maybe the bus belongs to someone who can help?" Harlot's voice raised an octave on the word help.

"Do we need help?" Yarok snapped back. The interior lights showed no shadows, yet he felt a presence.

"Shall we see who is on this bus, comrade?" The driver inched the Mercedes forward.

"Yes, let us meet our new friends. Perchance they can direct us to where our old friend Walter may be found."

The car inched forward to stop inside the bus's blind spot. Jimmy slipped back into the trees as two figures emerged from the front. One disappeared from view down the passenger's side while the other crept along with the driver. Jimmy tried to remember if they had locked the hatch after Alia took off. Stuck to the ground as he crawled more into the road for a better view.

The shadow hovered along the side, moving in slow motion. One arm raised in the silhouette of a hand that held a pistol. The hatch appeared open to break the movement pattern against the bus. Jimmy let out a sigh. The car made a slight shift as one of the backdoors opened. Another figure added to the mix. Less hefty than the two who circled his vehicle, this one stood and scrutinized. The spark from a lighter briefly illuminated his sharp features.

"Only an idiot would smoke in the middle of a forest fire," Jimmy shook his head. Low to the ground, he moved to a parallel position with the car. Inside the vehicle, another form moved. An outline of hair and hand gestures followed. The other leaned his forehead on the door and spoke too soft to hear. Small white puffs escaped on the side to punctuate each sentence.

The space between lay in semi-darkness brought on by a combination of the night sky and long shadows. The lights of the bus drew attention away from the weed-infested road. Jimmy stretched his arms into a full reach, at the same time sliding forward on his knees to rest his stomach on the gravel. With only a few transfers of rock underneath, his torso moved from side to side as his body slithered forward across the rugged pavement.

"Come on out, darling, and watch the fun." The voice had an east Slovak accent, yet the accent on the 'a' in 'darling' didn't allow for confirmation. It could be Russian or Chec.

"Shit," Jimmy started to back up as the back door clicked open. The wide beam from the overhead light left him fully exposed. Harlot slid out legs first. Her eyes widened as she and Jimmy gawked at each other. Without hesitation, Jimmy sprang to standing, turn 180 degrees, and started to run back into the brush.

BANG! The single bullet grazed against his ear. His body froze. Instinctually, arms raised up high in the surrender position. He made a calculated semi-circle to face the shooter. All three stared until Harlot's lips curved up to a smile.

"Comrade," she gave a head nodded at Yarok, "I think we hit the jackpot."

"Jackpot?" Yarok squinted at Jimmy.

"Yes, my Lyubov'[6]. Do you see who we have here?" Yarok moved his hands for her to continue. Harlot mumbled something in Russian then, very loud, added, "This is the Win Scout." Yarok's expression didn't change.

"I haven't been Win Scout for many years." Both Harlot and Yarok ignored the comment.

---

[6] Love in Russian

"Win Scout! The one who shut down the Central America operation for—"

"You are C.I.A.?" Yarok's voice rose.

Jimmy spoke slow, "I am not C.I.A.," he spat each letter out, "I am just a picker and a strummer whose bus tried to take a shortcut."

"Then why are you crawling towards my car like a government dog?"

"I went to take a piss," he tried to not smile, "and came out to someone circling my bus with a gun drawn. What would you have done?" When no one answered, he took a step in their direction and continued, "I watch too many spy movies. Crawling on the ground was the way the last one, some old Lev Gorn movie, ironically, anyway, that was the way he did it, so I thought…" Jimmy now stood a mere four feet from the car.

"How coincident you watched a great Russian actor," Yarok replied. "Let's see who else our friend, Win," he let out a cackle, "is traveling with. Maybe we have common friends."

Yarok waved the gun for Jimmy to move towards the bus. The steel rod of the barrel now pressed into his spine. Harlot leaned on the front of the car arms folded across her chest. She glanced inside the car and made a note of the keys, dangled in the ignition.

The Kid raced down the hallway, yelling, "ALISTER!" His high-pitched voice seeped through to the floors above and below. The screech penetrated through walls, doors, and concrete. He kicked open the Men's Room door. The two men standing at urinals turned. Both urinated on the floor as The Kid yelled out his boss's name. He banged open every stall door.

"ALISTER," followed his rush back into the hallway.

An office door slammed open. The worker's hands ejected a not bonded yet fifty-page report up in the air. The few doors banged against walls of empty offices. In the copy room, he caught a man and a woman embraced. "Stereotype!" he yelled along with "ALISTER!" Secretary's hid under their desks. Men in gray suits jumped out of his path.

A female dressed in gray pulled a gun on him, and yelled, "STOP!"

The Kid gasped for air as he stared into the barrel. "Crap!" he yelled to catch the agent off guard. He grabbed her gun and tossed it to the side. Instead of apologies, The Kid greeted people in his path with, "AHHHH!" or "CRAP!" along with occasional "SHIT! Oops, Sorry!"

Alister surveyed the mayhem leaning against the door frame of the opposite corner office. "Hey, Tippy, you need to see this." Both observed the wide-eyed kid as he yelled, pointed, and harassed Tippy's team. "I can't believe he just disarmed one of your agents."

"I don't think she can either," Tippy gestured towards the open-mouthed woman.

Alister let out a sigh, "Kid," he waved him over, "what is all the hoopla?"

"What's hoopla?" The Kid asked while in a struggle for breath. Tippy's secretary handed him a bottle of water. The Kid chugged down half before he exploded into a coughing fit. All the while, he pointed back towards his office. The wheezing noises bounced against the walls. The Kid slid down the wall onto the floor.

"Get a medic up here, stat!" Alister yelled.

The Kid held up his hand. "I am okay." He jumped to his feet. "But the dots—" Alister shoved him into Tippy's office and slammed the door behind. He put his fingers to his lips. High pitched shortness of breath, the only noise that remained. "Are you sure you are the good guys?"

"Why would you ask that?" Alister asked.

"I just, I just—"

"Have a seat," Alister gestured towards one of the two chairs near the desk. The Kid sat on his right leg as he pretzelled the left over it. He leaned his elbow on the desk to rest his head in the palm of his hand. "Why would you need to ask—"

"This isn't our office," The Kid stated. "I don't know you," he pointed at Tippy, "and my mother doesn't know I am here."

"All valid points," Alister acknowledged. "Your mother does know you are here," he crossed his fingers behind his back, "and we are the good guys." He sprinkled his answer with truth. "We have a problem at the other office—"

"Bald dude—" The Kid's voice just at a stage whisper.

"Yes, bald dude," Alister smiled. "We had to move here—"

"—but not tell nobody."

"Yes, I didn't tell anyone—" Alister repeated.

"Because of that girl who—" This time, Alister held his hand up to stop the conversation.

"Yes, partly because of Agent Price's status yet mostly to protect you," Alister said. The Kid gave Alister the wide-eyed stare. "No, you are not in any danger—"

The Kid started to chew on his right thumbnail. "Then what does protect mean? Is my mom okay?"

Alister and Tippy exchanged glances. Tippy spoke first. "I will have one of my field agents pick up your mom," he smiled as he gestured towards the chair in front of his desk. "We will make arrangements for both of you to stay in a nearby hotel, just for a few days—"

"Why can't we go home?" The Kid looked back at Alister. "And who are you?"

Tippy turned the family photo on his desk around. "Tiberius Josiah Waters. I am in charge of this division for the United States government," he stated at the same time he pointed to the photograph from Disney.

The kid leaned forward to scrutinize each member. "You vacation with this guy?" he head nodded towards Alister. "I didn't think you vacationed ever."

Tippy let a laugh escape before trying to cover it up with a cough. "Yeah, he's married to my sister. I work in a different branch of investigations, mostly internal." The Kid nodded as if he understood. "Alister and I, you may call me Tippy, by the way, work together."

"Is that how he met your sister?" Both nodded.

"Why were you shouting for me?" Alister interrupted the moment.

The Kid started wheezing again. "The dots!" His voice raised an octave. "I checked the locations again, and the dots are on top of each other, and—" All leaned in, "your guy just quit mid-game."

"Game," Tippy mouthed. Alister held his hand up.

Alister asked, "What do you mean, he quit?"

"He had my jester in a juggernaut and was going for the kill, and he just stopped. Typed in 'later' and left the game!" The Kid's intake of air audible.

"Shit!" Alister said at the same moment The Kid responded with, "Language!"

"What does this mean?" Tippy jumped in.

"I think that where ever the other people are," The Kid said, "they are all together."

Alister turned his attention back to Tippy. "Have your people landed?"

"They dropped within a three-mile range of your coordinates and are searching the area. And before you ask, they couldn't get in closer because of the forest fire. So far, nothing. Have you heard anything from Agent Price?"

All eyes went to The Kid, who shook his head no. "The last numbers I gave you—" he stopped. "I could look again." He pushed up to the leave at the same time Tippy stood.

"Please, use my desktop," he gestured towards his seat. The Kid slid in and began to run his fingers over the keyboard.

"This is a nice machine," The Kid noted as he typed. "Much more memory and a faster system." His hands froze above the keys. "You should get a system like this," The Kid directed at Alister.

"I will put in for an upgrade for you," Alister said. "But for now, can you—" He pointed towards the screen.

The Kid gave a quick salute with one hand. Both Alister and Tippy looked over his shoulder and waited.

Alia peeked through the resilient block of leaves to see Jimmy walking as some other guy lead him around the bus. The gun in the stranger's hand, invisible in the shadows. With a slight shift in the wind, she backed out of the brush and stood. A lone figure stood next to the car. Based on the curved outline, Alia surmised female. If she doesn't have a weapon, even in an unfair fight, Alia could take her.

That thought made her smile.

She melted back into the shadows to check on Marv and Brendan. The path still empty of other life forms as she retraced her steps. The landscape trajectory shifted right, towards the emptiness of a vast gray sky, filled with smoke instead of stars. On the horizon, the shape of one figure and a bench quickened her step.

Brendan slumped in the same position as when she had left. Her fingers went to his wrist. A small movement indicated he still had a pulse. Her hand moved to his chest. She felt long intakes of breath with a calm pumping of his heart. Thank heavens, the kid is still alive.

Alia placed her foot on the opposite end of the bench to raise her body up. In a slow, circular pattern, her eyes scanned the horizon for anything out of place. A branch that drifts too far without any wind. A rustle of leaves or possible scatter of rocks—all of her senses on high alert. A band of energy in motion from her set jaw out to her fingertips.

Without a sound, her legs slid out from underneath to squat down to a sitting position. "Some friend you got there, buddy," Alia said. "I directed that idiot to stay with you. He probably went after the mothership." Brendan's lips turned ever so slightly upward. "Don't waste your energy, kid," she said as her hand patted his. On the side of the valley, flames now shot up to the sky. She needed a plan. No, she needed a good plan. "Stay low key. I am going to get us out of this."

A bunch of 'if's' entered her mind as she paced, hand raised as if gripping a pen. *If I leave Brendan here, what happens if someone finds him. If I take him with me, I can't defend both of us. If Marv just stayed here, this would be easier.* The last *if* got Alia standing. She took a bottle of water out of her pack and placed it near Brendan's lips. She poured some into his mouth. Little droplets dribbled down his chin.

Thirst - another good sign. After a long sip, Alia focused her attention on Brendan. "I know you can hear me. I am going to get us a vehicle to get out of here. Stay still and quiet. I am coming back to you. If you see dipshit, tell him to stay." Brendan choked out a little laugh.

"Marv went—" Brendan started to speak. Alia shushed him. She placed the bottle, with about a sip or two left, tucked into his shoulder.

"I will be back." This time she walked straight into the brush. The vines tangled around her ankles. The thorns cut and scratched into her arms. "Damn it," escape from her lips. "Alister would have a field day with my language right now."

The wind shifted to bring a cloud of sightless smoke. Alia covered her face with her shirt while suppressing a slight cough caught halfway up her throat. The animals had now all scurried to safer ground. She followed the light draw into the night from the bus's wide door. Muffled shouts spilled out onto the asphalt, yet she couldn't see shadows in the windows or figures outside.

Alia moved with precision. She vanished behind old tree trunks; her body molded to each dimension. The closer her movements got to the bus, the brighter the path from its door extended. When her position paralleled, she made out a lone figure slumped on the ground. Based on the size, this wasn't Jimmy or Smoky.

She blew out a breath. Meticulously in without a sound, she slid around the tree for a better look. Smoky was nowhere in sight. The same with Jimmy, yet she could see his brother at the table. His hands gestured in all directions.

A shadow blocked the door as one of the stouter men carried the brother out of the bus. The tall one followed, gun in one hand, cigarette glowed in the other. The stout one dumped Fred's semi-lifeless body against the bus. The lanky one squatted down and to place his hands on Fred's shoulder, brotherly. They spoke, heads together, their voices that did not carry. The smoker laughed loud. His bellow echoed.

Now the lanky one stood up next to the slumped figure, who she now presumed dead. Both smiled now. The smoker leaned over to slap Fred's face. His head fell back against the bus as the smoker raised his gun. Alia jumped at the sound of gunfire.

Now two bodies lay slumped.

She walked back into the night. Once the bus's glow faded, Alia ran back towards where Brendan now sat on the bench. The bottle of water in the air above Marv's lips. Her hand raised up and slapped the plastic cylinder away.

"What the—"

Alia clamped her hands over his mouth. "Shut up before you get us all killed," she spoke with clenched teeth. "We have to move now." One arm reached into Brendan's armpit. She started to pull his body to a standing position. "Are you going to help me or what?" Alia said. As she tried to balance Brendan, his body slipped down her frame.

"You almost hit me," Marv whined.

"You left your friend incapacitated and alone."

Marv blew out a breath. "Nature called."

"The leak should have been completed fast and taken within view." Alia's words stung. Marv looked down at her. Tears made trails down his face through the soot.

Alia shifted her body to give Marv room to help Brendan move the bulk of his weight to him.

"Awaiting instructions," Marv stated.

Alia blew out a breath. "Look, Marv, I understand but—"

"Shouldn't we be getting out of here?"

"Right." Alia tugged in the direction of the old road. Through the trees, they had glimpses of the activity outside the bus. Jimmy now gestured towards the lanky one. "That can't be good," Alia muttered. The Mercedes and its occupant came into full view. Alia slipped back into the shadows.

"What now?" Marv asked.

"More than two-word communications, please!" Alia put Brendan down near a large pine tree. From a sitting position, the rest of the vegetation blocked them from every angle. "Stay here. Do not move. I will be back."

Marv nodded, and as soon as Alia disappeared into the night, he gave a one-finger salute in her direction.

Frustration levels hit the ceiling tiles as Yarok refused to be goaded back to the game. Other opponents approached the battle—a princess on a unicorn from the upper right corner. *You yellow-bellied sapsucker* was returned with *Stop relying on cartoons for your responses, you unable worms.* A wizard atop a dragon emerged from the lower-left corner started with *thy prick faced liver'd boy.* If you are going to quote from Macbeth, the kid replied, *use one that will get you a win, or have we eaten the insane root, you hurly-burly wretched fool.* An Aristotle clone, down to the strapped sandals, hurdled *moron,* to which *Zouderkite,* is thrown back. The ancient Greek figure exploded across the screen.

"Where is Yarok?" Alister interrupted his internet banter.

"Can't tell."

"What do you mean, you can't tell?" Tippy said.

"I can't tell! The dude was there, competing, and then poof, he disappeared. But he didn't log off, see," the kid pointed to a cartoon knight, sitting on a cloud with head in hands in the upper right corner of the screen. "Dude is just not engaging!"

Alister and Tippy exchanged glances while the kid continued to type insults. The knight neither replied nor moved. "Maybe his screen froze?" Tippy asked.

"Unfortunately, this game is more sophisticated than most," the kid's voice transitioned as if giving a lecture on video games. "See how the crawler stays in real-time," he pointed, "that is a built-in mechanism to keep players engaged. It is rather a genius feature because normally you can't do what he is doing. The word *terminus* should flash on both our screens to indicate that one is leaving the battle."

"Leaving the battle?" Tippy asked.

"The whole game is a battle of wits," Alister answered. "The kid here is king." The Kid smiled up at his boss. "Doesn't matter the genre, Shakespeare, Medieval insults, today's slang, he got it. I have never seen anything like it."

"I do have a weakness," The Kid confessed. "If he ever started quoting from Gilgamesh or Odyssey, I am screwed. I haven't got there yet, although I can do Aesop."

"Aesop wrote insults?" Tippy asked. "I never knew."

"Everybody wrote insults," The Kid went back to the screen. "His location in Pennsylvania hasn't changed." He threw his hands up. "I don't fathom what to do."

"Do nothing," Alister said as he placed one hand on the boy's shoulder. "Take a break. Can I send someone for one of those drinks you like?"

"No, I am over-caffeinated as it is." The Kid appeared pensive. "Maybe my mom could come to get me?" He sounded younger. "Like, can I go home? I feel like I have been away for days."

Alister chuckled, "That is because you have. I will give your mother a call and get you both set. Can you give me thirty?"

"Of course," The Kid said. "I'll just keep watch for movement, although Alister," The Kid stopped him at the doorway, "it is really weird that Yarok would put himself in a position to lose the game. He is really competitive and, well, based on past interactions, this doesn't feel right."

"Oh great, another gut person," Tippy mumbled.

"I appreciate your insights," Alister said as he squinted at his brother-in-law. "Please take a break, and if any new theories come up, find me." The Kid nodded and turned back to his screen.

Once out of earshot, Tippy asked, "Where do we go from here?"

"You guys are on the ground?"

"Yes, I got word they are currently blocking the old highway from both ends so parties can only escape through the park," informed Tippy.

"That's a huge escape route," Alister noted. He waited as a couple admins passed, earning a chin nod to Tippy then continued, "Do we have eyes in the forest too?"

"The fire is spreading rapidly, as you are aware. I have people coming in from the backside. Reports say they should be near the lot within twenty minutes."

Alister's head nodded as he took in this information. "Have you used any drones for surveillance?"

Tippy shook his head from side to side. "No. Too much smoke and flying under—"

"-- would trigger a reaction down below. I get it. On the other front?"

Tippy glanced around before he answered, "It appears that Morris is responsible for the leak."

"So, you arrested him?"

"Not yet," Tippy said. "Evidence is coming in much too clean, smells like a setup. I want to make certain to clear all the rat traps."

"I understand," Alister's head continued to nod. "Anything I can do?"

"Yeah, stay away from your office. Morris is freaking out, trying to find your whereabouts. I guess he doesn't like his team taking long lunches." Both laughed. "You remember the drill. Desperation will have him reach out to others. Alister, I want a clean sweep."

"As do I, Tippy, as do I."

Alia kept to the shadows as she made her way around the perimeter of the parking lot. A crack of a lone twig sent her to a crouch position that earned the addition of another crack from her right knee into the forest sounds. The tall one shouted in what sounded like Russian as the other man walked Smoky near the two bodies.

"Shit," escaped from Alia's lips. Smoky stood, arms crossed, with his face frozen in a pissed off at the world expression. The other man, devote of any emotion, modeled Smoky's body with one addition, a gun rested in his full hand.

Around the bus, a lone figure continued to lean against the black Mercedes. In Alia's mind, a good sign that she only had two to contend with at this juncture.

"The rumor on the street we heard, the ATF fired your ass because of our last encounter," the tall one baited Jimmy.

"Yarok, why do you listen to rumors," Jimmy replied. He now stood with his arms crossed. He wore the identical pissed-off expression as Smoky. "I retired from that shit. Decided I wanted to play guitar again, although right now, I can't figure why."

"You remembered my name. I am complimented. Now I see that I should have visited you behind the stage at that festival," said Yarok. Jimmy got a slight chill from his words. "Yes, I was there, but I hired your imbecile brother and his person to do work I should have, well me and my…" he nodded in the direction of the car.

"Yarok," Jimmy repeated his name, "my brother called me and asked for help. This is the first time I have seen him since the day I kicked his ass off my plane. You were there and heard me say never to show your face near me again."

"The day you started government work."

"Did I have a choice?" Jimmy's upper body frozen as he spoke. "That dipshit ran illegal drugs on my private plane! Listen, Yarok, I will admit that I was ready to get off that Rockstar bullshit but not the way it happened. Who volunteers to work in the hell holes we have seen? Come on, man, why would I go back?"

Alia noted Jimmy spoke to this man as an equal, even though one had the clear advantage of holding a firearm. She observed he took slow steps towards his foe as he spoke. She needed to move quickly, before both Jimmy and Smoky's bodies would be added to the pile.

Her current angle had Yarok's back to her. She calculated the chances of springing from the trees to tackle him from behind. As if reading her mind, Smoky now moved his head from side to side.

She nixed the tackle from behind plan. Every other angle lacked the cover she needed for some sort of success. She scanned the area with the hope of an idea. At the same time, she continued to move along the tree line, crouch-walking when fully exposed.

Smoky asked his holder for a smoke. She bounced out of both views with a quick move as the big guy turned to hand him a cigarette. With a silent thank you, she continued her moves.

Jimmy kept Yarok talking. "What about that time in Nicaragua when you shot me in the foot? Comrade, you should have killed me then," Yarok pointed out with a chuckle.

"Comrade, why would I have killed you? You meant me no harm. We both had a job to do, and we both finished that job."

Yarok jumped in. "You knew we would meet again."

Jimmy continued as if he hadn't spoken, "We were on the same side, no? At least I thought we were. We worked together—"

"To take out my competition—"

"To save a few of our countrymen's lives. Yarok, how did you go from that to this? Seriously, how did you get here?"

Yarok's laugh took a higher pitch. Alia ran her hands down her arms. Something flickered in the back of the parking lot. "How did I get here? Such a question, comrade," this time Yarok's voice took a hard turn. "I got here because, unlike my comrades, I was not satisfied with my work. I waited as idiots with fewer accommodations, whose fathers or uncles or neighbors," he spat on the ground, "get promotions over me because I am the son of one of the greatest chefs in Russian yet not an offspring of an aircraft commander or a nephew of Putin."

He took a long inhale. The gray sky just started to brighten in the distance. "Unlike in your United States, we have a hierarchy in Russia. If I wasn't put into the unit to work with you, then..." he shrugged. "So, now I have a, how you say, dilemma, no?"

"What dilemma, Yarok," Jimmy stood six feet away. "What dilemma could you have? I am nothing to you—"

"But you had a person I needed in that trailer. Maybe you saw where the others went?"

Jimmy shook his head and asked, "What others?"

"Please don't make me a fool."

"Yarok, I would never think you foolish." Neither men moved. "I don't know of any others. We left the festival, and the main road shut down. My driver over there," he motioned his head in Smoky's direction. "My driver thought this would be a short cut around. Once we saw the smoke..." Jimmy shrugged. Yarok stayed focused on Jimmy.

"There are others here. I can feel their presence," Yarok responded. He walked back a few steps and took a quick glance around. "My dorogoy," he shouted.

"Yes, my love," came a female voice from behind the bus.

"Do you see anything out of place?"

"No, my love. Same as when we arrived," she answered.

Yarok turned back to Jimmy, then spoke, "That was good for you."

Alia now stood diagonal to Yarok's trigger hand. The path between her and he left little for cover. The element of surprise would be the only advantage she possessed. A quick flash of light from behind the bus illuminated an area for a split second.

Something glinted against the pavement. Alia squatted for a better angle. Her eyes widened. A metal object lay in a patch of weeds. She glanced over at Yarok, who still babbled about unfairness in his country. "It happens everywhere, buddy," Alia mumbled. There would be one choice. She'd better make the correct option.

Louis Pilsner paced around Morris Webb's office. Agitation reverberated from every pore of his body. His red face inches away from Webb's. "What do you mean, Alister Reed is missing?" His arms held so much tension his biceps almost stretched out of his shirt.

"Him and the kid," Webb answered.

"No, I just saw the kid over at that fancy coffee shop he likes. Said Alister was supposed to take him to get something to eat-you don't think?"

"No, I don't think," Webb's voice a high whine. "Are you an idiot?" Pilsner drew his gun to point level with Webb's face. Webb blew out a breath. In a much calmer voice, he responded, "Pull that trigger, and you'll be in a pile of shit so deep that a troop of monkeys will not be able to eat you out of it!"

Pilsner raised his lips into a grin. "Troop of monkeys?" he laughed as he put his gun back into his holster. "Where did that come from?"

"Grandkids like Animal Planet." Morris Webb opened his top drawer, took out his standard-issue Sig Sauer, and placed it on top of his monthly desk calendar. "Do you think the kid is still at the coffee shop?" Pilsner answered with a head shake from side to side. "And he is not back here…" He absentmindedly picked up his cellphone. The screen had the time and date. No messages.

Pilsner observed the interaction. He said nothing as Webb typed on his keyboard. Both men stared at the screen. A map of Pennsylvania appeared. A red dot blinked in the lower-left corner, while closer to the center, a yellow dot did the same.

"Either the program is broken, or neither parties have moved in over two hours," Webb pointed. He typed in another series of numbers, letters, and symbols. The screen flashed then went to light blue. "Shit."

"Monkey?" Pilsner replied. The returning glare brought a more important question. "What happens to your screen?"

"Damn it! I have the blue screen of death," Webb replied. Pilsner clenched his jaw.

Webb continued, "Crap. I'll need the I.T idiots up here to fix this. It happened before, something with the way Microsoft runs." He ran his hand through his hair. "Dolores! Need I.T. up here right away!" Morris' assistant flashed by the door. Her hand raised in a salute.

The click of her heals faded as she ran down the hall. Within five minutes, a twenty-something with a ponytail sat in Morris' chair. "Hi, I'm Jack. Did you try unplugging the machine?" Morris shook his head no. "Okay, we are going to start there. This is probably something minor. I mean, you have auto-upload of your files, right?"

Morris and Pilsner exchange a shrug as Morris replied, "How the hell do I know?" Jack nodded and kept imputing different combinations of coding. His phone buzzed, and automatically he reached to see who was contacting. A quick swipe stopped the buzz sound.

"My girlfriend," Jack shrugged his shoulders. Two pairs of eyes squinted in his direction. "Not important." The screen flashed the same color blue, then died. "Dammit!" he yelled, adding, "excuse me," after.

"Problem?" Pilsner asked.

"Yes and no—"

"Well, which is it, son," Morris barked.

"There is a problem with your program, but I think I can get it working again. Do you remember if the remote access application is turned on?" Morris moved his head from side to side before meeting Pilsner's eyes. "No big deal. I can check here. Oh yeah." Jack typed in a series of codes and waited. "Huh."

"Huh?" Both men repeated.

"Well, I typed in the sequence, and it flashed remote access, and then it flashed again to show the application wasn't running." He stood up. "I apologize, but this is one for my supervisor. I can take your hard drive and get you another really quick to at least get you up and running again. Would that work?" No one moved. Jack rose up from behind the desk. His eyes now level with Morris' gun. "Umm, what do you think?"

"Would you go get the replacement, and we will fiddle with this until you come back?" Pilsner jumped in before Morris could speak.

"Yeah, no problem. I will try to bring Harry, my boss, back with me to try a diagnosis. He might be able to fix this without removing the unit." Jack jumped up and practically sprinted out the door.

Morris stifled a laugh. "He's not going to make it here if guns make him that nervous," he noted. Pilsner ducked under the desk, disconnected the small hard drive, then held it up for a show.

"You got a bag or something I can put this in?"

"Oh yeah, in the same drawer, I keep my purse." They searched the room with their eyes.

"A box? Something that wouldn't look obvious when we carry this out?" Pilsner plopped the unit on the desk next to the gun. "We need to get out of here and not leave evidence behind." He pointed at the unit.

Morris placed a wastebasket on top then moved the unit inside. In the process, he snatched up the gun with his opposite hand. "Now, we take out the trash."

Yarok raised the gun level with Jimmy's face.

"I want information about where the others are hiding," Yarok's voice changed back to the calm neutral tone he started. "I want that information now," he repeated in a much softer pitch. Alia noted his hand didn't shake. Jimmy kept eye contact.

Alia kicked her right foot back in a ready position and shifted her weight to her strong side. "There are no others," Jimmy repeated. "Only you and I are out here. My bus got lost," he retold the lie. "We need to get out of here. The fire—"

"I don't care about the fire! I care about that damn prosecutor in Connecticut because I went into business with imbeciles! I care about my enterprise, and I care about my Harlot Grace." He fired a shot. The bullet whizzed past Jimmy's ear. "Now you will tell me—"

"Dude, holy shit, a freakin' tour bus!" Marv's voice cut through the trees to draw both men's attention. Alia kicked back off her strong side to dive onto Fred's gun. She rolled over, pointed, and said a short prayer as she squeezed the trigger.

The bullet went straight through Yarok's hand. His gun flew in the air as Jimmy's left foot circled round to meet against his ear. Yarok fell to the ground in a heap. "Bros eto. Bros eto[7]," she shouted, followed by "Drop it!"

---

[7] "Drop it" in Russian

Smoky fist landed a strong punch into Yarok's henchman's gut. He added a knee to the face for good measure. The big man's body slumped against the two corpses, gun still in hand. Smoky pulled the arms behind to tie the wrists together with a piece of rag. He removed the gun, another Sig Saur.

"Where do Russians get these things?" he asked aloud.

Jimmy had Yarok on his stomach, knee rested in the swell of his back. Alia had disappeared around the blind side of the bus at the same time a hole shot rang out. He couldn't see it, yet he heard the sounds of another vehicle being gunned in the opposite direction.

A few gunshots, followed by a cluster of swear words. Smoky greeted Alia with, "I didn't realize that ladies used such colorful language, Althea." He let out a bellowing laugh after.

"Alia," she examined his facial expression. "Alia Price."

"Is that your real name?" Smoky asked. "I'll be damn, Zadie's gut strikes again." Both brought their attention to the pile of bodies.

Alia pointed, and asked, "Do you have any sleeping bags on this vehicle?"

"Why?"

She nodded with her chin back in the direction of the slumped figures. "We can't leave them here. They'll burn up." The wind made another shift that brought a burst of air, similar to an active oven door open.

"What about the others?" Jimmy's voice interrupted.

"Others?"

"The kid who yelled disappeared."

"Crap!" Alia took off into a sprint towards the spot where Marv had stood.

The Kid continued to try to engage Yarok in competition without any luck. His insults list ran the muck of reminding that this game is based on a logomachy and required a magniloquent language style. He even resorted to calling Yarok out as a muggle.

Nothing produced a response.

Alister entered the room and placed a frap down within The Kid's reach. He sat opposite and waited for a report. Without moving his eyes off the screen, The Kid reached out and raised the cup up to his lips. A long sip followed. He shifted his attention to Alister.

"Still no movement by Yarok," asked Alister.

"Have you checked the dots lately?" The Kid shook his head from side to side while fingers made tapping noises along the keyboard.

"Huh. The one attached to Yarok is moving away from the other," The Kid pointed to the screen.

"Dammit!" Alister stood as the door to the office flung open. A breathless Tippy entered.

"My men have reported gunfire in the area. They have the road leading out blocked and have begun to sweep the area. Any word from Price?" Both Alister and The Kid shook their heads from side to side.

The Kid brought the attention over to the screen. "Yarok's dot is moving away." The red dot blinked towards the main highway while the yellow didn't move.

"Come on, Al," Tippy grabbed Alister's arm. "I got the chopper waiting in the roof. Let's go." The Kid logged off. He opened his backpack, inserted his laptop, and stood.

All eyes fell on to the teenager. "What? I'm going too, right. I mean, you wouldn't have the locations—"

"Son—" Alister began.

"No, you can't leave me here. What about—" The two men turned away. Their voices so low the kid couldn't hear the conversation. When the hand gestures started, he jumped in, "Am I going or what?"

Alister started to say, "Or what," yet was immediately interrupted.

"I have a job for you," Tippy interrupted, "I need to be aware of who else had access to the coordinates you released. Is there a way to track that?"

"Did the Romans eat goat poo?" The Kid smiled. Both men returned the question with squinted eyes. "Yeah, they did, and yeah, I could. What do you need to know?"

Alister reached down and grabbed the kid's backpack. "Let's go," Alister said.

"Am I trouble?"

"You want to ride in the helicopter? Let's go. We are wasting our time arguing with a teenager which I found to be no win experiences," barked Alister.

The party of three rushed to the elevator. Alister and Tippy squatted low and ran over to the cockpit. The Kid froze in place. "For goodness sake!" Alister went back, grabbed The Kid's hand, and dragged him aboard the whirling creature.

The Kid jumped into an empty seat, reached up and spread the safety belt across his body, and snapped it into place as if second nature. The helicopter tilted a bit to the left, as it lifted above the building to disappear across the clear sky.

"We will see when we are close because of the smoke," the pilot informed. Alister removed the kid's laptop and handed it to him.

"We need a list of every party who had access to the locators. Do what you do." The Kid nodded and got to work. Alister turned his attention to the pilot. "How long until we reach the location?"

"Usually takes about fifty minutesoff, sir, yet I am taking the water route and pushing the throttle to get that down." Alister gave a thumbs up.

Tippy turned from the co-pilot seat. "I will have my people do a quick bank account search as soon as we get the list. We need confirming data, yet based on your recording from the stairwell, we have at least one, possibly two if either of those men talks."

Alister asked, "Do you need to go higher?"

"Not sure yet better, no stone unturned." Both men grinned.

Harlot heard a rustle in the bushes right before the culprit identified himself. The gunshots that immediately followed had her in the driver's seat. She stopped after doing a one-eighty in the car and pushed open the door.

"Hey, backstage, dude," she yelled to Marv, "remember me?" Marv gave a quick shrug. "Doesn't matter. Where's Brendan? I am supposed to take you two…" Marv glanced over his shoulder towards the tree then back at Harlot. She bolted from the car to his side. The steel rod of her gun pressed in his ribs.

"As I was saying," she continued. "Let's get Brendan and get out of here."

Marv hesitated. "Yeah, but—"

"Make a noise and die, comrade," she said as she pushed Marv towards the path. "Get Curry now."

"His mom will kill me," Marv stuttered.

"I will kill you." Harlot stared back at Marv. Brendan sat with his back against the tree, the same position as when he left. "Pick him up."

Marv crossed his arms. "What if—"

"Look," Harlot waved the gun in the air. "Either you both get in that car, or I kill you both now. Your choice." Marv reached down and moved Brendan's body over his shoulders. Hunched over, he scampered into the backseat—Brendan by his side.

Harlot watched the action on the bus. At least Yarok would no longer be an issue. The tires spun as she hit the gas. The Mercedes disappeared towards the main highway.

Alia sprinted through the vegetation. "Damn it!" Jimmy came up behind her. He stopped just short. "Shit!"

"Althea—"

"Alia," she shouted. "Damn it!" Alia circled the area. Her eyes went to the ground. "They dragged him," she muttered. Down on one knee, she ran her hand along the loose gravel.

"Do you think they took off in the car that left?" Jimmy asked. Alia turned looked up at Jimmy wide-eyed. He continued, "Newer black Mercedes with a satellite antenna on the top. There was a woman left behind—"

"Harlot Grace," Alia spat out.

"The Russian just referred to her as darling."

Alia stomped around, mumbling something incoherent. She switched to, "I am not drunk. I am not high. This is just my reality…" She grabbed Jimmy by the hand. "We need to get that bus turned around and go after—"

"Tour busses are big. They take time to get going. We will not catch—"

"We have to try!" Alia screamed before she took off through the trees with Jimmy on her heels. Smoky had draped the sleeping bags over the dead bodies. Yarok's hand covered in a blood-stained cloth. "We gotta go!" Alia yelled and pointed towards the bus door.

"What about—"

She glared at Jimmy. "You planning on using this bus again?" she asked. He gave a shrug back. "Throw anyone with a pulse underneath. Her eyes fell on Yarok. "Actually, I don't care if they still have a pulse. Put whoever in storage. If you are up to babysitting, the rest can go up top or in there too."

She paid attention to each as they struggled to move the bodies. "Screw it. Someone will come back for," she pointed towards the bodies. "Let's go! Now!" Jimmy, Smoky, and Alia boarded the bus. Smoky moved the large vehicle in a tight circle. One of the back tires ran over a foot in the process.

The headlights illuminated the many crevasses in the road. The pace went slow and steady. "Smoky, you need to move faster.

Screw the potholes!" Alia shouted. Smoky exchanged a look with Jimmy, who returned a slight nod.

"I needed a new bus anyway," Jimmy said. "Smoky, move it."

"You got it, boss. Hang on, y'all," he responded as he gunned the gas. The bus rocked with each hit of a tar canyon. Alia clung to the back of the driver's side seat. She looked out over the horizon line for a flash of red.

Snipers entered the old parking lot as visions in black. Yarok blinked a few times to see if it was the loss of blood or actual people moved towards him. The garbled sound of a two-way communication brought on a slight pounding in his temples.

"We have two dead bodies here. Both by gunshot along with a third victim with a missing hand." The sound of static followed. "Negative. Alia Price is not present."

The others scanned the area in a slow sweep motion. "Who are you, people?" Yarok choked out.

"I was about to ask you the same buddy," the one who appeared in charge replied. He squatted on the ground close enough to hear yet far enough away to avoid any contact. Another dressed the same, held Yarok's injured arm out straight. He injected something into the bicep. "You'll be out of pain in a moment," the man in charge continued.

Yarok's arm went numb as the line of cold moved from the injection site into both directions. A shiver ran through his entire being. "What did you give me?" Yarok's eyes grew.

"Nothing but a pain killer. We will get you wrapped up, and an evac crew will be here in a flash. Just relax, buddy."

The man rose to stand and began to point and yell in each direction. All but two took off in a fast jog down the road towards the main highway. Faced away from him, the conversation between the two remaining warriors continued to turn towards his position and then away.

None of their eyes meeting.

The bus lurched off to the left side. Tree branches scratched their tips to turn the purple paint into a trail of silver along the sides. Alia bounced from her seat to the floor. With the vehicle's movement against her, she brought her back against the wall. With her weight in her thighs, the rest of her body pushed up and plunged back into the cushion. The bus jerked forward, then rolled.

"What is happening?" Alia's voice rose above the screech.

"We hit something. The engine…" Smoky started to explain.

"Pop the door!" Alia yelled in his ear. She grabbed the white Sig from the sink and popped the chamber open for a quick check of ammunition. "Open the freakin' door!" she repeated.

"What are you—" Jimmy moved towards the sink.

"I can run faster than this. I have got to save Curry and Marv." Alia jumped out of the bus and disappeared into the night. Jimmy on her heels. Smoky took the remaining gun, along with the buck knife from under the driver's seat. He pressed the code to lock the door. Smoking moved in the shadows of the trees, parallel to the road.

Although only a short distance away, daybreak started to waken the land. Smoke still curved around trunks through its presence weakened. The thuds of helicopters heard overhead became part of the forest sounds. With practiced balance, feet hit the ground along the narrow wedge between tar and grass to create a steady beat matched by her pulse.

Alia heard the footsteps behind her yet did not take the time to look. If anyone besides Jimmy and Smoky were on her trail, she would contend with that if they caught her. A helicopter buzzed by a little lower than expected. Alia kept moving.

Alister motioned to the pilot he needed to land soon. The flight path buzzed by the rest area and possibly the tour bus. The pilot shouted coordinates over to the on-ground team. News of Yarok's capture alive brought on a short-lived celebration.

"There are two places I can land, sir," the pilot explained. "Back where the old rest area is one, yet there is not transportation in place at this time—"

"And the other?" Tippy asked.

"I can get near where the on-ground team has the road blocked. You are going to have to hike in about a mile to get to the exact spot."

Tippy motioned to Alister.

"Roadblock," answered Alister. Both looked over at the kid. Fingers flew across his keyboard one minute. He rose up in his seat to look out the window the next. This volley for attention continued throughout the trip, interrupted by a few "wow's" and "holy crapatudes" along the way.

"So, kid, what do you have for us?" Alister bumped his elbow to the kid's arm.

"You won't believe what I found," The Kid said. "You are not going to arrest me for hacking, right?" Both gentlemen nodded as a laugh turned into a cough escaped from the pilot. "I found an off-shore bank account for the cranky dude—"

"That would be Morris," Alister explained.

"—that has about five mil in it."

"When was the last deposit?" Tippy asked, phone positioned in hand.

"Um, let me see. It looks like he got, no, that can't be right."

"What?" both Alister and Tippy shouted.

"What I see here is that he got fifty thousand dollars yesterday, but that is small compared to the rest." The Kid shifted his screen towards both men. "I can screenshot this and send it to you." Both men nodded. A few clicks later, "Done."

The Kid inspected the wings movement from the sky to treetops down to the trunks.

The craft bounced to a stop. Tippy jumped out and ducked off to the side. Alister hesitated. He tapped the pilot on the shoulder. "Can I leave junior here with you?"

The pilot looked at the kid, who now met his gaze with a full-on smile. "I guess… this is irregular… maybe I should check?" Alister just shook his head from side to side.

"You can come—" Alister gestured towards the ground.

The Kid hesitated, then asked, "Do you want to hear the rest?"

"The rest of what?" Alister shifted his body back inside.

"That creepy dude—"

"Pilsner?"

"Is he the cop?" The Kid asked. "He has matching deposits from the same bank along with three others. I can—"

"Send me a screenshot and then follow me." The Kid started typing as Alister shouted instructions. "The laptop comes too, in your backpack. You will stay close by me and Tippy and will be quiet. You will listen and follow my instructions without question, and if I tell you to run—"

"I will run, got it." The Kid slipped his laptop into the backpack. He swung the bag over his shoulder and waited for Alister's next instructions. The pilot turned towards both.

"The Commander just communicated he can see the blockade, and you two should move it."

Alister nodded. Both jumped from the doorstep and disappeared out of view.

Harlot drove as fast as she dared. The tires bumped and rubbed against the car's steel frame. A custom rim flew off the road to disappear into the thick green vines off to one side. Sunrise brought out gray skies. The car slipped around a ninety-degree turn to slow at the sight of a single police car.

She decelerated on the gas. "If either of you makes a move, I will blow this car into so many pieces, your bodies will disintegrate."

"Nice," Marv mumbled.

"You play along with me, and I will let you go. My game. My rules," Harlot stated.

Neither man spoke. The officer had moved from a rest position against his car to stand with feet spread, one hand on his gun, the other in a stop position. He approached the car with a measured stride.

"Remember what I said," Harlot's voice changed from just above a whisper to almost a shout. "Officer! Officer, I am so glad you are here!" Her hand brushed against her blouse to unfasten a few more buttons. With shoulders back, her cleavage rose into view. "We were so lost and smelled smoke and—"

Marv noted that the cop had moved his hand away from his gun and now leaned in the window. Eyes going straight to the loose canyon that escaped from Harlot's blouse.

"Calm down," he said, in an almost friendly voice. "How did you get back there?"

"I don't have no idea!" Harlot exclaimed. She turned away to point at the road and gave Marv a wink. "We got stuck in traffic after a concert. My GPS said this was a short cut." Harlot looked up at the cop to meet his eyes. "And then the smoke!"

The cop stood and looked past his car. "Everything is blocked beyond here. I guess I can call ahead and see if you could get by. There is so much emergency equipment." He bent back in the window. "Can you hang here a minute? I am going to see if I can get you back to the main highway."

"That would be lovely," Harlot said. She waited until he walked away before revving the engine. The car leaped forward to clip the man in his hip. He fell to the ground. Harlot opened the door and jumped on top of his body. One hand removed his gun from the holster, while the other pushed down on his wound. With his gun in hand, Harlot stood to look down at the officer.

"I decided that you shouldn't call anyone," she said. "I also decided not to kill you. You should thank me for this." The silence lifted in the air at the same time Harlot's foot raised. The move delivered a swift stomp on his hip. The officer screamed with pain. "I said you should thank me."

"Thank you," came out barely above a whisper.

"You are welcome." She turned her attention to the car. "Don't even think about it."

"Think about what?" Marv said.

"Think about anything." She waved the gun. "Actually, I need you. Get out of the car." Marv moved to helped Brendan. "No, not him. Just you. Now!" Marv hesitated as Harlot fired a shot in the air. The car door slammed opened. Marv stood just outside the car. His entire body vibrated.

"Please don't kill me," he begged.

"Do I look like a killer?" Harlot waved the gun in his direction. "I want you to move my friend here over there, out of my way." She waved the gun towards the side of the road. "And after I want you to move that," the gun points at the state police vehicle, "out of our way. If you do these things for me, I will not kill you now."

Marv bent over and tucked his hands under the cop's armpits. He dragged the body a few feet and stopped. "Over there," Harlot repeated.

"Dude is not that light," Marv commented back. Again, he took the officer by his armpits and dragged a few feet further. When he looked back, Harlot now leaned against the car, swirled the gun in the air while she made a show of tapping her foot. In a much quieter voice, Marv said, "Dude, I am trying. We are not together. She wants my friend. We need help."

The officer gave a slight nod at the same moment Marv pulled. Both remained only seven feet from where they started. "Never mind," Harlot shouted. "Leave him. We take his car. Now move your friend." Marv went to the back door. Brendan lay across the seat.

"Come on, buddy," he said, "stay with me." With a tug, Marv moved Brendan from lying to a sitting position. From there, another tug got him standing. One arm hung around Marv's shoulders as his arms hugged his friend's back and waist. They slumped in unison towards the cruiser.

Alia heaved into a sprint at the sound of a gunshot. She rounded the bend to catch sight of the wounded police officer's body on the ground. Another couple of feet brought the idling Mercedes into view. Harlot Grace stood just outside the state police cruiser as two bodies disappeared into the back seat.

Without hesitation, Alia got down on her hands and knees. Rocks imprinted into her palms as she scurried along the ground, the Mercedes positioned to shield her from view. The heat from the exhaust pipe gave the trail. Out of earshot, Harlot yelled something. A cackle followed, this loud and clear. A quick shuffle brought her within ten feet of the cop.

Their eyes met. Alia mouthed, *are you okay?* The cop gave the slightest chin nod in her direction. *Can you move to?* A thumbs-up followed. She shimmied around the side of the car. Her body hugged against the steel. The police cruiser's engine now revved.

"Harlot Grace," Alia yelled as she stood, gun drawn. No answer followed. She could see Harlot's body turned towards the back seat. The shot would be clear, yet the bullet would not penetrate the glass. "Damn it." With measured steps, Alia moved into the open space in a measured circle towards the driver's side of the cruiser.

Behind her, the state cop made a slow progression towards the shelter of the Mercedes.

Alister and Tippy made a direct path through the vegetation. Their progress slowed by the kid. "Come on, we got to move!" Alister pulled him by his backpack strap.

"I think I want to stay with the helicopter dude, maybe do more research," The Kid answered as his hands flew down his head and along the shoulders.

"What's he doing?" asked Tippy—the view of the helicopter now hidden away by long vines. The vegetation had returned to its natural stance once all three moved through.

"Spiders, man," The Kid answered as he swatted at the air, "and bugs. I feel bugs on me."

All froze at the sound of a gun followed by a loud female cackle. Tippy grabbed the kid by his backpack straps back into the foliage. The Kid started to slap his hands up and down. Alister caught his eye. He froze, hands mid-air.

"Stop. It. Now," Alister commanded through tight lips. He pushed the kid down to the earth. "Stay here—"

"But—"

Alister held up one finger. "Please stay here and be quiet." A small hand grabbed his arm as he turned to leave.

"Please don't abandon me here," the small voice stopped both men. "Please."

Alister got down on one knee at the same moment Tippy took off towards the noise. "You need to stay out of harm's way," he started to explain. "Go back to the helicopter or stay put. Do not proceed after us." Alister stood and ran into the woods. The kid looked down in time to see a small spider crawling up his pants leg. He swatted it away.

The two men left a trail of broken vines in both directions.

Alia took a slow step towards the cruiser. Her finger pulsed on the trigger. Harlot sat in view. "Come on out, Harlot Grace," she shouted louder. In the front seat, she saw movement, and a hand leveled a gun out the side window. "You are not that good a shot," Alia kept a sequenced stride towards her target.

A bullet whizzed by to end in ping as it sunk into the Mercedes. Harlot let another fly, followed by clicking sounds. "Harlot Grace, fight like a girl and cut out this gutless man crap." The front driver's side door open. Harlot dunked just beneath the window, the barrel of her gun visible between the glass and metal frame.

"I always fight like a woman," Harlot answered. "I should have killed you at that festival?"

"And I should have killed you at the drug raid," Alia replied. She stopped ten feet away. "But I didn't. We all make mistakes. Like Salvi." Another bullet whizzed by her right shoulder. "Sore subject?"

"Ah, my Salvi," Harlot replied. "Too bad, he is so pretty. Jail will not be kind if he makes it there."

"Harlot, Salvi already threw you under the bus—"

"He wouldn't," Harlot shouted back. "I ruined him for other women—"

"You ruin something," replied Alia. Both women stared at each other. Maniacal laughter followed from both. Alia added, "This isn't about Salvi."

"We could make it about Salvi. He was so dumb he didn't even realize that you are F.B.I."

"I am not F.B.I." Alia stated.

Harlot's lips curved up into a slow smile. "Not F.B.I., huh? Then what are you?"

Alia took another slow step. Her eyes not leaving Harlots. "I could be a friend—"

Harlot's voice softened. "Friends don't participate in drug raids—"

"Or escape from a hospital with bullet wounds—"

"Friends. Ha!" Harlot yelled as she fired the gun.

This time Alia dropped to the ground at the same moment a bullet grazed along her upper bicep. Shadows moved inside the cruiser.

"Move one more inch, and I shoot your face off," Harlot instructed.

As if she didn't hear, Alia pushed herself up to a squat.

Harlot continued, "I have no issue killing you. As a matter of fact, I might enjoy this." Gun barrel first, Harlot slipped her body around the cruiser door. In a wide, balanced stance, she lifted the barrel and pointed it towards Alia. "We are done here."

The cruiser lurched forward to tap Harlot off balance. Her body twisted as she fell forward. Alia jumped to her feet and lunged to spring on top of Harlot. With the hit to her chest, Harlot's gun flew off to the side. Both women rolled on top of the gravel.

Alia kneed Harlot in the stomach while Harlot held tight upon her hair. "Let the freak go," Alia shouted. At the same time, she pulled back on her head. With full force, Alia's forehead met Harlot's nose. Blood splattered all across the pavement, their arms, hands, and down the front of Harlot's blouse.

"AHHHHHHHHHHH," rang out of Alia's mouth. The primal scream came as a warning. A soft bounce brought her body from a squat to a full stance. The left leg came around hard as it connected with Harlot's right side. She fell to the ground.

Alia rose again to deliver the final blow. Two hands linked across her stomach, to pin her arms against her body. Alia shimmied and shook to land an elbow into the ribs of her handler. A loud grunt blocked the sound of impact.

"Come on, darling, we got this. Take a break." The words sung into her ear through clenched teeth. Jimmy felt Alia's breath slow as her body slumped in his arms. "That's my girl. A couple more deep breathes, and I will release you."

Still, on high alert, Alia slowed her breath further. Her capture's arms loosened just enough for her to slip out. With precise aim, her elbow connected to his ribs a second time. A quick hopped turned her face to meet her assailant. She cocked her leg back for a roundhouse kick. Target missed.

Jimmy ducked out of the way just as her foot caught air in the space he stood. "Darlin'," he said. One hand rested on his bruised rib, the other held out in front in the stop position.

Alister, Tippy, and Smoky stood off near the abandon Mercedes. Laughter spilled out of the area.

"So, you all are old friends with my boss," Alia said. She and Jimmy sat off to the side. An EMT attended to the scratches on her arms and legs along with the new black and blue marks on her elbow.

"Yeah, me and Al and Tippy go back to the old days," Jimmy glanced in the direction of the laughter. "Smoky actually hung with those boys more than me, though."

"Huh," Alia said. "And when was the last -OW!—" Her arm swatted away the medic's hand.

"Look, lady, this is going to sting. Build a bridge or stop fighting. Pick one or the other," the medic barked back. Jimmy turned a laugh into a cough as Alia's glare turned on him. "Seriously, you agents are all alike."

Jimmy raised an eyebrow and waited. "Yes, I work for Alister. My job was to find Brendan Curry—"

Jimmy nodded in the direction of another ambulance. "The kid over there in the other ambulance—"

"Yeah, the kid in the other ambulance. I work mostly on drugs," Alia started to explain. The medic pulled the syringe away. "Not that kind of drug," she waved her hand in his direction, "the illegal supply. We had a problem with our last bust. I will leave it at that."

"One more question—" Jimmy held up one finger.

Alia nodded and asked, "Then, it's my turn?"

"Then it's your turn," Jimmy smiled. "How do you know Johnny DeLuca?"

Alia sat with her mouth hung open. Alister joined the two. "Excuse me?" Alia said.

"How do you know Johnny?" Jimmy repeated.

"Agent DeLuca was my trainer at the academy," Alia explained. "A real prick. How do you know Johnny?"

"He's my other brother," Jimmy answered. Alia's mouth drop for the second time.

"James," Alister injected, "We tell the truth here." Both men started to laugh.

Jimmy gave Alister a nod, then continued, "Johnny was my partner down in Nicaragua. He and I have been chasing Yarok for a while. He'll be happy to hear we finally caught the bastard."

Alia considered how this could have played out if she knew that Jimmy and Smoky were on her team. "You know Alister—"

"Don't say it, Alia. As crazy as this may sound, this situation," Alister held his hand out to sweep across the scene. In the immediate area, three ambulances, two state police cruisers, and half dozen soldiers milled about, while across the field, a helicopter idled. "Would not have happened if the kid over there played a different video game."

"You tracked us through a game?" Alia looked over at the kid, by himself on his computer. He glanced around every few minutes then brought his eyes back to whatever had his attention on the screen.

"Yes, a game that Yarok apparently fancied." Alister waved to the kid. "He found the leak."

"No shit," Alia said.

"Language Alia—"

"I mean, no kidding," she said with a smirk.

"Tippy's boys are rounding them up as we speak," said Alister. The three watch Marv sit down next to the kid, who looked up and smiled at the company. Both sat, heads together, faces lit by the screen. "Do I need to be concerned?"

"He may start spewing about aliens..." Alia replied.

Smoky joined the group. "I got Zadie on the phone. She says her gut is acting up and wants to find out if she missed anything?"

L.M. Pampuro

This book came to life at a music festival. My husband and I sat ten rows back from the main stage and I felt the overwhelming urge to write a story set here, at one of my happy places.

I am fortunate to have a community of musicians, artists, writers, and even a few non-artistic folks who inspire, encourage, and at times, motivate me to write.

I am humbled to have this incredibly honest group of humans as family, friends, and colleagues.

I appreciate my Beta readers, Maura Troy, Evelyn Pampuro and Robert Calegari who came through for me, again, with kind suggestions and constructive comments. I would also like to thank a new mentor, Ron Samul, for his feedback. Ron, along with Christine Archer, Kay Janney, Jamie Cat Callan, and others, are part of my writers' journey, each as primary mentors at the perfect time.

I have a fantastic tribe who help my creative bubble. Thank you to Terri Meigs, Renee Stevens, Faith Campbell-Powers, Terri Coe, Carrie Lombardi, and Laurie Beth Roberts.

Along with Shayna B's by The Sea, The Pure Alchemy Café kept me in vegan cookie dough balls and energy bars.
To the loves of my life, my hubz, who understands that silence is my best medicine, and our son, who just is an incredible human.
And finally, I want to thank my readers, booksellers, and everyone who is part of this craziness. Read a book and go on an adventure!
Peace.

L.M. Pampuro

***Get Social to Stay Updated:***
Facebook.com/LMPampuro
Instagram.com/LMPampuro
Pampuro.com

CPSIA information can be obtained
at www.ICGtesting.com
Printed in the USA
BVHW032346210221
600569BV00005B/1